PURE EVIL

A MAFIA ROMANCE

THE DARK LORDS

STELLA ANDREWS

Copyrighted Material
Copyright © Stella Andrews 2023
Stella Andrews has asserted her rights under the Copyright, Designs and Patents Act 1988 to be identified as the Author of this work.
This book is a work of fiction and except in the case of historical fact, any resemblance to actual persons, living or dead, is purely coincidental.
All rights reserved. No part of this book may be reproduced or transmitted in any form without written permission of the author, except by a reviewer who may quote brief passages for review purposes only.

18+ This book is for adults only. If you are easily shocked and not a fan of sexual content, then move away now.

NEWSLETTER

Sign up to my newsletter and download a free eBook.

stellaandrews.com

BE CAREFUL WHAT YOU WISH FOR!

All I want is a room somewhere
Far away from the cold night air
With one enormous chair
Oh, wouldn't it be loverly?

Lots of chocolate for me to eat
Lots of coal makin' lots of heat
Warm face, warm hands, warm feet
Oh, wouldn't it be loverly?

Someone's head restin' on my knee
Warm and tender as he can be
Who takes good care of me
Oh, wouldn't it be loverly?
Loverly, loverly

Eliza Doolittle
My Fair Lady

THE DARK LORDS

PURE EVIL

I breathe vengeance and taste pain.

Beneath the tailored suits and silk shirts beats a heart with no mercy.

My billions lie on top of broken souls and tortured endings.

I am evil and I accept I always will be.

My plan. To hide behind innocence to play my enemies at their own game and bring them down.

I have the perfect weapon.

I rescued an angel who believes I am a good man.

Noble, charitable, fair, and true.

She desires me, craves my wicked touch, and drowns in my depravity.

She is pure. I am evil.

She is my fair lady — my Eliza Doolittle if you like. A blank canvas on which I will create a masterpiece. Somebody to fool the most discerning eye.

But I am no gentleman. I am the man she fears the most. The devil waiting behind the mountain range.

I will teach her how to be my perfect woman and she will thank me for it.

I am the master of the game.

She doesn't even realize we are playing one.

She signed a contract inked in tears and sealed with blood. Now she is mine and there is nothing she can do about that because hidden in the small print — she gifted me her soul.

Revenge, a marriage contract, and a devastating betrayal.

For fans of dark mafia romance and hard-fought happy endings. Mad chaotic scenes and devilish behavior. Steamy, intense, and shocking. You have been warned.

CHAPTER 1

KILLIAN VIERI

SERENITA

When death comes knocking, it makes its presence known. It lingers as a promise of retribution for all your past mistakes and deeds. Waiting with the cold fingers of everlasting damnation, promising you an afterlife far more torturous than the one you left behind.

I sense it now, circling, waiting, anticipating and it angers me that I can do fuck all about it.

My gaze falls to the open window where the merest hint of a breeze makes its way inside, reminding me that life goes on.

The unusual sound of emotion disturbs the air, and my gaze falls on my sister who was named after the very place we wait for the grim reaper to show his face.

I offer no words of comfort. No assurances that he lived a good life because we all know those words would be empty ones.

"What's taking them so long?" The irritated growl from my brother's impatience switches my attention to him instead, and I wonder if he really expects an answer. It falls to our father to bother to try.

"He always was a belligerent bastard. He will die on his own terms and in his own time."

Nobody smiles. Nobody reacts and nobody cares what he thinks anyway because Benito Vieri turned his back on his father many years ago and doesn't deserve to crack jokes around his deathbed.

The door opens and we stare expectantly at the person who, of anybody present, deserves the right to her grief. Ariana Vieri, previously Torlioni, appears like a weary vision before us.

We stand and she smiles tremulously.

"He will see you now."

Serena is the first to her feet and as she reaches our grandmother, she pulls her in for a hug and I watch her whisper something in nonna's ear which causes the woman to smile, a strange twinkle in her eye being the only indication she likes what she hears.

It intrigues me and I catch my brother's eye, knowing he has seen it too. It's an interesting reaction from a woman who is about to lose the love of her life.

We have no time to ponder this because our father stands and says, slightly irritably, "Come. Pay your respects to your grandfather."

He hovers beside nonna and it's almost as if he doesn't know what to do in the circumstances, which again is a strange reaction from a man who was brought up to cherish family above everything. I wonder when that changed for him because Benito Vieri turned his back on this family as soon as he was granted his freedom. Something I have yet to experience for myself.

Shade raises his eyes and I exhale wearily. It would be nice to respect our father, but we both lost that ability years ago. Not that he was a bad one, he just never measured up to the role he was set to inherit. Luckily for my grandfather, all three of his grandchildren share his own sense of duty.

Our father stops and glances at the silent woman in the corner who never says much, but when she does, we all listen. It's almost as if he forgot she was there at all, and he stops and nods respectfully.

"Giselle, we should go in together."

Giselle Matasso is our aunt and a far stronger woman than he is a man and the fact she has just buried her husband must make for an interesting Groundhog Day.

She stands and nods, serene and regal, as she moves toward her mother and kisses her respectfully on either cheek. Nonna nods and smiles and once again it strikes me how devoid of grief her expression is. Something feels wrong about this and for a man who likes to know everything ten steps in advance, I wear my unease beneath the countenance of indifference.

Once again, Shade glances my way and his expression of helplessness has been replaced by excitement, telling me that, as always, my brother and I are on the same page.

My father stands aside for his sister and as they leave the room, nonna says softly, "Follow them. He wants to see you all together."

Shade offers Serena his hand, and she smiles at him with a puzzled frown, telling me she has felt it too. There is something happening none of us anticipated and as I follow them out, I stop by my grandmother and whisper, "It appears that my condolences will not be required any time soon."

The only reaction I get is a small nod of appreciation and a soft chuckle from the woman who deserves all our love and respect.

"You are so sharp, Killian, just like your grandfather."

She reaches out with a small loving smile and grasps my large hand in her small one. "Forgive him. He only has your best interests at heart. He always did."

"I know." I squeeze her hand, which shocks her a little because emotion isn't something I care to show–ever. It causes her to chuckle softly.

"There is hope for you, after all."

I shake my head. "Hope is an emotion for fools. It means you have lost control, which we all know is the beginning of the end."

She says with a dash of irritation. "You will learn that hope is the one thing that gets us through. It drives ambition and makes you stronger. Never lose hope, Killian, because if you do, you have lost everything."

"If you say so, Nonna." I turn away and am surprised when she pulls me back and stares at me with a hint of sadness in her beautiful green eyes.

"Open your heart, Killian. Let emotion inside and stop trying to control every aspect of your life, your feelings included. Only then will you be as powerful as your grandfather, because without love or emotion, you are weak."

I say nothing and stare at her with indifference, not believing a word she says because since when did emotion play any part in my life? It certainly didn't get me where I am today.

I shrug it off and turn away, her soft sigh accompanying me and as she follows behind, my mind turns to what's waiting behind the closed door we head toward.

CHAPTER 2

KILLIAN

My father knocks respectfully but waits for no command to enter and as we head inside, I don't question the choice of room.

Don Vieri's den.

The place he classes his sanctuary and not the location of your usual death-bed scene, but not surprising given every meeting we ever had with him has happened inside these four walls.

The light is dim, the heavy drapes closed against the glare of the sun, and I make out his figure sitting in his chair behind the walnut desk.

My father steps forward and says in slight disbelief, "Father."

"Benito."

If anything, the tone of my grandfather's voice is amused and sounds nothing like the one of a dying man.

"What's going on?"

My father sounds surprised, which makes me want to roll my eyes because surely he knows his own father by now.

"Sit."

The short sharp command etched in the rumble of authority causes us all to drop silently into the nearest available chair, and I note my aunt's small smile that she quickly disguises with a small cough.

Nonna moves to stand beside her husband, and he reaches for her hand and stands, holding out his chair so she can sit there instead. I feel my heart beating faster, which is the only reaction I have because this is not the meeting of a dying man with his children. If anything, it appears to be an intervention and I wonder what the occasion is.

My grandfather stares at each one of us in turn and as his eyes fall on me, I stare back with no expression, causing him to nod as if he is happy about that.

"I'm dying."

He states the obvious as he glances around the room and then says with a sigh, "But not today. Probably not tomorrow and I expect not next week either."

"I don't understand." My father dares to speak and is rewarded with a curt, "Listen, Benito. For once in your life, shut the fuck up and listen before you speak."

My father glowers at him but has the sense to remain silent and my grandfather exhales slowly.

"I brought you here for a reason and knew that my death is the only one you would react to."

He glances at nonna and laughs softly. "Ariana said it was cruel. I disagree. I have spent a lifetime molding cruelty into business, and this is just another day at the office. I had to be certain of your attention and it appears my calculations were correct as always."

I doubt anybody in this room cares that we have been summoned here under false pretenses and, like me, are merely curious as to the reason why. If anything, it surprises me that he felt the need for the theatrics because when Don Vieri speaks, we ignore him at our peril.

He turns to my father and says wearily, "Benito. You have enjoyed a relatively easy life, purely of your own choosing."

He shakes his head. "You turned your back on the family business to create your own and we all know to what you owe your success."

My father is bristling with indignation, which is almost amusing to watch because we all know my grandfather is speaking the truth.

He peers at my aunt and growls, "At least your miserable husband departed this world before me. I can die happy knowing your debt has been paid."

"*My* debt?" My aunt is probably the only one in this room, nonna aside, who could interrupt Don Vieri and she says irritably, "My debt was yours. You used me to settle it and we all know it."

She glares at him with delicious fury, causing him to say with a small shrug, "It was business. You were required to play your part."

My aunt says nothing and just directs a hostile gaze his way, and I expect we're all surprised when nonna stands and says icily, "Giselle. Don't ever question your father's motives. It was necessary, and you weren't complaining at the time, if I remember rightly. In fact, I distinctly remember your own demands and, as always, you were granted every single one. So don't play the victim card because we know there is not one victim among us."

She sits down and my grandfather rests his hand on her back and his eyes shine as he stares around the room with pride. It always struck me that Ariana Vieri was the power behind the throne and that intrigued me more than the man who sat on it.

My aunt fades back into black, the place she prefers to exist in, and we turn to my grandfather as he says in a strong, unwavering voice.

"The Dark Lords are turning against us."

I straighten up because now we're getting to the reason we're here.

He hisses. "They are turning against the founder member and trying to edge our family out."

He begins to pace behind his desk, and I sense his building fury as he spits, "Respectability. That is the reason they give to erase us from their honor roll. It appears the very organization that kept them out of trouble is no longer required as they strive to distance themselves from the dirtier side of the business."

I sense his rage and it excites me. It always has and as if we are of the same mind, I sense the connection with Shade and Serena as we hang on his words because like me, my siblings live for this shit and whatever he wants, he always gets from us.

My father obviously doesn't share our love of the family business and says foolishly, "Then let them have it. We don't need them anyway and if I were you, I'd call it quits and enjoy my retirement."

As if he tossed a grenade, tension explodes in the room, and I watch with eager anticipation as my grandfather turns to stare at his only son with an expression of murderous rage, making me wonder if I will witness my own father's death instead of his own.

"Let. Them. Have. It."

His eyes flash with fury as he slowly recites the words my father used back at him, causing him to shrivel in his seat as he realizes the mistake he just made.

Nonna glares at my father with disappointment and rage

that is rarely seen on her face and my father says with a catch to his voice, "What? I'm only stating the obvious."

"Silence!" Nonna stands and faces her son with a twisted expression of anger and disappointment, and we stare at her in surprise as she snarls, "You will not disrespect the organization your father created that has enabled you to live like a king and assured you of richness. I will *not* tolerate the lack of care for something this family should die to protect. There have been many times in your life that you have disappointed me, Benito, but none even come close to this. Well, enough. You no longer have the right to offer an opinion, so pack your bags and leave this island. You are no longer welcome here."

If anything, my grandfather stares with interest at a scene none of us expected and certainly not my father, who stutters, "But…"

"Now!" she yells, causing my father to scramble to his feet and say angrily, "I'll go but don't come crawling to me to sort this shit out. I'm not interested."

He storms out without a backward glance, leaving a shocked silence behind him. As the door closes, my grandfather says with a deep sigh. "That wasn't unexpected. He is inconsequential anyway, and he always has been."

Nonna returns to her seat and her eyes flash as she stares around the room, her rage feeding my own tarnished soul and filling it with happiness. I love this shit. I always have and if you go against family, you ensure the wrath of the woman who has dedicated her life to it.

All eyes turn to Don Vieri as he says with a growl.

"The Dark Lords are about to learn that the Vieris have sat at the head of it for a very good reason. You will all play your part and if necessary, we will bring them down, along with our great organization, even if I must delay my own journey to the afterlife to see it through."

Danger, excitement, anticipation, and revenge are the most delicious ingredients for something that I crave more than air. This is what I love. What my family thrives on and as we wait for instruction, I bask in the most massive surge of adrenalin as I wait for the storm to break.

CHAPTER 3

PURITY

This city terrifies me. I'm the fool who believed she could pull this off, but coming from a small town wrongly named Heaven, never prepared me for life outside it. I thought it would be easy. I was very wrong.

I stare up at the skyscraper rising before me majestically into the heavens and I catch my breath as it threatens to derail me from my mission. I must see this through. It's all I've thought about since that day I met *her*. The woman who changed the direction I was heading in and the woman who promised to make my life better.

Her crumpled card lies hot in my palm, the creases disguising the address printed on it. I have memorized the place she told me to call on for help. It was my only hope of life away from the hell I was heading toward.

As soon as the chance presented itself, I snatched it eagerly and now I'm standing before my destiny, uncertain if I should proceed any further.

The sounds surrounding me are alien. Loud noises coming from the building works nearby. The screech of tires on the dirty road and the chatter of passers-by as they hurry to get to their destination. An aircraft adds to the confusion and the blare of music from a passing car is gone as quickly as it came.

I shiver as I stand on the sidewalk, gazing up at the steel and mirrors hiding a world of possibilities.

I stumble as somebody pushes past me and feel a faint tug on the strap of my purse. I react without thinking and turn my arm, ready to defend my property from an assailant.

"Excuse me, ma'am."

A woman murmurs apologetically as she removes her shopping bags from my side and I smile.

"It's fine."

She nods and hurries away and I take a deep breath as I admonish myself for believing everything is a threat in this hostile environment.

I suppose I am so out of my comfort zone rational thought has been left behind because I am so freaking scared right now, but the pull of a better life is hard to ignore.

Mustering courage from somewhere, I take a deep breath and head through the revolving doors of a building I never really believed I'd witness first-hand.

The interior is even more impressive than the outside, and I stare in awe at a space that is completely alien to me. The marble floor appears endless and the black leather couches set around a huge glass table make me blink at the decadence of this place.

Huge arrangements of interesting flowers dominate with color and the glass and mirrors set all around me create the illusion of more space that is definitely not needed. I gaze in awe as crowds of people rush toward huge glass elevators that make me gawp in amazement as they lift their passengers to the heavens, and I gulp as I stare at a scene I never really expected existed.

"Ma'am." A uniformed man approaches, and I grip the

card in my hand a little tighter as he gazes the length of me, his expression confirming he is less than impressed by what he sees.

"May I be of assistance?"

I can tell he is already preparing to dismiss me to the street outside and so I paste an imperious expression on my face and stand a little straighter, wishing the plain navy cotton dress I'm wearing was even halfway a match for the outfits surrounding me now.

"I'm here to meet with Gabriella Sinclair."

My voice wobbles a little and I curse it under my breath.

"Is she expecting you?" He raises his eyes and I say politely, "She is."

He nods and points to a gleaming marble counter that is set against a wall of mirrors.

"Check in at reception."

He turns away, dismissing me already, and I take a deep breath of relief, thankful I'm not tasting the air outside. The first hurdle has been cleared, however, the next may not be as easy.

As I head toward the counter, the dismissive gaze of the woman watching me makes me stand straighter and grit my teeth. I never thought these people would be so cold and yet a lifetime of treatment just like this, causes me to brush it off with disdain.

"Good morning." She smiles as I approach, her insanely white teeth causing me to run my tongue against my own, wondering what it takes to have a smile as bright as hers.

"I'm here to meet with Gabriella Sinclair."

I repeat my sentence and watch as she raises a perfectly drawn eyebrow in apparent confusion.

She glances at her computer screen and says with a smile. "Do you have an appointment?"

"I do." I brazen it out because I may have been told to come here, but it wasn't with a firm date or time in mind.

"May I have your name?"

"Purity Sanders." I say abruptly, and she glances at the screen.

"Where are you from?" She enquires and I say without missing a beat.

"Heaven."

She raises her eyes and I shrug. "The town Heaven, not the well… you know."

"Of course." She smiles but I can tell she thinks the wind blew the crazy in off the street and she peers at the screen and says, "There's nothing in her diary."

She appears thoughtful and I prepare to be sent packing, but then she glances up and says with a smile.

"I'll call her. If you would like to take a seat, it shouldn't take long."

I smile gratefully because this woman is the first person I've met who is being kind to me, which means a lot to a girl who has spent her entire life expecting the worst of people.

I retreat to the black couch and sit perched on the edge with my hands clasped together on my lap, not really knowing what to expect now that I'm here.

I notice the woman talking into a headset and wonder about this place. Where I am from, there is no technology, no comfort and nothing that is considered unnecessary. Even the flowers here would be frowned on in Heaven, despite being a thing of such natural beauty, it should be celebrated.

Not there.

Not in a town that rules through fear and demands complete devotion to the lord and the reverend who delivers his teachings. Having been here for less than four hours already, I already know I prefer Chicago, despite how scary it is.

PURE EVIL

I glance up as the woman stands before me and says with a hint of pity in her expression. "Miss. Sinclair has asked that you wait. She may be some time, though."

"I have time." I reply with determination, and she nods.

"Okay. Would you like me to fetch some magazines? A coffee perhaps."

I am disarmed by her kindness, and smile with relief, causing her to stare a little harder.

"I would like that, thank you."

"Consider it done."

As she turns to walk away, I say quickly, "Thank you."

Her heels clicking on the polished floor is my response and as she heads back to her desk, I congratulate myself on being one step closer to my new life.

CHAPTER 4

KILLIAN

Gabriella is seriously pissing me off, reminding me why I have rules, ones I broke with her and am now suffering the consequences of that.

"Just once more, Kill."

She purrs as she lies entangled in my sheets, peering up at me with suggestive eyes as I sweep my fingers through my tousled hair.

"We're late." My response is curt because I hate the fact I continually allow myself to fuck this woman. Then again, it's better the devil you know, and I happen to know Gabriella Sinclair extremely well indeed.

"It can wait." She whines and I snap.

"Business can *never* wait, and I am disappointed you even said that."

She sighs and stretches out, her legs falling open in a move I'm convinced is to tempt me into defying my own words and I growl, "Close your fucking legs and stop acting like a greedy whore."

My words have the desired effect and the frown on her

face excites me way more than the sensual one as she says through gritted teeth. "You're a bastard, Kill."

"Deal with it." I turn away and head to my bathroom, and it irritates me when says hopefully, "Do you want me to scrub your back and suck your dick clean?"

Once again, I wonder what the fuck I see in this woman, and I snap. "I don't want anything from you other than your ass at your desk doing the job I pay you extremely well for. You can use the guest bathroom. Be ready in fifteen minutes."

I slam the door behind her and lock it for good measure because I wouldn't put it past her to try her luck again.

As I stand under the cold jets of a hard wake-up call, I resolve to end any further intimacies with my willing executive. It should never have happened, but she was convenient and has provided a reliable fuck whenever I say so.

My grandfather's words are coming back to bite me as I scrub that woman from my skin.

"You are becoming a joke, Killian. Reckless, undiscerning and a playboy. Your name is rarely out of the tabloids and your list of fucks is thicker than a copy of Who's Who. Clean up your act and become a saint, because the only way we are going to win is to be spotless. So, shine up your principles and unpack your scruples because you must become whiter than white itself if we are going to beat them at their own game."

I hated every word he spoke but owned them. I am out of control sexually and use any willing woman who flashes her eyes in my direction. It's become the candy that is threatening to choke me, and I am awash with the effects of gluttony. I have over indulged and hate the fact I have lost control of my libido. Sex is my release and the rougher the better. Violent, destructive sex feeds the beast inside me and powers my soul. The harder I fuck, the more I want, and I'm never satisfied. I'm an animal with no moral compass and yet when I pull on my business suit, any passion inside me is replaced by cold cruelty. There I get my kicks another way and I tear down my enemies and ruin lives — just because I can.

As I dress, I think about the life I live and can't imagine it any other way. It is controlled, meticulous and satisfying and I congratulate myself on having my shit worked out. Why should I let my grandfather dictate my basic requirements but even I realize he has a point? I must calm the beast to kill the one threatening our livelihood and if it means I fall into line, I'll do whatever it takes. I will become a saint disguising the devil I really am just to win this bloody war. If it means cloaking my red soul with light, I will do it all in the name of victory.

Gabriella is waiting by the door and without even a look in her direction, I head into the elevator and press for the basement.

As the door closes, she says belligerently, "You're a fucking bastard, Kill. Would it hurt you to show a little affection once in a while?"

I am so close to removing this woman from life forever, but realize Gabriella is too much of a business asset to replace anytime soon, so I guard my tone and say dispassionately, "We have a job to do. There is no room for anything else."

"Until tonight." I detect the hope in her voice and fix her with a dismissive gaze as I say cruelly, "That was the last time, Gabriella. From now on, you do your job, not me. Understand."

"What the…" Her mouth drops open as I adjust my gold cufflinks and say in a bored voice. "I am cleaning up my act and that includes putting out the trash. Find some other distraction when you're not doing your job."

"You…" She steps forward and raises her hand to strike me, and I catch it easily and sneer, "Not a good move, Miss.

Sinclair, if you value your life. Go gracefully and you will survive another day. Do anything to upset me and it's game over. Understand?"

She nods miserably, knowing I'm a man of my word and as the elevator doors open, my protection moves forward, and I wave to the second car. "Miss. Sinclair will be traveling alone from now on."

She can't even object as she is ushered toward the second car and as I step into the first one, my bodyguard Saint closes the door with an approving nod. He always hated Gabriella. I could see it in his eyes and as always it reminds me he knows me better than I know myself sometimes.

* * *

ON THE JOURNEY, I work. I always do and usually spend it briefing Gabriella on what is expected. Now I'm alone and for a very good reason. I am going to become whiter than freshly fallen snow with a view to bringing our enemies down. There is much to do, so I spend the time wisely and work hard on formulating a plan that will deliver everything we want.

I don't register the journey time at all and as the car stops outside my building, I am mildly irritated that I must waste precious minutes relocating to my office.

Saint opens the door and glances around to check the surroundings and after a nod, I step from the car and take a deep breath of normal life before I head inside the building that offers a distinctly abnormal one.

The name on the brass plate never gets old and I gaze with satisfaction at the company I created from scratch. Gold Hawk Enterprises. An acquisitions business that buys and sells, making a gigantic profit between transactions. This is the legitimate face of my business, which hides the dirty one that lies beneath the cracks.

Extortion, murder, drugs and intimidation. Money laundering and illegal activities that would make a lifetime behind bars a certainty if it wasn't for one impenetrable shield protecting us.

The Dark Lords.

The organization my grandfather started when he was a young kid in college has grown exponentially to become the largest secret society in the world right now. At least that's what we believe, but the trouble with secret societies is, they don't publish the minutes of their meetings to the nation. Who knows who is waiting in our shadow, which is why we need this organization like an IV line.

I head inside the building and stare straight ahead, not risking any eye contact with people I wouldn't be able to pick out in a crowd. My employees are paid well but have no loyalty from me and I couldn't name anyone outside of my own close team.

Gabriella follows me inside and only the receptionist calling her name distracts my attention from my desire to get to my office.

"Miss. Sinclair."

It makes me look, but as my eyes turn, it's not the receptionist I see in my vision but a curious sight instead.

Sitting on the couch waiting is a young woman. Not unusual, but the sunlight streaming through the glass is surrounding her in brilliance. It catches on her white hair and bounces off the curious aquamarine eyes that are staring at us with interest.

Even from here, I can tell she is a cuckoo in this particular nest because she is sitting straight-backed, her hands clasped on her knees and her feet crossed at her ankles. As our eyes lock, I witness a morbid curiosity, but nothing else. She stares back at me, showing no fear, no sexual interest and nothing but polite indifference, and that holds my attention more than anything.

It happens in a split second and then Gabriella moves past me and stops before her, blocking my view and I keep walking, but it's as if my steps are forced and slow. For some reason, this woman has the ability to slow me down and I'm surprised about that.

I wonder who she is.

I'm not sure why, but it's as if that was a pivotal moment because something is telling me my reaction is unusual. She was a pretty girl, that is undeniable, but it was her reaction that intrigued me.

Ignoring everyone who nods in my direction, I storm to my office and as Saint follows me inside, I say gruffly. "That girl with Gabriella. I want to know everything about her. Who she is, why she's here and what her business is with Miss. Sinclair?"

Saint nods and leaves, no opinion offered, and as I shrug out of my jacket and hang it on the hanger in the cupboard, I can't prevent my thoughts from returning to the intriguing woman downstairs.

The only comfort I have is that Saint will have everything I need before my coffee arrives in approximately ten minutes time. What I do with that information, though, remains to be seen.

CHAPTER 5

PURITY

I have never seen anything like it before. It was as if God himself walked into the reception. Before they arrived, there was a general murmur that echoed through the building. Almost as if the occupants were preparing for an approaching storm and so, as the door opened and four men entered, my eye was drawn there at once.

It was like a scene from a movie as two men dressed all in black came through it first, closely followed by another man who was walking beside one that definitely stood out from the crowd.

He is important.

It's obvious just from the reverent glances thrown his way and the hushed awe that surrounded him.

I am intrigued and fascinated and can't help staring, even though I know it's considered rude. It is more surprising when he stares back and as our eyes connect, a shiver ripples down my spine as if ice enters my veins.

He takes my breath away but not from desire. It's fear because those eyes have a million hard stories locked inside them. I can see them swirling around as if jostling for position and yet I could drown in those eyes. They are so dark, deep and filled with torture, and I wonder what sort of life is the result of such madness. I am mesmerized and only break eye contact when the woman I came to see blocks the view and stares at me with curiosity.

"Purity?"

She smiles with interest, but no recognition, and I stand awkwardly, offering her my hand.

"I'm pleased to meet you, Miss. Sinclair. Thank you for asking me to come."

"I'm confused."

She steps away because it's obvious she doesn't recollect our meeting and my heart sinks.

"You gave me this." I uncurl my hand and wince at the appearance of the worn card that lies on my outstretched palm and say quickly. "You came to meet my father, Elijah Sanders, from Heaven." I falter, suddenly unsure of what I've done, and she cocks her head to one side as if she's thinking. Then she smiles and nods.

"Of course. I remember now. You have grown since then. I hardly recognized you."

"It was four years ago, ma'am, and I kept your card."

"Wow, that's amazing."

She chuckles softly. "So, how can I help?"

"Um …" I falter slightly because this isn't what I imagined. To be honest, I don't know what I expected but certainly not indifference.

"A job." The words come out in a rush, and I say without catching a breath. "You, um, told me that if I was in Chicago to look you up. You would help me and make sure I was looked after. That you had a job with my name on it and the possibilities were endless for a girl like me."

"I remember." She appears almost amused as a spark

lights her eyes and she looks me up and down.

"Turn around, Miss. Sanders."

"Excuse me."

I'm unsure what she means, and I detect a hint of steel in her voice as she snaps, "I said, turn around. I need to look at you."

Slowly, I do as she says and for some reason, I don't like how it makes me feel, especially when I catch the expressions on the faces of the people standing nearby watching the scene with interest.

"Does your father know you're here?"

Miss. Sinclair says quickly, and the fear strikes me deep as I say in a rush, "No. I, um…"

I falter, and she laughs softly. "Say no more. This will be our secret, Purity."

She nods toward the elevators. "Come with me. I'll take care of it. I have just the job in mind for you."

My heart sags with relief because I knew I was right. From the moment I first met Miss. Sinclair, her kind smile told me I would be safe with her. Now she will set me on my future path that is heading in the opposite direction to Heaven, and I feel the excitement stirring as I contemplate a brave new world opening up before me.

We join several other people in the elevator, and they stare at me with a curiosity I throw right back at them. They intrigue me because I have never met people like this. My life was sheltered, controlled, and dictated by my parents and the only friends I had were ones I snuck out to see. I never really knew that a world like this existed outside my own and as I drown in the euphoria my escape created, I am excited for what lies ahead.

Our journey up is obviously further than most because the elevator empties the higher we go. I stare around in amazement as I spy the diminishing ground beneath us through the glass walls of the elevator. I have seen things like this in the movies I watched in secret, which told me there was more out there than my parents had me believe. Now I'm living the dream because I made it, and Miss. Sinclair is the angel God sent to help me escape a fate worse than death.

We reach our stop and as we step into a hallway, my heart is banging so hard I'm sure she can hear it. You would never know because she has ceased to make conversation and is more interested in her phone and so I follow her to a huge office at the end of the corridor and hover nervously by the open door.

"Take a seat outside, Purity, and wait. I won't be long."

She says dismissively and I nod as I step back into the outer office and perch nervously on the edge of the chair set by the wall.

There are a few people working who glance at me with interest and then return to their computer screens and start tapping away, making me wonder if I'll work here. I'm not sure what I can do that I'm qualified for because I wouldn't know how to operate a computer if I tried. Such things weren't available to the women of Heaven, only the men, and despite trying hard to make it work when my father was out, I never managed to see what all the fuss was about.

As I wait, I shift nervously on my seat, wondering what happens now because this is my one shot at a future of my own choosing. If it doesn't work out, I have one number to call. The last resort I suppose which would take me to stay with the only friend I have who also escaped from her childhood home. Faith is the one person standing between me and Heaven and if this dream turns to dust, at least I can rely on her to help me.

So, I wait for my life to get interesting and as the clock ticks the seconds past, it soon becomes apparent that I'm in for a longer wait than I first thought.

CHAPTER 6

KILLIAN

The door opens and Saint heads inside.

"Purity Sanders."

"You're kidding me. Really, that's her name?"

He nods and I shake my head at the twinkle in his eye.

"Interesting." A wry smile touches my lips because what are the odds? Purity.

Saint carries on. "She turned up with Gabriella's card in her hand and told Yvonne she had an appointment. She didn't."

"And…" I fix him with a calculated look, and he shrugs. "It's not uncommon. Gabriella hands out business cards like confetti to pretty girls. Occasionally, they come on the promise of a job and end up working at one of the clubs. A pretty girl like that is probably heading that way or as an escort for some of the higher priced parties."

"A whore."

He nods and I think of the girl I saw sitting straight-backed and curious and, for some reason, the thought of her working at my clubs, providing entertainment for men with more money than conscience, leaves me cold.

Saint adds, "She said she came from Heaven."

I raise my eyes and he grins. "That fucking weird-assed town Gabriella spoke about when she was sent there to meet the guy supplying the opium."

"I remember."

I cast my mind back to the place Gabriella told me gave her the creeps. It's been a good source of opium for us over the years and there is never any drama or comeback. I'm guessing she took one look at Purity and sensed a different kind of business for the poor, unfortunate, delusional girl.

I glance at Saint, who is waiting for instruction and say gruffly, "Where is she now?"

"Waiting outside Gabriella's office while she finds her a placement, no doubt."

"Bring her to me."

Even I'm surprised at the words that made it out into the open, but Saint merely nods. "Of course, boss."

He turns and I spin around and stare out through the clouds, down to the street below. I love this view. I am like a king up here and it's my sanctuary. It's the perfect place to interview an angel from Heaven and it makes me smile as I turn my attention to what the fuck I'm going to do with her.

This is a first for me. I have never been in this position before, and I expect it's because of my grandfather. Shutting things down with Gabriella earlier was the start of that, and as I wait, an idea begins to form in my mind. I need to act fast. That's obvious because the stakes are too high to ignore the consequences of inactivity. I'm known for dealing with problems and finding a satisfactory conclusion to them—for me, anyway.

My instructions were crystal clear. Clean up and paint a very different picture to the world of who I am. Be fucking Santa if I must and become a major benefactor to worthy charities, disguising the real motive behind my actions. I am set to become the most powerful businessman in the state, if not the country, and it begins today. The people I surround myself with must be loyal, beyond reproach and fucking saints if I want to polish my own halo and who better than an angel from Heaven to help me bring my enemies down.

I will dress my evil in purity and as luck would have it, she's waiting downstairs and completely unaware of the turn her life is about to take.

* * *

A GENTLE KNOCK on the door shifts my mood and as the door opens, Saint ushers the girl into the room. I take a closer look and assess her for the role I have assigned her and am pleased to note she will be perfect. It's as if a breath of the purest air accompanies her as she heads into my office, showing none of the nerves I would expect from a woman in her position and those amazing eyes are focused on mine with innocence, an enquiring mind and nothing else.

Perfect.

I stand and extend my hand, pasting a warm smile on my face that causes Saint to smirk and lower his eyes to the floor with a wry twist to his lips. He is fully aware I can turn on the charm and disguise the devil that is fully in charge of my soul.

"Miss. Sanders. Welcome to Gold Hawk Enterprises."

Her small hand rests in mine but is surprisingly strong as she shakes my hand and stares directly into my eyes with a sweet smile.

"It's a pleasure to meet you, sir."

She cocks her head to one side and peers at me with interest and as we shake hands, it's as if I am holding a delicate flower in my iron grip. Soft hands with short fingernails and no polish, almost childlike and yet the woman staring at me is definitely no child.

I'm guessing she's early twenties at the most, her youthful appearance mainly due to the fact she is bare of make-up and, quite frankly, she doesn't need any. A blank canvas that is a masterpiece.

Her astonishing eyes give color to a pale complexion, a hint of pink dusting her cheeks put there by mother nature. Her soft pink lips hide an even set of white teeth with none of the cosmetic artistry of the dentist.

Purity indeed because this woman is just as nature intended, which suits me fine because I will mold her into my perfect woman and there is nothing she can do about that.

My Cinderella if you like. Pretty Woman if you want a more modern fairy tale. But I am no Prince Charming and no Richard Gere. I am pure evil, and I almost pity the angel who has fallen into my pit.

Reluctantly, I drop her hand and nod toward the chair set before my desk.

"Please take a seat, Miss. Sanders."

She drops with ease into it and sits straight-backed, once again with her hands clasped in front of her resting on her lap. She says nothing and I like that–a lot. She obviously doesn't use words unnecessarily and has none of the nerves I would expect from a woman in her position.

"You are looking for a job."

I get straight to business, and she nods, looking hopeful.

"Miss. Sinclair gave me her business card a few years back and told me if I ever needed a job to come and find her."

I lean back and stare at her with a contemplative expression.

"What were you hoping for?"

I ask a question that I have no intention of honoring, and

she shakes her head and smiles softly. "I won't lie to you, sir. I am not qualified to work in an office. But I am honest, hard-working, and desperate to learn and would welcome the chance to enter a training program or start at the bottom and work my way up."

"I see."

Once again, I catch Saint's eye and his smirk tells me even he knows this poor girl doesn't stand a fucking chance and I pretend to consider my options without speaking a word by return.

I'm impressed that she doesn't try to fill in the silence with unnecessary conversation, just stares at me with a blank expression as she waits for me to speak.

After a while I nod and tap my fingers on my desk and say slowly, "There is no position for you at Gold Hawk Enterprises. We employ the best there is and have no time to train a woman with no experience."

I watch for her reaction, but I get nothing back except the silence that tells me she is waiting for me to speak first. This is refreshing because most women would be flirting like crazy with me now and doing everything in their power to ensure their position in my company, or in my bed. Not Purity Sanders. She is giving nothing away.

I know she has no options. She is wearing a tatty dress and probably only has the things on her to her name. She will have no place to go, no money and no friends. She is taking her shot and hoping to score a direct hit, and she has. She just doesn't know that hit will backfire on her and cause her more harm than good. I am going to have so much fun educating her in life in the real world. Not some cult town in the middle of nowhere where life was frozen in time and the women treated like third-class citizens. She is so perfect I can't believe my luck.

I pretend to contemplate further before saying,

"Although…" She stares at me with no emotion as I say slowly, "I do have a position for an assistant, but it's a live-in one."

"I don't understand."

She appears confused and I lean back and say casually. "It requires no experience because full training is provided. You will be paid well, and your living accommodation and meals are included. I offer a clothing allowance and a personal grooming budget. The catch is, you are on call twenty-four seven."

I watch for her reaction, but once again she says nothing and just appears to be considering her options. The silence that hangs in the air gives nothing away, and I watch with interest to see where her decision falls.

"An assistant?" She cocks her head to one side.

"What exactly does that involve?"

Saint smirks, enjoying the scene a little too much and I stare at him pointedly, causing his smirk to disappear fast, before smiling at the woman hovering on the edge of my web.

"It involves accompanying me to events and charming my guests when I entertain, organizing my diary and fetching what I need. You will be the person closest to me and will help organize my day. You see, Miss. Sanders…"

I lean forward and stare her directly in the eye and get a similar direct gaze thrown right back at me.

"I am a busy man. I have no time for anything other than business and yet normal life gets in the way of that. I need someone beside me who is professional at what she does. Doesn't question, just follows instruction, and conducts herself with poise, elegance and grace and I think you will be perfect for the job."

I take out my fountain pen and write a figure on the notepad and slide it across the desk to her.

"This is your salary, and it doesn't include living expenses that will be provided by me."

I watch with a hooded expression as I wait for her to jump headfirst into my trap because there is no possible way a woman in her position could turn down this sum of money. The way she blinks her eyes as she stares at the figure before her is the only clue that I have already won.

CHAPTER 7

PURITY

I have never seen a figure like it. To be honest, I don't even know what it equates to, but I guess it's a lot. More than usual, which raises a few red flags. To be honest, this man is one giant red flag, and I don't know what to do about it. He is offering me something that I'm almost positive hasn't been advertised and I wonder about that. There is something very wrong with this and I need time to think about it.

I study the figure and wonder what is happening. When I came to see Miss. Sinclair, I thought it was to apply for a job. She left me waiting with no indication of what that would involve, and then this man's assistant came and told me to follow him.

When I walked into his office, the man waiting scared the panties off me. He fills the room with a dark presence. The air is tense, acrid, and stifling, and it's difficult to breathe. His personality is dark, but those tortured eyes mesmerize me. There is so much power in them, so many dark secrets that I *never* want to unlock.

He tries to be polite, but I sense the anger inside him, the power, and the expectation. He is extremely bad for me; I already realize that, and I've spent a lifetime being warned of the Devil taking on many disguises. Is this my test? Is this man one I should avoid at all costs?

Then again, what choice do I have? Miss. Sinclair perhaps. Will she offer a better alternative?

My mind is racing, and I need time to breathe, so I stare directly into his dark gaze and say firmly, "Thank you for your offer, sir. I will need time to consider it."

He doesn't react. Perhaps the darkness intensifies a little in his eyes, but other than that, he remains impassive and merely nods.

"You have one hour, Miss. Sanders. Saint will direct you somewhere private to contemplate your decision."

I nod and stand, offering him my hand as a show of respect.

"Thank you for the opportunity, sir. I will give it my consideration and let you know."

I drop his hand and turn, the door already open and his assistant waiting to show me out and as soon as I leave the tense atmosphere, I take a deep breath, hopeful the oxygen will bring clarity to the situation.

As I follow the man, I say quickly, "If you please, will you take me back to Miss. Sinclair?"

He says nothing and presses the door to the elevator and ushers me inside.

As we travel down, we do so in silence. There is no easy conversation, no general chat, just cold, sobering, silence.

He returns me to the seat outside her office and leaves as quickly as he came, and I try to steady my heart that is racing frantically as I consider what happened.

I grip my purse a little tighter because everything I own in the world is inside it and wonder what my Plan B is because I was so assured Plan A would work out. It still might and as the office door opens, I peer hopefully at Miss. Sinclair who exits with a smile.

"I'm so sorry to keep you waiting, Purity. It took longer to arrange your position."

She points inside her office, and I follow her inside, hopeful she has a different kind of occupation in mind.

Once again, I take the seat in front of her, and she fixes me with a bright smile.

"Good news. I managed to secure you a position that comes with accommodation."

It's a little like Deja Vue, but I smile politely, and she says briskly, "We can head over there now. They are preparing your room. It's a nice house in a quiet area that is clean, and you will have your own room with ensuite facilities."

She takes my silence as agreement and smiles. "The job itself is an easy one. Hosting parties for influential people and arranging entertainment, food and making sure they have everything they require."

She leans forward and says with a wink. "You will be sharing with four other women. It will be fun. They are great girls, and it will be a blast. The money is basic because you are provided with food and lodgings, but the real money is in the tips."

"Tips?" I'm not sure what she means, and she laughs softly. "The visitors have a lot of money and if they are happy with the service they receive, they pay well. Make them happy and you are happy. I'm almost certain a pretty young girl like you will make a killing, so all that remains is to welcome you to our family."

I'm a little confused, but she is being so nice it would be rude to question her and as I weigh up my two options, I prefer hers. At least I would be with other women, a kind of freedom I've never enjoyed until now, and that man scares the hell out of me. I'm almost positive I'll take Miss. Sinclair up on her offer and so, as she stands, I do too, and she nods toward the door. "Shall we go? It's not far."

"Excuse me, Miss. Sinclair."

She stops as I speak, and I say with an anxious smile. "I wonder if I may have thirty minutes to think this through."

"What's there to think about?"

She appears genuinely confused and I feel a little foolish even asking.

"It's just, well, I could use the bathroom. It's been a long day already."

She nods, glancing at the gold watch on her wrist and it strikes me how polished and assured she is. There is not anything out of place on Miss. Sinclair and that was partly why I wanted to take her up on her offer. When I met her in Heaven, I was mesmerized. I had never met a woman like her before and it made me re-evaluate my own life. She is the reason I'm here because if I get one wish in life, it's that I become half the woman she is.

I wait for her response and with a deep sigh, she says in a rush. "Okay. I have some work I need to catch up on. I'll meet you in reception in thirty minutes' time."

She flashes me a soft smile. "This is a good opportunity, Purity. You would be a fool to pass it by."

I smile gratefully and head back to the elevator, praying I remember the way back to the reception.

As I take the short journey, I try to make sense of my jumbled thoughts. Two offers of employment, but very different to the one I had in mind. I have nothing to compare them to and I am running out of time. The scary man told me I wasn't qualified for office work. Maybe organizing parties would be more interesting, anyway and female company would be better than his—surely.

The doors open and I head back into the marbled reception area and waste no time in heading over to the polite receptionist, who smiles as I approach.

"Excuse me, ma'am, but may I leave a note for someone?"

"Of course."

She slides a pad of paper across the desk with a pen and as soon as I begin to write, I feel like an idiot. The pen hovers in mid-air and I say apologetically. "I didn't catch the name of the man I just had an interview with."

"A man?"

She looks confused. "I thought you were being interviewed by Miss. Sinclair."

"I was, but while I waited, another man told me to follow him, and I was shown to an office where a rather frightening man was waiting."

"I don't understand."

She shrugs and I say quickly, "It could have been on the top floor. There were no other floors for the elevator to stop at and when we got out, the interior was more spacious. A little more luxurious."

"The top floor."

Her eyes widen. "This man you met, is this him?"

She taps on her screen and turns the monitor to face me, and I nod, intrigued at the photograph of the man I just met. "That's him." I glance at her with a nod, and she appears shocked for some reason.

"Mr. Vieri. He is the owner of Gold Hawk Enterprises. Our boss."

"Is he?" I'm mildly interested, but not surprised.

"Well, if you could give him this note, I would be most grateful."

Her expression turns to suspicion, but I don't dwell on it and merely scribble a few words on the paper and fold it in four pieces. I slide it toward her and smile.

"I'll wait over there for Miss. Sinclair. Thank you for your help."

She nods respectfully and as I leave, my heart thumps mercilessly inside me. The boss. Why am I not surprised by that?

CHAPTER 8

KILLIAN

*P*urity Sanders irritates the hell out of me already. What is there to think about? I am offering her a position most women would kill for.

'I need time to consider it.'

What the hell!

Ordinarily, I expect an immediate answer. Not to be kept waiting while *she* decides. What the fuck. I don't let people decide. I tell them. I am irrationally pissed about this and as Saint returns, I snap, "Give her one hour and then drag her back here if you have to."

"Drag her?" He arches his brow and I growl, "Fucking woman, making me wait. I had her down as clueless; she hid that well."

Saint shrugs. "Maybe she cleverer than you think. You've got to hand it to her. She's cool under pressure."

"She doesn't know the meaning of pressure."

I tap my fingers angrily on the desk, anxious to wrap this up quickly so I can devote my attention to actual business that makes me money. Not costs me.

"Where did she go?" I don't know why I even care.

"To Gabriella's office."

My head snaps up and I stare at him with an expression that could cause an instant cardiac arrest.

"Ga-br-ie-lla's off-ice." My words come out slowly and are laced with anger.

Saint shrugs. "She asked to return there. I'm guessing she is waiting to see what else is on the table."

"Did she now."

Knowing exactly what is on the table, I'm confident she will be hauling her ass back here pretty damn quickly when she learns what Gabriella has in mind for her.

Confident of that, I turn my attention back to business and wait for the lamb to come to slaughter willingly.

It must be half an hour later when Saint heads back inside and from the look on his face, it's not good news.

"What?"

He slides a folded piece of paper my way and I snap, "What's this?"

"Read it."

He appears concerned and the words swim before my disbelieving eyes.

Thanks for the offer, sir, but I would like to consider my options before I make my decision. I will give you my answer tomorrow.

"Is this for real?"

I stare at Saint in shock and his smirk doesn't help my temper.

"What!" I yell and he shrugs.

"She's not as naive as she looks."

"You think?" I shake my head with a scowl fixed firmly on my face.

"The girl's a fool. A misguided, clueless country hick who doesn't understand what her options are. I'm almost tempted to withdraw my offer and throw her to Gabriella to ruin for me."

I thump my fist down hard on the desk and yell, "Fucking options. I'll give her options. Does she realize the only other option is fucking guys for money? Is she so stupid she doesn't see that?"

I start to pace, so angry I can't think straight, and it takes every ounce of control I have not to instruct Saint to take her to my mansion and lock her up until I am of the right mind to deal with her.

Saint is my bodyguard for a very good reason because he is the only person outside of family who can speak the truth to me, no matter how much it angers me.

"Think about it."

He drops into the chair before my desk and leans back, staring at me with a calculating expression.

"You've met the girl. She's awash with innocence. She hasn't got a fucking clue the mess she's in and I'm guessing as soon as the penny drops and she realizes exactly what her shiny new job involves, she'll be beating a trail to your door and hammering on it with both fists. Let Gabriella terrify her first, and then you will have a broken angel to play with. I'm guessing she'll be a lot more grateful for the opportunity then."

Let Gabriella terrify her first.

Why don't I like the idea of that? Picturing her soft expression and trusting eyes. The innocent edge to her words and the curiosity in her expression makes me want to preserve it forever because I have never met the like of her before.

Do I want to allow her innocence to be crushed with the prick of a needle, drugging her into acceptance?

Do I want her innocence torn from her body by a man with no regard for her feelings?

Do I want her to be passed around like a rag doll at a party with drugs and orgies just to prove a point?

Like fucking hell I do, so I snarl, "Follow them. When Gabriella leaves, head inside and drag that woman out and take her to my mansion. Against her will, if necessary, just make certain no one touches what's mine."

His sharp look makes me consider the words that just told him how weak I already am around her.

Mine.

Since when was she mine?

Since when did I want her to be?

I don't claim women as mine – ever. Any woman I've fucked has been around the block enough times to make them dizzy. It's my rule. It keeps emotion from my door because I owe them nothing they don't already know about. They expect nothing but a depraved fuck and a fistful of dollars and we both leave happy.

Mine.

Since when did she become mine?

From the moment that sun kissed her shoulders and directed my gaze her way.

From the moment I set eyes on a pure and natural beauty that has remained untarnished in perfection.

From the moment she sat before me with interest, but nothing more.

From the moment I realized I need Purity Sanders in my life more than anything else because she is the woman who will bring me revenge.

Delicious revenge on the Dark Lords. Yes, Purity Sanders was mine the minute she blew in off the sidewalk and it will be intriguing to see what she thinks about that when the realization dawns on her innocent, trusting spirit.

CHAPTER 9

PURITY

We are met by a large car with a chauffeur holding open the door. It reminds me of when I first knew my father had visitors. I came home from school and saw the car waiting outside. The chauffeur smoking a cigarette and hiding behind black sunglasses.

When I saw Gabriella, I was spellbound. She was the most exotic person I had ever met in my life, and I was in awe of her. I still am and as I sit beside her in the luxurious interior of the car, a shiver of excitement passes through me.

I did it. I escaped Heaven, and I knew coming to Chicago was the best option for me. She promised she would help me, and she is. This job sounds appealing, fun even and I can save for an apartment, perhaps. Start my life on my own terms and work my way up and maybe someday I will be qualified for a job in a place like Gold Hawk Enterprises.

I'm trying not to think of the man who owns it. Hopefully, I won't ever see him again because working for him was a scary proposition. Spending twenty-four seven with a man who scares the shit out of me wasn't even worth the ridiculous amount of money he offered me.

No, this is better. On my own terms and in my own time, I will work from the bottom up. I'm free at last. This is what I came here for, and I'm confident my decision is the right one.

* * *

WE HEAD out of town and the landscape changes to countryside and fields. This is more like it. What I'm used to even and I relax for the first time since I came to Chicago. I have somewhere to live and a job and a friend in Miss. Sinclair. She is kind and I really do believe is helping me find my way.

We soon reach our destination and I'm not surprised we never spoke at all. She is obviously an important woman because she spent the entire journey on her phone. Mainly texts and emails but the occasional call too and now I know why Gold Hawk was no place for me. The only phone I have is one loaned to me and there is only one number programmed into it. My one-way ticket out of here if I need it. Protection against danger, that's what this is and so I sit happily in the knowledge I'm probably never going to need it.

The car pulls up outside a huge mansion house and I stare in awe at luxury the like of which I have never seen.

The chauffeur opens the door and Miss. Sinclair says quickly. "We're here, Purity. I'll introduce you to Mrs. Collins. She's the housekeeper and in charge of the girls."

I nod, grateful for someone to show me how things work, and as we head inside, I stare around in awe at the crystal chandeliers and decadent furniture that welcome us in.

The walls are mirrored and make the interior appear ten times its size and I wait nervously beside Miss. Sinclair, as an older woman, approaches us.

"Mrs. Collins." Miss. Sinclair says abruptly. "Meet Purity. I trust you will make her feel at home."

The woman nods and looks me up and down, almost as if she is assessing me.

"Perfect." She smiles and yet I notice it doesn't reach her eyes.

The two women exchange an expression I can't make out and Miss. Sinclair says quickly, "I'll leave her in your capable hands. Good luck, Purity. You know where I am if you need anything."

I'm a little worried that she leaves, but as soon as she does Mrs. Collins says abruptly, "Follow me. I'll settle you in."

We head toward a room set close by the entrance and I note we are in an office of sorts. A glass desk is positioned in the center and there is a wall of white cupboards behind it. Another huge chandelier hangs from the ceiling, and she gestures to the chair in front of the desk and says curtly, "Please sit."

I do as she says, expecting her to explain the job role and how things work, and I'm surprised when she reaches into a drawer and removes a leather case.

"We have some procedures to follow before you enter the premises."

"Procedures?" I enquire and she nods, snapping open the lid of the box.

"I need to inoculate you against a virus we are currently experiencing high levels of. It keeps you safe, along with the rest of us."

"I don't understand."

I wasn't expecting this at all, and Mrs. Collins says with exasperation. "Don't question me, Purity. This is for your own good."

She takes out a needle and a phial of liquid and approaches, grabbing my arm roughly.

"I don't…" I make to pull away and she says sharply, "Don't resist me, girl. This is for your own protection."

"No!"

I shake my head because I am not agreeing to this until I know what it's for and then I scream as she plunges the needle directly into my arm and empties the contents into my veins.

"How dare you!" I shout and she shrugs and returns to her seat, calmly placing the needle back inside the box.

"I don't hang around, Purity, and what I say goes. Now. Your uniform."

"Uniform?"

She nods. "Remove your dress."

"No."

Once again, I shake my head and she sighs heavily. "You are not making this easy for me. Do you want me to restrain you and rip it from you instead?"

"Why are you doing this?" Something is very wrong, and I wonder why Miss. Sinclair brought me here and then I discover the hard facts when Mrs. Collins snarls, "You will strip, wear this uniform and when the men arrive, you will entertain them. You live in this house by our rules and do everything we tell you to. Your whole existence is to pleasure our visitors, and if they like it, they pay you well."

The tears pour down my face as I stand and say with a sob, "No. This isn't the job I came here for."

"Sit down."

She snarls and I ignore her and head to the door and wrench it open. I run straight into a broad chest and scream as two arms lock tight around my waist and I am carried back into the room and held against the wall.

"Strip her." Mrs. Collins says with no emotion in her voice, and I scream when the dress is torn from my body, along with my underwear.

I am crying and struggling to breathe with the giant's hand around my throat and as Mrs. Collins stands before me, she says critically, "She'll do. Are you a virgin?"

"Of course." I gasp, because what's that got to do with it? Then I'm horrified when she says coldly to the man holding me, "Deal with that."

I gaze in disbelief as he tugs down his pants and I gasp in horror as his huge cock springs free and he growls, "Spread your legs."

I don't even register what happens next because suddenly, the door crashes open and I hear a gruff, "Move away now."

I am dropped immediately and as I slide down the wall, I note the horrified expressions on the faces of Mrs. Collins and the brute who held me.

I turn to see the murderous expression of the man who escorted me to Mr. Vieri's office as he holds a gun out in front of him. Another man tosses me his jacket, which I use to cover my naked body, and I tremble at the animosity in the room as the first man speaks.

"Come with us, Purity."

I need no further invitation and scurry to his side as Mrs. Collins says fearfully, "I'm sorry, Miss. Sinclair brought her here. I wasn't aware she was protected."

The man doesn't even answer her and just lowers his gun and says darkly, "Nobody must ever know she was here. I am holding both of you responsible for that."

"But Miss. Sinclair…"

"Will be reminded of her position." He says gruffly and then he turns, and I note the gleam in his eye that doesn't make me feel any safer with him.

"Come. There is no job for you here."

"My purse." I say slightly breathlessly, and he nods to the man who tossed me the jacket, and he retrieves it, pressing it into my outstretched arms.

"We're leaving."

I am ushered between them, and once again bundled into a black car, making me wonder if I just swapped one bad experience for another one.

CHAPTER 10

KILLIAN

I took the call, and for the first time since meeting Purity, I relax. She's safe. For now, anyway.

Saint told me they reached her just in time and imagining what would have happened if they were a few minutes later, causes the rage to boil inside me.

"Where is she now?" I growl into the phone and Saint answers, "Sleeping. Locked in the guest suite of the mansion. They drugged her. She should be out for a few hours."

"Get the doctor. Make sure she's comfortable."

I cut the call and feel my blood boiling. Fucking Gabriella. She is making a habit of this little sideline she's got going on. I warned her not to involve Gold Hawk in the less respectable side of my business. Vulnerable women sold to organizations like the one Mrs. Collins runs. Drugged and exploited and imprisoned in a mansion in the middle of nowhere. Gabriella sells her girls with no ties, and they are never seen again all the time they are useful. I warned her not to risk the legitimate side of my business, and now I am pissed.

I make the call.

"I want you in my office now!"

I cut the call, caressing the ball of rage inside me as I wait to dispose of the woman who is now well past her use by date.

As expected, she knocks on my door inside five minutes and I bark, "Enter."

I stare with a blank expression as she walks into the room, her hips swaying from side to side and her eyes laden with suggestive intent.

"You called, sir."

"Sit."

I point to the chair in front of my desk, and she sits, crossing her legs, her skirt revealing she is wearing nothing underneath.

"Did you miss me, Kill?"

She licks her lips and leans forward, her chest bravely trying to stay within the stretched fabric, and I say with cold fury.

"You're fired. Effectively immediately."

"I'm sorry." Her head snaps up in shock and she stares at me with disbelief.

"Clear out your desk. You have five minutes. Security will escort you from the building."

"Why?" Her eyes fill with tears, and I lean forward and snarl, "Mrs. Collins."

Her face pales.

"What about her?"

"You ignored my wishes and are still trading with her. You broke loyalty, so you're out."

"Just one." The tears roll down her face as she says pleadingly, "It was just one more. A girl from a backwater hick town who came to me for help. What else was I supposed to do? She will probably thank me."

"Is that what you believe?"

I shake my head. "You're a fool, Gabriella. You wasted everything for a quick buck. Now get out."

"Are you sure about that, Killian?"

She sits a little taller and her eyes flash as I stare at her with a dead expression.

"I know too much for you to cast me out on the streets with no respect for everything I have done for you."

She leans forward and hisses. "I know everything about you. Your life. Your perversions and your business. Do you really want to lose control of all that?"

I say nothing, and she twists her lips into a sadistic grin.

"I have an insurance policy if you ever thought of double crossing me. Anything happens to me, and you will be arrested for first degree murder and all your crimes are well documented."

I still say nothing, and she laughs softly. "You know how it works, Kill. We protect one another and I have learned from the master. I am just taking out an insurance policy to protect myself because I know how you operate."

I fix her with a dark expression and say slowly, "Are you threatening me, Gabriella?"

I note the pale tinge to her skin and the sweat bead on her forehead, but she maintains a blank expression.

"Of course not. I'm just protecting myself."

"Nothing has changed. You're fired and I never want to see you again."

She stares in disbelief, and I say as an aside, "There is a current vacancy with Mrs. Collins. So, it's not all bad news."

I watch as the penny drops. "Purity. You're talking about Purity."

Her eyes are wide, but I don't react and say roughly, "Time's up."

The door opens and my security guards enter and

Gabriella yells, "Fuck you, Killian. You won't get away with this."

As she is hustled from my office, I hear her screaming abuse all the way to the elevator, and I sigh. Fucking Gabriella. I should have disposed of her years ago. She got too familiar, too caught up in her own self-importance.

Her threats will be extinguished, but her life remains because she is going to play a huge part in bringing down my enemies. She just doesn't know it yet.

* * *

It's dark before I head home and as the car stops at the entrance, I take a minute to consider the reception I'm liable to receive. Women don't come here. I conduct my liaisons at my penthouse in the city. Not my mansion and so it's strange knowing there is one here now. I surround myself with paid bodyguards and I employ an English butler, James Carrigan, who is a blessing because he manages my affairs and I rarely acknowledge his presence.

Now we have a house guest and I wonder what he thinks about that.

However, Purity is here for a different reason entirely, and she doesn't realize how much trouble she is in. I need her for my plan to work and she will have no choice but to comply.

For some reason, I'm relishing the challenge because I love making people do what I tell them, against their wishes if necessary. Money usually helps, but threats and intimidation can change people's minds just as easily.

James meets me at the door, and I say roughly, "Where is she?"

"Still sleeping, sir."

"Still?"

I'm surprised, and he says softly, "Doctor Ramen guesses she had a huge dose of a drug designed to knock a person out for hours. She won't regain full control for a while."

"I see." I'm incensed because I know what Mrs. Collins' plan was. Drug Purity and allow her guests full use of her body while she couldn't react. Some men love that shit, and she always uses it on the new recruits to break their spirits and bring them in line.

James says reverently, "Your supper is waiting, sir."

"I'll be twenty minutes."

He nods and fades into the shadows as always, and I head to my suite of rooms to shower and change. This is my routine when I'm home. Shower, eat, work and end the evening with a night cap and a movie. Wake early and train before breakfast and leave at six am for the office.

I am a creature of habit, but my timetable is very different when I stay in my penthouse in the city. That usually involves an evening of socializing followed by depravity. The women I choose know what to expect and the night is spent testing their limits and honing my skills. Lately it's become more frequent as I struggle for satisfaction, but nothing is doing the trick which is sending me feral.

As I shower, I picture the angel lying a short distance away. I imagine her white hair framing that perfect face. Her untouched body sliding against the silk sheets I always insist on. I imagine her small gasps of pleasure as I work her body to an orgasm, and I wonder what it would feel like to hold such innocence in my arms. I am hard just thinking of it and as I hold my cock and pump furiously, it's with Purity's face in my sights.

Such a pleasure, so untarnished it's a delicious anticipation to claim such a beauty. And I will. Make no mistake about that because Purity Sanders has been brought here for one reason only.

To become my wife.

CHAPTER 11

PURITY

My limbs are heavy, and my brain is foggy. It's a struggle to open my eyes and I strain to listen for any sigh of life. There is nothing. Pure silence.

Something feels cool and soft against my skin, luxurious in fact, and I stretch my limbs tentatively, testing if they still work at all.

I open one eye and then the other and stare at a painted ceiling. At least I think it is, and I gaze in awe at a scene of cherubs and clouds. Am I in heaven? The real one, that is. Did I die? It's a possibility.

I struggle to remember what happened and as the dots connect, the pain of betrayal brings me to my senses, and I gasp with fear as I sit up and stare around me wildly.

Where am I?

For a moment I think hard, and everything comes rushing back. Am I inside that mansion? Did they — he…?

I glance down at my body, that is dressed in a simple cotton nightdress. Who did this?

Peering around me, I notice the grandeur of a room that I never imagined could be real. I'm in a huge bed with silk sheets and fur throws. Chandeliers hang from the ceiling and the walls are decorated in silk paper. Heavy drapes with fringing hang at the windows and glass furniture hold huge flower arrangements.

Beside the bed is a table with a huge lamp and a tray with a pitcher of water and a glass.

Is it safe to drink? What are those pills beside it?

I was drugged. I remember now. It happened so quickly and–

I swallow hard when I remember what happened next and then I was rescued. Or was I?

My legs tremble as I slide them over the side of the bed and, as I attempt to stand, they give way beneath me, causing me to land with a thud on the carpet below.

Almost immediately, the door flies open and as I glance up, my soul shivers when I see who has entered. Him!

My heart fills with terror as he prowls across the room, looking angry somehow.

He says nothing and as he reaches me, in one swift move, he lifts me into his arms and places me carefully back into the bed, glaring down at me with an enigmatic expression.

"I don't understand." My voice wobbles and he surprises me by sitting on the edge of the bed and fixing me with a strangely kind expression.

"I'm sorry, Purity."

"For what?"

"Gabriella."

"Is she here?" I glance past him fearfully and he says angrily, "She's been fired. You won't be seeing her again."

"Fired?" I am so confused, and he exhales sharply. "Gabriella was acting on her own when she took you to Mrs. Collins. She knew exactly what the job would involve, and you were about to be drugged, raped and imprisoned, all to earn money for Mrs. Collins, who would give Gabriella a cut."

I can't take it all in and hate the tears that slide down my stricken face as I stare at him, a broken woman.

"You saved me." I stutter, not understanding why, and he surprises me again by reaching out and dragging his finger across my face, wiping my tears away.

"I did."

"Why?" I'm confused, and he says softly, "I'm still figuring that one out."

His stare alone could slay a million soldiers, and I am struggling to place it. Those eyes fascinate me, and I wonder about the darkness that swirls inside them and the events that placed it there. For a second, we lock eyes, and I couldn't look away if I tried. He is gazing at me with the most intense stare I have ever received in my life, and it surprises me how much I like it.

Then he looks away and says with no emotion. "You are now a guest in my home while you consider the offer I made you. If I'm guessing correctly, you are still without a job, and I have one on the table."

He shakes his head. "You will be incapable of walking for the rest of the day, so I have remained here to assist you."

"Assist me?"

I'm shocked and he nods, turning to face me with a wicked smile on his face.

"I live here alone, Purity. James is my butler, and my bodyguards are men. There is no other person to help you but me because the hell I will let anyone near you after what happened yesterday."

"Why not?" I'm so confused, and he hisses, "Because I trust no one, Purity. I never have, and you are too important to me for that."

"I don't understand. Do you need that vacancy filled so desperately?"

It raises a small smile to his lips, and he nods.

"Yes. I do. There is only one woman who qualifies for the job though and I'm looking at her."

"But why me? I'm not qualified."

"You are the *only* person qualified for the job."

He stands and frowns down on me.

"I expect you are hungry. We will take lunch on the terrace."

"Don't you mean breakfast?"

He laughs softly. "I mean lunch. You have slept for close on twenty-four hours. You need to drink and eat to regain your strength."

Before I can even process this disturbing information, I am shocked when he reaches down and sweeps me into his strong arms and holds me tight against his broad chest. The same chest I have been struggling to ignore ever since he walked into the room because the tight T-shirt attempting to cover it is fighting a distinctly losing battle.

"What are you doing?" I say with embarrassment.

He chuckles softly, "You can't walk, remember, and this is the fastest way to get there."

"But I'm heavy. You'll injure yourself."

"Do I look as if I'm struggling?" He chuckles some more, and I must admit, he doesn't appear to be.

I hold myself rigid and he whispers in my ear, "Relax. You're safe with me."

"Am I?"

I really don't believe I am, and he nods.

"To a point, that is."

"What does that mean?" I reply and he turns and stares deep into my eyes and whispers, "All the time you do as I say."

"And if I don't?"

"You discover who I really am."

"You speak in riddles."

I roll my eyes and for a second, he almost seems amused. It feels strange being carried like a baby and especially by a man like him, and I'm not sure what to think about it. Part of me is scared shitless, and the forbidden part of my soul likes it a lot.

I say nothing more and as he carries me effortlessly down the huge grand staircase, I peer around me with interest. If I thought the room I woke up in was decadent, this place reinforces it. It appears to be lined in gold and polished with silver. There are so many riches, which is sensory overload to a girl who had very little as a child. Possessions were frowned upon, and material things considered the temptation of the Devil.

As I glance up at my ride, I kind of wonder if he knows a lot about what makes the Devil tick. That should scare me senseless, but somehow it makes me even more interested in discovering the man behind the mask of secrets.

We head outside onto a light-filled terrace, and I gasp at the beauty before me. Endless lawns lead down to infinity and a stone terrace sweeps as far as the eye can see along the back of the most colossal mansion.

"Wow."

I gaze in wonder and long to run through the grass and discover the delights around me and as the warm sun kisses my face, I take a deep breath of delightful, cleansing oxygen.

"You have a beautiful home, Mr. Vieri."

"Now you know my name."

He appears amused at that, and I shrug. "The receptionist filled me in. You could have introduced yourself; it was kind of rude."

He arches his brow and appears a little shocked at my

words and I say, "I'm kind of guessing nobody ever calls you out on anything."

"What makes you say that?" He hovers by a deep cushioned chair, and I wait for him to drop me in it, but if anything, his arms tighten around me as he stares at me deeply. It's almost intimate and for a girl who has never experienced any of that, it's confusing.

I must blush because his eyes flash and he whispers, "You are so innocent, Purity, just like your name."

"I am."

I state the obvious and sigh. "Not by choice, though."

I quickly change the subject. "Anyway, you never waited for my answer. That's neglectful, by the way. Questions should always be answered, otherwise they remain questions and you don't progress."

He stares at me as if confused, and I nod toward the chair. "Put me down and tell me why nobody calls you out. Or do they? There must be someone."

To my surprise, he does as I say and as soon as his arms leave me, I am strangely disappointed about that.

I watch as he pulls out the chair beside me and lifts a carafe of water from the table and pours us both a glass and as he hands it to me, he says nonchalantly, "My family make it a habit of calling me out on everything. They are the only ones who get that privilege."

"Your family?"

"My grandparents mainly. My siblings try, but they don't get very far."

"Tell me about them."

I am so hungry for information because family wasn't something that meant a lot in Heaven. There were no siblings because there was a strict one child policy and I wonder what it's like to have a brother or sister.

He says nothing as a man appears with a tray and I stare

61

in wonder as he sets it down and nods respectfully to Mr. Vieri and smiles at me.

"Good afternoon, Miss. Sanders. It's good to see you up and around at last."

"Thank you, um…"

"James, ma'am. If I can assist you in any way, please call."

"Call?"

He smiles gently. "Every room has a control panel, and you only have to press service."

I stare at him in astonishment, and he nods respectfully. "It's my job, ma'am. I like to be kept busy."

He smiles warmly, which is probably the only sign of any warmth around here, the sun excluded, and I watch in silence as he sets two plates of salad before us with a platter of fish and meat on the table to share.

He fills our glasses with a cool crisp wine and says to Mr. Vieri, "Will that be all, sir?"

"It will. Thank you, James."

As he heads off, I whisper, "Why don't you get your own food?"

He shrugs. "Because I pay somebody else to do it."

He nods toward the plate. "Eat. You need to rebuild your strength."

I say nothing and just enjoy the feast before me, marveling at the hidden flavors that have made an innocent salad into a gastronomic pleasure. Occasionally, I steal small glances at the man beside me and wonder about him. He gives nothing away and appears quite brooding, almost as if his mind is working hard even though he rests. There must be a myriad of secrets behind those eyes, and I have always been fascinated by secrets. It's why I'm here now, I suppose, because from an early age I knew I would never be happy living the same life as my mom.

Almost as if he can read minds, he says suddenly. "Tell me about yourself, Purity."

"Is this my interview?" I say with a smile, and he shrugs. "If you like, or it could merely be polite conversation."

"I doubt you do a lot of that, Mr. Vieri, or can I call you by your name?"

He raises his eyes and I shrug, "You call me by my first name, it's only fair."

"I don't believe in fair, Purity."

"What do you believe in~"

I raise my eyes and he grins. "Killian, Kill for short."

"That's an interesting name. I hope you don't live up to it."

For a second his eyes flash, causing the words to stick in my throat because right at this moment, I truly believe that name is well deserved. I don't know why, but there is an underlying sense of evil surrounding this man and yet he has shown me nothing but kindness.

"Do you live up to your name, Purity?"

He says with an amused smile, and I shake my head.

"It's rude to answer a question with a question."

"Then my answer is yes." He says, as if it means nothing, and I swear the blood drains from my face as he raises his eyes, "Your turn."

"Yes." I say, staring him directly in the eyes and I swear they deepen to dark pools of danger.

For a moment we say nothing, our admissions between us both quite shocking in their own way.

Kill.

That is the one word I can't let go and then he breaks the silence by leaning forward and saying huskily, "Good answer."

CHAPTER 12

KILLIAN

The more time I spend with Purity, the more interested I get.

I've never met a woman like her in my entire life. She is so innocent. Unspoilt with a naivety that's adorable. The women I am used to have none of those qualities. They are hard, refined, elegant and sexually aware. She is none of those things. Almost childlike, with a sharp edge that tells me she knows her own mind.

I like that a lot and as I stare into her eyes, I am intrigued by what lies behind them. I want to dive in and discover all her secrets. I want to educate her in what life offers and I want to awaken her sexuality. Reach in and draw it out, every delicious bit of it, and I want to mold her into my perfect woman because of all the women I've ever met, she is the first one who has even come close.

So, I decide. I will have her, own her and ruin her. I will marry her, control her, and keep her. She is my Eve who has tempted the devil this time because now my sight is set on her, she will never escape.

Now my decision is made, a sense of calm washes over

me. It is done. I've found her. The woman who will share my life and bend to my will. The one my grandparents urged me to find. To clean up my act and she is the only one who can help me with that.

"Do I scare you, Purity?"

I'm mildly interested in her response, although I can already guess the answer.

"You interest me, Killian."

"Interest you." It makes me smile because this is refreshing. I like that she isn't afraid when she should be. If she realized what I was capable of, I'm convinced she would look at me very differently.

"In what way?"

"I have never met a man like you before."

"And you have met many men in your life."

I doubt it, and she nods. "Not really, but the ones I am used to aren't worth my interest."

"Why not?"

"Because they don't see past their own needs and believe women are there purely to serve them."

"What makes you think I'm different?"

"I don't." She shrugs and takes a sip of wine, and grimaces. "This stuff is disgusting."

She grabs the water and I think of the price of this wine, and it makes me raise my eyes. "Disgusting?"

"I prefer water. It's what I'm used to."

"So, you don't drink alcohol."

"No. I was never allowed."

"What else weren't you allowed?"

"Freedom." She says it with no emotion and her answer only reinforces how perfect she is for me because freedom won't be something she enjoys with me, so she won't miss it.

"Freedom is overrated."

"Says the man who has his freedom."

65

"You think I am free."

"From where I am sitting you are."

"Then you know nothing, Purity."

"I know my own mind. They can't take that from me."

As I glance her way, she stares at me with an honest expression, and I have an overwhelming urge to keep her. The thought of her enjoying her freedom is not a pleasant one because a woman like Purity wouldn't last five minutes in the world I live in.

I remind her of that by saying cruelly. "Your desire for freedom nearly backfired on you. There are unscrupulous people who trade on women like you. I hope you're aware of that."

"Women like me." She cocks her head to one side and fixes me with her astonishing eyes.

"Innocent. Naive and foolish."

"You don't have a high opinion of me, Killian. Or is that women in general?"

It makes me laugh out loud, and she stares in surprise. "That made you laugh. Why?"

"Because you don't give a fuck what you say, Purity and it's refreshing."

"I speak the truth. Why hide it?"

"Because the truth is sometimes best hidden."

My phone rings and I glance down, noting the number and say with a sigh. "Business calls."

I make to leave because my business is not for innocent ears and then I change my mind because I am interested in her reaction.

"Saint."

"Jefferson Stevenson wants to do a deal."

"That didn't take long."

"Are you surprised at that?"

He laughs softly. *"Shall I arrange a meeting?"*

"Arrange dinner. The dining room. Seven tonight. Tell him to bring a plus one. It will be a social occasion."

"Consider it done."

As I cut the call, it reminds me why Saint is invaluable to me. He arranges everything with no questions attached. If he disagrees, he re-words it differently, causing me to think again. He is a Master of Planning, and always operates ten steps ahead, which is why I value him so much. To others, he's my bodyguard; he is way more than that. He is my defense, my conscience and my confidante.

I turn to Purity and fix her with a blank expression. "The job."

She looks interested.

"After your attempt at finding your own employment, I would consider this very carefully. My offer remains on the table. Do you accept?"

"No."

I shake my head. "A strange choice of word when there is no other option. Explain."

"Who said I don't have options?"

"Which are?" I'm calling her bluff because I know she ran away from home and it's the last place she probably wants to return to.

"I can go and stay with my best friend in Washington. I only need to call, and they will come and get me and allow me to stay with them."

"Your best friend."

This is interesting, and she nods. "You underestimate me, Killian. Most people do. You see, I ran away from Heaven after a carefully considered plan. I wanted a better life and the last thing I want is to be controlled by a man. I have watched the women in Heaven lose their identities the moment they marry a man their parents choose for them. I never wanted that and so I planned my escape. Miss. Sinclair gave me a starting point, but it didn't work out. You are offering me money, but not a lot else. It's obvious you buy people, Killian. I know that already. People to serve you both in the office and at home. I'm not interested in that. I can do that in Heaven, so thank you for your help, but I'll decline your kind offer and call my friend instead."

"Then what would make you stay, Purity?"

She stares across the terrace to the view below and says slightly wistfully, "Freedom of choice, I suppose. Opportunities to live my best life. To explore, to discover and to learn."

She turns and stares directly into my eyes and says, slightly sadly.

"I never had that chance. Never hoped life would be any different from what I had in Heaven. I heard talk of it. I snuck into a neighbor's home and learned through his television. I listened to conversations I shouldn't have, and I kept an open mind. I want to discover what life is really about, Killian, and stuck here with you is quite restrictive of that."

It makes me smile because if only she understood what I could offer her.

"There is also the moral reason why I can't stay with you?" She adds with a slight shake of her head.

"Moral?" This I must hear because morality isn't something I ever consider.

"We are not married. It would be a sin to share a home with a man. If I worked for you, I would need my own apartment. My own life outside of this one."

Now this is refreshing and so I decide to change direction as I discover the weakness in her argument.

"What if we were married, Purity? Would that change anything?"

"If we were married, Killian, you would control me, and I will never be happy with that."

"Even if the marriage was a business arrangement and nothing more."

"I don't understand." She is genuinely confused, and I lean back and say in a firm voice.

"We become husband and wife, as a contract. I need a wife to help me secure business and you want to travel, to explore and to live your best life. You will have all of that with me and more. I won't curtail your freedom, but I will protect you from what that can mean. We live here and work together for our mutual benefit."

"A business arrangement. Nothing more."

I can tell she's interested, and I nod.

"A partnership."

"And you will pay me for that."

I can sense her mind working hard and I nod. "The sum written on the paper stands. I will deposit it into your own bank account, and you will have full control over it. All I ask is for your help in accompanying me socially."

"Is that it?"

She chews on her bottom lip and appears to contemplate my offer, and then she sighs heavily.

"It doesn't seem right."

"Why not?"

I lean forward. "It is no different to the married life you described back in Heaven. However, this time you are in charge."

"Of you." She appears a little excited by that and it makes me laugh.

"Of *you*, Purity. You decide. You are not required to cook, clean, bear my children, or bow to my wishes. This is business and nothing else. Now, do we have a deal?"

"I'll need time to consider it."

This time, I roll my eyes.

"You had time and look where that got you."

"Exactly. I need time."

It makes me smile.

"Then you have one hour, Purity."

It makes her smile.

"May I sit here and consider it?"

"Of course."

I stand.

"I will return in one hour's time. Do you need anything before I leave?"

"I don't think so."

"The bathroom perhaps."

She blushes a pretty shade of pink.

"No. I'll, um, wait. How long before I get my movement back?"

"Anytime now, Purity."

"Then I'll wait. Thank you for asking."

I nod and as I turn to go, she surprises me by saying softly. "I appreciate the offer, though."

I turn. "I don't need your appreciation, Purity. I need the answer to be yes."

As I walk away, I am almost interested to see what happens if she says no.

CHAPTER 13

PURITY

I like it here. As the sun kisses my skin, I turn my face to welcome it. The fact I've slept for close on a whole day has sharpened my mind and dealt with any demons I may have brought along with me for the ride.

I remember what happened yesterday with a mild curiosity rather than fear. If anything, it has taught me not to trust a kind smile and a well-meaning gesture. The devil comes in many forms, and it appears Miss. Sinclair was cloaking hers with kindness and concern. I will not make the same mistake again.

The possibility of what may have happened terrifies me. That man was a brute. Cold, emotionless, and rough.

I've always wondered what happens between a man and a woman in private. Wondering what those strange feelings are when I'm alone. My reaction to an attractive man makes me hope there's more to life than what my family told me.

Sex in Heaven happens between a married couple for the purpose of procreation. Do they only do that once? I doubt it.

When Faith told me what it was like with Jonny, I hung

on her every word. She had a dreamy expression on her face and her eyes shone with happiness. My mother has never looked like that.

Then there's Killian Vieri. A man who wants to be my husband for whatever reason he has. That thought alone causes my skin to tingle and my heart to leap inside. Is it through joy or fear? I am yet to figure that out. Will he expect that privilege as a benefit of our contract? I wonder what I feel about that.

I'm curious, definitely, but scared at the same time. I'm guessing he knows what to do. I don't.

Will he require a child from me? Is that part of the deal? He has that right and as his wife, I will be unable to deny him. I've been educated my entire life in what a husband expects from his wife, and I never questioned it.

I am now.

The breeze tickles my face and I glance down at my outstretched legs. There is a slight tingle in my left one and I tentatively test it out. My toes move and I breathe a deep sigh of relief as it shifts a little. Feeling brave, I test the other one and almost weep when it responds.

I edge slightly to the edge of my seat and test the ground. They are wobbly, but I'm able to stand and I clutch the side of the table for support.

It feels good to stand. Good to be me again. Independent and free. Isn't that what I wanted, but now I'm faced with the same contract I ran from. Marriage.

I sit down and reach for the jug of water, pouring the crystal water into the glass and sip the contents as I consider what I want.

It would be so easy to head inside and make the call that would end this adventure and take me on a new one. Call the men that rescued Faith to do the same for me.

They were kind. I was safe with them, but that was Faith's salvation. Not mine.

I've always wanted more. I deserve more and Chicago was the land of opportunity that would deliver me from evil.

I always believed that, and perhaps this is God's intervention. He always intended me to find Killian Vieri because he is the man who will deliver what I want.

The opportunity to live life on my terms.

So many doubts surface when I think about him. He scares me – a lot. His dark, brooding eyes and strong jaw tell me he's a man who is used to getting what he wants. That chest that smelled divine when I snuggled against it and those strong arms that held me so tenderly caused a reaction I am still struggling to understand. I felt something in those arms. More than one thing. They were safe, strangely addictive, and I was disappointed when he freed me.

His personality could sure use some work and this place may as well have tumbleweed blowing through it. He's a strange one for sure, but maybe I could work on that.

When he fired Miss. Sinclair, I was delighted. I admired that about him. He didn't agree with what she did and acted accordingly. That proves he is a good man. An honorable man. He has acted courteous, polite, and is a gentleman. Could he also be my husband?

I glance around at the mansion that sprawls in the countryside like a majestic jewel. It is the biggest, most magnificent building I've ever seen in my life. Is it a home, though? Will I be happy here?

There are so many questions causing me to switch between decisions and the hour passes quickly when I see the man himself heading out into the sunlight.

My reaction to him astonishes me because it's as if my body wakes up and is anticipating his return. A soft shiver of pleasure ripples through it as I react to his appearance.

He is possibly the most attractive man I have ever met, and it appears I am attracted to him. Is that enough, though?

My grains of sand have hit the bottom of the timer because he approaches and fixes me with a calculating expression.

"Your decision is…"

He drops into the seat he vacated what seems like seconds ago and fixes me with a brooding stare that heats my blood curiously.

"With certain conditions, I believe I have."

He smirks, causing me to laugh softly.

"You have already guessed my answer?"

"Your conditions gave it away."

"I haven't told you what they are."

"You didn't need to. The fact they are a consideration means you will accept, but require negotiation. I like that."

"You do?"

"It's best business practice and we both know this is a business arrangement, so I would be disappointed if you had no conditions."

He leans back in his chair and studies me through deepening eyes, and it fascinates me. My mouth dries as I stare at him, but I can't say the same about the heat that spreads through my body like a bush fire.

He affects me, but I don't understand why, and I shake him out of my head and fix him with cool regard instead.

"The contract will be drawn up professionally with the conditions attached."

"Of course."

I take a deep breath.

"We work together as equals."

"In our marriage, of course."

"Good. Um, children?"

He raises his eyes and I say quickly. "Will you be expecting me to provide you with one?"

"One?" He appears almost amused.

"Well. Do you?"

He appears to consider his answer and then says with a wicked smile.

"Yes."

"Oh" I am hot at the thought of being intimate with this man for that purpose.

"So, we will, um, be intimate, once."

Now he openly smiles and then leans forward and says almost tenderly, "Only once, Purity? It takes quite a bit of practice to produce a child."

"It does?" I'm shocked at that, and he appears almost sad and surprises me by placing his hand over mine, an act that shocks me a little and says kindly, "We won't do anything you are not happy with. It is not the purpose of this marriage."

"Oh."

I take a deep breath and nod, trying to regain control and stop my heart from beating so fast.

"I would like my own room, if possible."

He appears amused. "There are ten bedrooms. You can take your pick."

"Ten!"

I'm shocked and he shrugs. "They came with the house."

It makes me giggle because he is surprising me. Somehow, he is different from what I first expected. Softer perhaps, and I like that.

"The job, what would it involve? I may need training."

I say innocently and his eyes flash as he rubs his chin and stares at me through darkening eyes.

"I will train you personally."

Again, a shiver passes through me as his gaze runs the length of me and I know I should be extremely afraid right now. But somehow, I'm more excited than afraid and it's as if I am falling into a deep abyss that has no bottom.

There are so many emotions inside me and sensations I have never experienced before, and it's all because of him and the opportunity he is offering me.

"Will we travel?"

I'm eager for details and he nods. "I own a private jet. We can go anywhere in the world. Just ask."

"The world!" My eyes are wide because this is unexpected.

He will give me the world.

That is an offer I would be a fool to refuse.

He leans forward and says in a deep, husky voice.

"I can offer you a life you could never imagine. There is nothing I can't give you. The only thing I expect in return is loyalty. You will enjoy freedom in our marriage to an extent as you desire, but it must always be business first."

"What extent?" My heart is beating furiously, and I recognize it's excitement and he says with an intensity to his expression that takes my breath away.

"You trust me. Don't question me and accept that everything I do is for your safety and comfort. I will educate you, teach you how to be the perfect woman, and build you into a strong one. You will push aside everything you think you know because you know nothing, Purity. The world is a dangerous, amazing place that can be beautiful with the right man beside you, or it can be brutal. You have already experienced that brutality. Let me show you the beautiful side."

"Okay." I nod my head slowly, knowing I couldn't say no if I tried. He is telling me everything I ever wanted to hear and is staring at me as if I am the most important person in his life. It's intoxicating, intense and addictive, and right in this moment, I trust this man with my soul.

"Okay?"

He raises his eyes and I say slightly breathlessly. "I accept your offer in principle. Draw up the contract and I will read it through and if I am happy, I will sign it. Thank you for the offer, Mr. Vieri. I won't let you down."

For some reason, he smiles but the expression in his eyes doesn't match. If anything, they are even more turbulent now as something flashes in them I can't quite place. It strips the breath from inside me and causes my heart to race and I couldn't look away now if I tried because it's as if he has cast a deep spell over me and my soul now belongs to him.

CHAPTER 14

KILLIAN

She said yes. I am almost disappointed about that because I relish the kill. The fight and the ultimate win. However, the most delicious part of this contract is ruining her soul and molding her into my perfect woman to slay my enemies.

Tearing away her innocence and crushing that hope that sparkles in her eyes. She belongs to me now and I must tread carefully until she signs on the broken line. I will be Prince fucking Charming until I reveal the devil inside because Purity Sanders has just agreed to be my weapon, to forge a dynasty that will ensure the Dark Lords is brought back firmly under the control of the family who created it in the first place.

Clean up your act, my grandfather said. Become whiter than white and control your enemies, giving them no weapons to use to create your downfall. Purity will shroud my dark edges and radiate light in the darkest world. She is my salvation and my revenge, and I will enjoy every second of it.

She looks so happy I bask in it. Women don't look like

that when they do business with me. There is emptiness in their eyes as they sign their soul over to me, knowing they had no other choice. They know the price. She does not and so I drown in her innocence, loving how it runs like a sweet balm over my battered soul. I want to reach out and touch it. To caress it, savor it and inhale it. Pure innocence doesn't visit me often and now it's here I am never letting it go.

I extend my hand and as her small soft one settles inside the power radiates through me. It calms the vile blood that runs like an evil virus through my body. The blood of the damned that met their ruin through what I want. Hers mingles with theirs as I smile into her eyes, loving the pure honesty in her eyes as she smiles into mine.

"Come. I'll show you around your new home."

She nods with an excitement that makes me smile. So eager. I wonder how long it will take for that light to dim in her eyes when the full reality of her situation reaches out and socks her hard.

I cling onto her hand, loving that I have conquered her already, and she doesn't even know it, and as we walk back into the house, I make easy conversation.

It takes a while to show her around my home. It's rare I do the tour myself and seeing it through her eyes is refreshing. Every room we head into causes her to gasp and squeeze my hand a little more and the light in her expression makes me smile.

"I love your home, Killian." She smiles as we head upstairs, and I nod. "Thank you."

"How old is it?"

"Three years."

"Really, it seems older than that. In a good way, of course." She adds quickly and I shrug. "It suits me."

"But it's so large. Don't you get lonely?" She enquires, and I shake my head. "I don't. I sleep, eat and work out here.

Catch a bit of television before I head to bed. I work most of the day and into the night and occasionally head out to functions."

"On your own?" She adds hesitantly and I shake my head.

"No. I have companions."

"Oh." She falls silent and I say dismissively, "They are convenient. Women who enjoy an expensive meal in the finest restaurant or attending the most sought-after show in town. They make up a space beside me. That is all."

"Is that what you're paying me to do?"

Her voice catches and I know how desperate a woman like Purity is for the fairy tale. It's just a shame she opened the wrong book.

"Yes." I turn and note the disappointment clouding her eyes and taking her face in my hands, I adore her startled expression as I hover close to her lips and whisper, "Your job is very different to that. I've never had a wife before and that affords you my respect."

Her lip trembles and her eyes sparkle as her breathing intensifies and I say huskily, "Our relationship will be a more intimate one. Are you okay with that?"

She is like a frightened animal caught in a trap and she trembles in my grasp causing a rush of power to surge through me as I hold pure innocence in my hands.

"Yes." Her answer is slightly breathless, and I can't help myself as my lips gently touch hers, tasting sweet against my seasoned ones. Her lips part easily, and I inhale the sweet scent of fresh air and honey that promises to become my addiction. So fresh, so pure, like an unwrapped book of secrets waiting to be told. Untouched and pure, something I never knew would be intoxicating until now.

For my own self-preservation I pull away and love the disappointment that clouds her eyes and say firmly, "Allow me to show you the bedrooms."

Her breath is racing, and I love the pink tinge to her cheeks as she scampers after me as I head toward the nearest bedroom. She appears almost distracted as I show her around and then as we step inside my own suite of rooms, I sense the tense atmosphere as she stands in the doorway and whispers, "This room smells of you."

"Interesting." I turn and smile softly. "Tell me what I smell of."

"Sandalwood, musk, and temptation."

She stares straight into my eyes as she says it and I have a renewed respect for Purity Sanders.

"Temptation." I cock my head to one side, and she nods slowly. "You wear your masculinity like an aftershave. It's intense, intriguing and potent. This room smells like that. It feels forbidden, almost as if I shouldn't be here. Intimate even and as if it holds a million secrets. Like you."

"You are correct." Her eyes widen and I sit on the bed and stare at her malevolently, causing her to shift on her feet and clasp her fingers together as if in prayer.

"I am ruthless, Purity. It goes with the job."

"Acquisitions?" she says nervously, and I nod.

"I take things and either tear them apart or build them up to be more magnificent. If they have potential, they become better, if there is no hope, I put them out of their misery."

"Am I an acquisition?" She says bravely and her direct gaze heats my blood as I say huskily, "I suppose you are."

"Which category do I fall into?" She says with bated breath. "Will you build me up or tear me down?"

"That depends on whether I see potential or not."

She nods, glancing around the room and then, smiling, says softly. "Maybe I should steal a page from your book and do the same to you."

"That would be interesting."

"It would."

She moves closer with small baby steps and says with a slight hitch to her voice. "I'm guessing you don't like to lose, Killian. I imagine you get everything you want in life and anything you don't have you didn't want in the first place. I wonder what you would do if something was so far out of reach you couldn't grasp it. What would you do then?"

She is closer now and, in a flash, I reach out and grasp her wrist, tugging her sharply onto my lap and pulling her arm behind her back with one hand and tilting her face to mine with the other. Then I whisper against her lips, "I reach for a ladder."

Her soft laugh makes me smile and I am so tempted to take her now. To unravel the innocence and watch it drift from her soul forever. To turn the innocent into the starving wanton slut women become around me. To crave what I can do and beg for more. To ruin it and crush it under my depraved ravenous appetite and to hear her scream my name as she comes so hard it shatters her soul.

It would be so easy. To deal with something that is inevitable. However, the fun is in the chase, and I am having way more fun than I've had in ages, so I release her and smile respectfully.

"Come. The contract is ready to be signed."

"So soon."

She appears amazed about that, and I laugh softly, "I gave you one hour, Purity. I used that time wisely and had the contract drawn up. It has arrived in my inbox, so we will print it out and sign it. Then we can begin."

"Begin?"

Her face is flushed and I fucking love it and as I stare at the excitement shining in her eyes, I wonder if somehow, in one twisted fucked up way, fate has delivered the better half of my soul.

CHAPTER 15

PURITY

We head downstairs and toward his den. I remember it from my tour and although I gained a swift glimpse, I already knew it was an intimidating place. Dark paneled walls are illuminated by subdued lighting. The thick dark blue carpet appears brand new, and the bookcases set along the far wall are bursting with books that look as if they have never been read.

Three chairs are placed around a desk behind which is one huge leather studded chair that provides a throne for the king, and I really do look at him like that because Killian Vieri conducts himself as a ruler. He has an aura and a presence that commands attention and respect.

There is an oil painting above a huge fireplace of a beautiful house surrounded by orange groves, and I love the peace in that painting. I can sense the warmth of the sun and feel the breeze causing the leaves on the trees to sway. I stare in awe, wondering where on earth this place is and I'm surprised when he stands by my side and whispers huskily, "Serenita."

"Is that what it's called?"

I'm in awe of it and he nods, a certain pride in his voice.

"It is home."

"Where you were raised?"

"No. Where my family live. My grandparents."

"Is it far?"

"Italy. An island off the coast. Nobody goes there but the Vieri family."

"Your family owns their own island?"

I'm shocked and he laughs softly. "You will soon learn that my family owns a lot more than one small island. Not all of it is good. Serenita is special, though. We will marry there."

"In Italy?"

I must sound shocked because he nods, turning to face me with an amused grin.

"I will show you the world, Bella. We will explore it together."

His hand finds mine and as we stare at the painting side by side, a warm sensation floods through my entire body. I have never been so happy. So cared for and so needed. To experience those feelings with a man like Killian Vieri is unexpected and not altogether unwelcome. I can't believe how lucky I have been because he is everything I want and a lot more besides. I am just astonished he isn't already married because who wouldn't be ecstatic about marrying a man like him?

I am in so deep I couldn't clamber out if I tried and I turn to face him with a broad smile and whisper, "Then I should sign your contract."

He nods, his eyes gleaming as if they are on fire, and my breath hitches when he directs that powerful gaze in my direction.

"Come."

He leads me across to the desk and instead of directing me to one of the two seats set before it, he leads me around to the throne and holding it out gently, guides me inside.

I see a pile of paper on the desk covered with small print and I raise my eyes.

"Is this it?"

"Yes. You may read through it, and if there is anything you disagree with, we will negotiate."

"Okay." I lift the first page and he says with amusement.

"You may need longer than an hour to read through this."

"Then you will allow me an extension even if it takes all week." I say in a hardened voice, causing him to laugh out loud.

"Spoken like a true Vieri, Purity. Are you certain we're not related already?"

"Unless your family was brought up in Heaven, I doubt it." I say quickly and he replies with a dark whisper against my ear, "My family would be more at home in hell."

It causes a shiver to run through my entire body and I can't decide if it's his words or his proximity that caused it.

I am so confused by my reaction to this man and as the words swim before my eyes, I realize I am out of my depth. Numbers, figures and weird foreign words don't make any sense to me and after a couple of pages I am so bored I really can't face reading the rest.

In a show of bravado, I flick through the pages and say firmly, "You asked me to trust you, Killian. This will be the first test of that. If there is anything in here that I don't like, I trust you to change it on an ad hoc basis."

"Ad hoc." He laughs out loud. "Where did you hear that from?"

"I'm not stupid, you know." I say tartly, and he smiles. His mouth betraying him as it twists into an amused grin.

"You are far from stupid, Purity. In fact, you are many things, but stupid is not one of them."

"What things?" He is so close now we could touch lips and I wouldn't mind seeing what that would be like, and he whispers against them. "You are beautiful, courageous and bold. You aren't afraid to speak your mind and you are honest. I can tell you have a caring side and yet question everything. You are pure like your name and untouched. That makes you more valuable to me than any of the riches I own. You. Are. Everything."

My eyes burn as I turn away and stare at the contract resting on the blotter on the polished wooden desk.

He whispers in my ear. "All I require is your signature, and then we can begin."

My fingers hover over the pen and a moment's doubt filters through my mind. I should read it thoroughly. Dissect every word, but I'm new to this. I don't understand contracts and business speak. I work on gut instinct and my own judgment. He is a good man. I can tell that already because he saved me from the bad ones. He has been a gentleman and I do believe I'm safe with him. If anything, I feel a little foolish even hesitating and so I grasp the pen and boldly sign my name with a flourish, confident that I am doing the right thing.

"Good girl." His husky voice is soft against my ear and his lips dust my cheek as he whispers, "You are mine now."

His. That word doesn't scare me half as much as it should because wasn't that always my destiny, anyway. To belong to a man. However, I have *chosen* this one. My parents had nothing to do with it. I am no longer under their rule, I'm under his and he has assured me of a freedom I would never get from them. Definitely not from any husband they choose for me in Heaven and so a thrill runs through my entire body knowing I have changed my path in life. Me. Purity Sanders. I took a chance, and I ran from home. I knew Chicago would deliver, and it has. Him.

He pulls away and lifts the pen that resides by the leather blotter on the polished wooden desk.

I gaze up into his eyes and swallow hard at the dark menace in his expression that wasn't there before. It surrounds him and consumes me, and I stare in wonder as he changes before my eyes. If anything, the soft edges have been sharpened and there is a power to him that intoxicates as well as terrorizes and I can't tear my eyes from his as he pulls me from my chair and into those strong arms I desire so much.

He tilts my face to meet his and almost growls as he lowers his lips to mine and sucks my bottom lip into his mouth. My heart pounds and my breath deserts me as he crashes those lips against mine and positively devours me. His tongue edges inside and claims mine, the rough scuff on his jaw scratching against my skin. His hand pushes my back closer into his chest and his leg somehow positions itself between mine.

He is hard, dangerous and intimidating, but it doesn't scare me. It should. I know that now, but as he fists my hair and holds it tight, there is a sensation passing through my body that tells me it likes this. It likes him and as he deepens the kiss, I shift a little closer. Wanting something I don't know anything about.

His hand runs down my side and presses against my breast, the thin fabric of the cotton nightdress no defense against it. With a deep growl, he lowers the straps from my shoulders and, as the top falls, I jump a little because this seems wrong. It must be, but why don't I care?

I am curious. Faith said she felt an intense urge to experience something unfamiliar when Jonny touched her, and now I'm feeling it too. With him.

I gasp when he lowers his lips to my breasts and takes one into his mouth. Biting down forcefully on the tiny bud, causing me to gasp with pain but desire it more.

He presses in and the thin cotton becomes an irritant that he deals with swiftly as he tears it from my body, leaving me naked against him.

I yelp into his mouth because this is a sin. We are not married, despite what the paper says, and he pulls back and hisses, "You belong to me now, Purity. You gave me the right."

I can't argue with that, but is this what was written in the small print? It must have been, otherwise he wouldn't be doing it.

He shocks me by stepping back and staring openly at my naked body that trembles before him. He is fully dressed, and I feel vulnerable and exposed.

"You are beautiful." He says with appreciation, and I blush like a furnace as he drags his gaze over every part of my body.

"Turn around," he commands, and I do as he says because then I can't see him. That's better, surely, and yet as I stand shivering in the center of his office, I catch his reflection in the mirror on the wall and it excites me all over again.

He is removing his T-shirt and I can't tear my eyes away. That huge chest is covered in dark hair that only makes him even more masculine somehow. His muscles dance in the reflection and I hitch my breath because he is magnificent.

I jump when his belt is torn from his jeans and they drop to the ground, revealing a tight pair of underpants that leaves nothing to the imagination. Then I squeeze my eyes tightly shut when he tears them off and I see what he was hiding beneath them.

I should be so afraid right now, but I am too far gone for anything than to go forward. I want to discover what is spoken of in low tones and hushed whispers. I want to become a woman, and this must be what happens when the contract is signed. I don't want to appear naive to that and I trust him. He told me to.

CHAPTER 16

KILLIAN

I couldn't stop myself if I tried. As soon as she signed the contract, it lit a fuse inside me that went out of control pretty damn quickly. I am burning up because the thought of owning such a beauty is like pouring gasoline on a naked flame.

I will have her now, in this room, on top of that fucking contract and she will soon learn that I do what the fuck I like, whenever I like. I don't consider her feelings. I don't think about how scared she must be. She has given herself to me and that is all that concerns me now. Purity may have feelings, desires and needs, but I am not wasting time considering them. I am starting as I mean to go and doing whatever I god-damned like.

I advance and fist her hair in a cruel hand, flinging aside the fact she's a virgin and deserves a vanilla kind of experience. I'm not vanilla and I never have been, and she gets the man I want her to get.

She feels so good against my rough hand. So soft; tantalizingly so. I could caress her skin all day and plant soft kisses over the whole of her. Perhaps I will, but not now. Now she must become mine before the ink dries on the contract. It will be brutal and savage and if she can't deal with that, she will soon learn.

I drop my greedy lips to her neck and suck in hard, savoring the taste of her sweet flesh as she trembles in my arms.

I cup her breast with my right hand and squeeze her nipple hard, loving the groan that spills from her sweet lips. Then I drop my hands and spread her legs, leaning her back against me, my cock pushing hard against her ass.

She moans sweetly and as my fingers play with her clit, she cries out as her first orgasm hits her hard. Perfect.

I sense her throbbing against my fingers, her sticky heat coating my fingers, and I raise them and stuff them into her mouth, growling, "Taste your desire on me."

She sucks my fingers clean, which causes me to growl because this is the most potent drug I have ever had. Innocence is addictive it seems and so I spin her around and push her back on the desk, lifting her hips so her ass is against the contract.

She is flushed and her eyes sparkle as she gazes at me and I press down on her chest, so she falls back on the desk, my legs sweeping hers aside as I position myself between them.

"Trust me, Purity." I say with a wicked grin, and she nods, too far gone to stop this if she tried.

As I ease in a little, I hiss at the pleasure it creates. Knowing she is untouched and that no man has been here before. It's as if I have found the Holy Grail and for a second, I savor the anticipation.

The sweat is sliding down her brow and I can smell her arousal. It sends the blood rushing through my body as I prepare to conquer and as I thrust in hard, her agonized scream is the sweetest sound in the world. I tear through her innocence, relishing every single fucking second of it as she cries out in pain and alarm.

I love it. I love knowing I have discovered new territory and lean down and lick her tears that fall with my greedy tongue.

Her sobs are music to my ears as I thrust harder, scraping her virgin walls, making my mark. Then I touch her clit and press down on the throbbing bundle of nerves, loving how she relaxes around my hard cock, a fresh burst of wet heat driving away the damage.

As I stare into her stricken eyes, I move slowly, building up her expectation once again and as her body relaxes and welcomes me in, her gasp of desire replaces the tortured one.

We are closer than two people can be and as I fuck her slowly and deeply, I stare into her eyes the entire time. She bites down on her lip and in a feral haze, I lean down and do it for her in a far more brutal way. The blood that spills is nectar on my tongue, and she cries out as I growl, "Those lips are mine now. You only get to taste them when I fucking say so."

I thrust deeper, harder, punishing her for taking what was mine and as her back slides against the contract, I hope every fucking word of it is imprinted on her back. She signed her life away to me and she doesn't even know it. I own her body and her mind, and she will do everything I tell her to. She is mine to ruin and I can't fucking wait, so I tear through her body like a wild animal as she struggles to keep up.

As my release hovers on the edge, I grip her neck with one hand and roar as I spill my seed deep inside my woman for the very first time. It comes on huge waves of ecstasy and to my delight, her own isn't far behind.

Her screams tear through the air like the cries of the damned and it makes my soul sing. Her orgasm hits her hard, and she sobs as her body betrays her and delivers wave upon wave of euphoria, coating her with desire for me. She can't fight it.

Her body is screaming for release, and it overpowers her rational thought. I grip her hair and fuck her until I have nothing left, and she lies like a crumpled heap on an extremely crumpled contract.

As I pull out, my cum spills onto the paper and I smirk with pride. There is no going back now. Purity knows no different and everything I do to her she will think is expected. How lucky am I?

I pull out and move away fast, tossing her the cotton nightdress to clean herself up.

I love seeing the blood staining the fabric and I almost consider continuing this pleasant pastime.

However, we have dinner reservations, and I must find her an outfit, so I say coolly. "Come with me. You need to clean up and take a nap while I arrange your outfit for tonight." The fact she is naked as I open the door doesn't concern me. If the cameras pick her up, they will all know she belongs to me now.

She peers around her nervously and whispers, "I can't go out there. People will see me."

"What people, Purity?" I say with amusement, loving the angry flush that stains her cheeks.

"James. Your bodyguards."

I shrug.

"They won't care. Neither should you."

I pull her from the room, her hand locked in mine, and as we take the stairs, she says with a slight hint of anger, "What just happened?"

"We sealed the deal, Purity. It's what happens when two people are engaged to be married. Didn't you enjoy it?"

"I, um, well..."

I spin around and face her, causing her to stumble and as I lift her chin, I stare at her with a malevolent gaze.

"Did you enjoy it?" I say with a dark edge to my voice, and she nods, despite probably wishing she could deny it.

"Yes." she says in a whisper, and I smirk.

"So, what's the problem?"

I turn and pull her after me, stopping outside her room and as I open the door, I say coolly, "Take a shower. I'll be back with your outfit for tonight. Grab some rest. We are in for a busy night."

Before she can answer me, I slam the door behind her and turn the lock. She can't escape me now. No matter how much she may be regretting her decision right now. Once again, I have got exactly what I want, and I am looking forward to teaching her every single fucking rule she must follow when she becomes my wife.

CHAPTER 17

PURITY

I can't believe what just happened. My body has been torn apart as if a wild animal was let loose on it. It hurts — everywhere and I can hardly walk. My insides are on fire and my lips are bruised. My head hurts where he pulled my hair, and I can feel the blood trickling between my thighs.

How did I not know that happens? Why didn't my own mom warn me about that? It hurt like hell, but I loved every minute. I craved it in fact and when the initial pain subsided, I wanted more.

I am wicked. A sinner and yet I have a smile on my face because of *him*.

As I wander toward the door at the end of the room, I can already tell it leads to a fully equipped bathroom. It's open and the gleaming tub is welcoming me in.

I stare at my refection in the full-length mirror and marvel at how different I look. My hair is tousled and my skin on fire. My lips are swollen and there is bruising on my neck and body. I am bleeding and broken and yet I'm ecstatic. Euphoria is washing away the pain that tells me I'm a woman now.

His woman.

The fact he roared my name as he planted his seed in my womb made me smile. I did that. I pleased him. Me. Innocent Purity Sanders. The virgin from Heaven who was destined to be a man's wife. I will be *his* wife and if that's what's involved, I'm more than happy about it.

As I run the bath, I empty a bottle of lotion into it and feel slightly alarmed when the foam spills over the edge onto the tiles below. Will he be angry? I've messed up the bathroom.

Spying some huge white towels rolled up under the vanity, I grab them and attempt to dry the floor. All it does is cause me to slip and fall heavily on my back, causing me to cry out in pain.

Fuck, that was bad. It's almost as if I've broken something. I'm winded and as I stare up at the ceiling, my own reflection stares back at me.

A mirror. On the ceiling. Whoever thought of that? However, it makes me giggle when I see the woman staring back at me. I did it. I made it happen and I have no regrets at all.

Running my hands over my body, I wonder if it's changed somehow. It feels a little fuller, more like a woman. Would it happen that fast?

I'm a mess. A bloodied tousled mess and yet I feel more alive than I ever felt in my life. I did it. I made my own decision and I'm convinced it's the right one.

Gingerly, I use the tub to pull myself up and close off the taps. Aching to dip in the hot sweet water to wash the fluids away. As I lower my body into the tub, I groan with appreciation because this feels so god-damned good.

I submerge myself, allowing the water to wash over my head and it is so peaceful under here. Like a serene land that only I inhabit, and I let the warm water attend my wounds while I remember every delicious second of saying goodbye to my virginity.

Am I pregnant now? Was that the one and only time I will go through that? I am disappointed if it is. Hopeful that it didn't work so we could try again. It happened the first time for Faith. She grew the result of that, and I wonder what it would be like.

So many thoughts run through my mind as I come to terms with what just happened.

As my body adjusts, my mind does too and it's with a smile on my face that I creep into the silken sheets and hug the soft pillow, drifting off to a delicious dream where everything in my life is perfect.

* * *

I'M WOKEN by a soft touch to my face and as I open a weary eye, I see Killian staring into my eyes with a darkly intense expression.

"Bellissima, Bella." He says huskily, stroking my face gently and gazing at me with a turbulent expression.

My breath hitches as I stare at him openly and he smooths the hair away from my face and whispers, "You are sleeping so peacefully, it is a shame to wake you."

"What time is it?"

I make to sit but he presses me down against the pillows and tosses the silk sheets to one side.

I blink in surprise as he lifts the satin slip I am wearing in the absence of the cotton nightdress and exposes my tortured body to his lustful eye. He obviously approves of the damage he inflicted because his hand strokes my body with an ownership that doesn't escape me and he says huskily, "I love seeing my mark on your skin."

I don't know what to say because his words should be waving red flags in my direction, but all I do is shiver with excitement.

He bends his lips to kiss my abdomen and inhales deeply, causing me to squirm a little. He is so intense, like an animal as he gazes the length of my body with proud ownership.

"Are you sore?" He asks in a soft voice, and I shake my head. "A little but the bath helped."

He strokes my skin and then eases my legs gently apart and I gasp as his head nestles between my thighs and he takes a long swipe with his tongue, flicking my clit and sucking it gently into his mouth.

"Oh God." I cry out as my legs tremble and my breath deserts me because so many sensuous sensations are passing through me right now.

He sucks gently and then bites it harder and I scream as an orgasm hits me so hard, I swear I'm about to take my last breath.

My body convulses as if I'm having a fit and I hear a low chuckle as he watches me with interest.

I am so ashamed of my lack of control, and he leans in and whispers, "I like watching you come for me, Bella. Get used to it."

Then he pulls me up against him and says softly, "You have half an hour to change for dinner. The car will be waiting at seven. Don't keep me waiting."

He pulls away and dropping a light kiss on my trembling lips, he turns and leaves as quickly as he came.

CHAPTER 18

KILLIAN

I am fast realizing the benefits of having someone close. A woman on hand to distract my attention in such a delicious way. The fact Purity comes from a crazy half-assed cult run town has done me a favor. She knows nothing of the real world, and I can make her believe anything. She will be grateful and desperate to please me by the time I've finished with her and keeping her by my side will ensure she never discovers any different. She is my perfect woman already, but unrefined. A man of my standing and future self needs a poised, sophisticated woman by his side, so educating Purity is high on my to do list.

If I wasn't so angry with Gabriella, I would thank her because inadvertently she has delivered my ultimate prize and she would hate knowing that.

I pull on my customary black suit with a black silk shirt and tie, loving how black is the perfect choice to shroud my soul. The silver cufflinks and my black leather belt complete the outfit and my polished shoes are fresh from the box.

I maintain the rough edge to my jaw because it hides the

scar gifted to me by a surprise attack. It taught me many things and I have never been 'surprised' again.

Everything in my life is planned and calculated, and my marriage is no different.

Purity will become the perfect wife and mother to my children and if she believes she will get away with only bearing one, she is about to receive a wake-up call. I intend on fathering four children, hopefully boys. I am building an empire and she will be my queen. Yes, Purity Sanders is pure perfection, which is good because I am pure evil.

I head downstairs and am met by James in the living room. He pours me a glass of whiskey and hands it to me in a crystal glass.

I nod my thanks and he steps to the side, waiting to offer Purity a glass of champagne when she appears.

Saint heads into the room and I nod to James to offer him the same refreshment and as he takes the glass, he says softly, "Jefferson will be accompanied by Gina Di Angelo."

"Good." I grin because Gina has been on our payroll for years and will play her part perfectly.

A movement by the open door distracts our attention and I swear I stop breathing for a split second when I see the woman heading into the room. Gone are the rough edges of the girl from the countryside. The woman who stands before us deserves the title of my queen.

She stands tall on the highest heels of the soft leather shoes that complement the dress I chose for her. Pure white silk that molds to her body like the finest glove. It falls just above her knee and my eye travels to the diamond choker sparkling against her throat, causing the beast inside me to growl with desire.

Mine.

She won't understand the significance of that, but my

guests will. I own her. It will be obvious, and I feel a smug sense of satisfaction that things worked out so well.

She has tried to make the best use of the box of make-up I had delivered, and her hair is freshly washed and tumbles around her shoulders like spun silk. The fact it's white means she radiates innocence and the feral beast inside me is sharpening his claws.

The rosy tinge to her cheeks is heightened as she attempts to walk in the shoes and fails miserably. I note Saint's small smile and James' concern as I bark, "Walk tall, Purity. Those shoes will not bite."

She blushes and tries so hard to walk normally and as she takes a few more steps, James heads toward her and hands her a flute of champagne, guiding her by the arm to a waiting chair. A kindness that causes her to smile at him gratefully with a soft, "Thank you."

It amuses me when she takes a sip of the champagne and visibly winces before setting it down on the table by her side, causing me to say roughly, "Drink the champagne, Purity. You will develop a taste for it, but only if you practice."

She looks up and I note the fury in her eyes, which almost makes me dismiss my staff and show her who is in charge around here. However, she is a polite woman and merely grasps the glass and tentatively takes another swig, grimacing as the cool liquid attacks her uneducated taste buds.

There's an awkward silence as we watch her and then as she drains the glass in one and slams it on the side, Saint turns away to disguise the broad grin on his face. I nod to James, who appears worried but knows better than disobeying me. He refills her glass much to her horror and I say evenly, "You appear to be thirsty, Purity."

"I'm good, thanks." She smiles at James and shakes her head and I say darkly, "Drink it."

She looks as if she's about to argue, but then notes the

expression on my face and reaches for the glass with a trembling hand.

This time she takes a small sip and holds it in her hands as she peers around her and says softly, "I'm looking forward to tonight. I have never eaten in a restaurant before."

James glances up and the pity on his face causes me to roll my eyes and he looks away, knowing how there is no room for sympathy under my roof.

"I promised you an education, Purity and the heels and the drink are part of that."

"They are." She stares at me through those astonishing eyes, and I wish I could cancel this interminable evening to spend it educating her in a much more pleasurable pastime. Instead, I nod and swirl my own glass around my hand and knock back the contents, relishing the burn.

"You have much to learn. Do not question me, just know I am doing this to educate you in social graces. You will be offered the finest champagne wherever we go. It would be impolite to refuse. Mastered well, the heels give you a poise and presence that could command an army and you would be wise to practice walking effortlessly in them. Tonight, we will be eating in the finest restaurant and as it's your first time, you must follow my lead. Do not react, do not have an opinion just do as I say, and you will pass the test."

"The test?"

She appears worried and I nod. "You are in training to be my wife, Purity. I like the best. I *demand* the best and you *will* become the best. There will be no small-town girl accompanying me but a poised, sophisticated woman that makes me the envy of everyone. Do not let me down."

She nods, her eyes lit with excitement, which makes me smile inside. Purity is ravenous for experience, and I can't wait to show her everything. An innocent let loose in the world who has stumbled down the darkest hole. I will teach her everything I want her to know, and she will enjoy every fucking second of it.

Reaching out, I take her hand and pull her to my side and say to Saint, "Is the car ready?"

"Of course."

He heads out of the door, and I nod to James and, with Purity's hand firmly in mine, we follow him outside.

CHAPTER 19

PURITY

I am so nervous. When I discovered what Killian had ordered for me, I was like a kid in a candy shop. I have never seen such luxurious clothing in my life and for a second, I didn't even know how to dress myself. The silk underwear was decorated with lace and sparkles, and fastened around my body like a corset, pushing my breasts up, making them appear fuller somehow. The panties don't even deserve the name because half of them is missing. They cover the front of me, with hardly anything behind. The dress itself was so luxurious it made me gasp with pleasure and as for the diamonds in the red velvet box, they dazzled my eyes.

Of everything, it was the make-up that I was most excited about because I have only seen women wearing it on the television, I stole time with. It transformed me and I had to blink several times to test it was my reflection staring back at me.

However, those heels are my mortal enemy because how the hell do women walk in these things?

They are painful, uncomfortable and awkward and I long for my flat sensible shoes.

If I thought Killian would take pity on me, I was wrong, and he was sharp and slightly cruel when he told me to master them. I must remind myself he is doing this to educate me so I don't fail, and I should thank him, really. However, I didn't like it and am a little hurt that he shamed me before his employees. As for that ghastly drink. Why do people drink stuff like that? I only drained the glass to get it over with. Much like the medicine my mother used to make me take when I was sick.

When he demanded I drink another glass, I wanted to fling it across the room at him, but he reminded me of what normal people expect and he was right. The last thing I want is to embarrass myself – to embarrass him – so with determination, I tried to get a taste for it.

I am a little light-headed as I take my seat beside him and as the car pulls away from the house, I say nervously, "I don't feel so good."

"That will be the champagne. You haven't eaten for hours, and your stomach is empty. We should be there soon, and I suggest eating everything placed in front of you."

"Okay." I take a deep breath and then almost jump out of my skin when his hand snakes under my dress and he says huskily, "I'm glad to see the panties fit. I will admire them more openly later."

I gulp as he slides the thin fabric aside and his finger dips inside me, causing me to gasp. He plays with my clit and the wet heat drenches what fabric there is of my panties, and he chuckles softly, "I want to know you're wet for me, Bella. When we sit in the restaurant, I want your body aching for mine."

He pushes in harder, and I groan as he plays with my clit and my eyes roll back as an orgasm hits me hard. As I open my mouth, his hand slams against my lips and I scream into it as my body reacts to a violent wave of pleasure that he created.

As he pulls out his fingers, he reaches for a handkerchief and dips it between my legs, cleaning me up and then pocketing it with a wicked grin.

Then he rearranges my clothing and whispers, "Good girl."

I really can't answer that and my face flames with mortification.

How does he do that? Play me like an instrument and make me desperate for more. He gives me no warning before he strikes. It's as if I'm his plaything to do with what he likes and part of me loves it, craves it even, and the part of me that wanted her freedom is horrified by it.

I take a deep breath and muster some courage from the jagged ruins of my respectability and say softly, "What does marriage mean to you, Killian?"

"Power." He says simply, which surprises me a little. I'm not sure how I found this bravery because just his presence beside me is like a nuclear bomb waiting to go off. He is brooding, mysterious and secretive and I wonder about that. I suppose the darkness in his eyes is what intrigued me in the first place and so I only have myself to blame, and I shift slightly away from him and turn, causing him to sigh heavily. "Purity."

He says my name as if it's an irritation and then turns to me and the expression in his eyes could make a strong man cower to his knees but me–it excites me, and I shift on my seat with excited anticipation.

"Marriage is nothing like the one your parents enjoyed."

"How do you know? You've never met them and have never been married before." I say bravely, or some may say, foolishly.

His face twists into an amused grin, and he nods, reaching

for my hand and holding it carefully, as if it's a butterfly who has injured its wing. He raises it to his lips and kisses it softly and I swear I melt inside.

"Marriage to me will be like no other. There is no set of rules, nothing to compare it to because we are writing our own script. You are naive, but not stupid. I like that. You are weak, yet stronger than most women I've ever met. I like that too. Your beauty is unsurpassed, and we will fit well together. You have many qualities I admire, and I expressly like your enquiring mind. I am different to any man you will ever meet and any in your future. Marriage to me will be a journey of exploration and excitement. We will share many things and not all of them will make you feel comfortable. But I promise you will live to the extreme. To explore the world and enjoy the best of what it offers. I will be loyal and expect the same in return. That is why I am taking your training seriously because if we are going to make this work, we must become the perfect machine, working effortlessly to stand any chance of a long and happy life together."

The glittering eyes that stare at me have trapped my soul. I am falling with no safety net because he is saying everything I burn to hear. He is speaking to my innermost desires and promising they will be heard and there is nothing I don't like about this man except his cold indifference sometimes. Then he does something that sparks that indifference into a deep emotion that sucks me in and draws me deeper under his spell.

Since the moment I met Killian Vieri, it's as if I'm struggling to breathe and for a girl who has seen and experienced so little, it's intoxicating, devastating and too good to be true.

* * *

THE CAR PULLS TO A STOP, and he smiles, a dark edge to it that tells me I'm about to unwrap a little more of his soul tonight. I am interested in watching him interact with this man he seeks to do business with. I heard the conversation; I realize this isn't a double date in the usual sense and I'm excited about that.

Most of my life has been spent in the shadows, listening to conversations I shouldn't. It's how I learned that life in Heaven was different from the huge world outside. My father conducted many business conversations on behalf of Reverend Peters, and I realize those meetings weren't strictly what God would have approved of.

It fired up my curiosity and made me long to discover those secrets for myself and tonight will be an education that has been a long time coming.

CHAPTER 20

KILLIAN

Purity is quiet beside me and as she holds onto my arm, I know it's because of the heels she is wearing, and it makes me smile. She is trying so hard to walk normally, however, she stumbles a little as we head toward the door of the restaurant when a flash of light from the waiting crowd disturbs us. There are many paparazzi that hang around the Dining Room, hopeful of getting their picture on the web and this one will be eagerly sold because of her.

Purity is an enigma, the unknown and the fact she is on my arm will cause fruitless investigation. She is a woman with no past, my own beautiful secret and so I whisper, "Stand up straight, Bella. Act as if you belong here."

Her astonishing eyes gaze at me with an innocence that disturbs the beast inside me. When she peers at me with those trusting eyes, I want to tear off her clothes and bury myself deep inside her innocence. I want to ruin, to corrupt and to explore and I have never in my entire life felt so passionately about a woman as I do her.

She nods and the tentative smile on her face does something to me inside. It's as if I hold the most treasured secret in my hand that only I know about. It makes me possessive and desperate to protect and so I grip her hand and squeeze it reassuringly, gazing into her eyes with a softer look than normal and leaning down, kiss her lips in full view of the waiting paps.

The explosion of light around us tells me this is the photograph that will make their evening a successful one. It is one of a kind, just like her and as I pull back, I drown in the lust sparkling in her eyes and the smile of happiness on her face. It appears a little affection is all it takes to bring her back in line, which is yet another weapon to store in my arsenal against her.

We head inside and she wobbles beside me, the concentration on her face adorable. The head waiter bows reverently and says respectfully. "Welcome, sir, ma'am. Your table is ready, and your guests have arrived."

"Thank you." I say politely and as we follow him I believe every pair of eyes in the extremely crowded restaurant turn to watch our progress. A couple at the nearest table stare in awe and I'm pleased to note it's not directed at me. It's Purity. She walks as if a light has entered the building. She virtually shines beside me, from her astonishing white hair to her stunning eyes. An enviable slender figure that isn't the result of a fitness regime and a diet of salad leaves, but the beautiful creation of mother nature at her finest.

The diamonds that sparkle at her throat dazzle and I glare at the men who openly stare at my woman. I am a possessive bastard over my things, not usually women though, which is curious in itself.

Gripping her hand a little tighter, we make our way to the best table in the house and I see Jefferson Stevenson stand to attention along with Gina Di Angelo, a woman I have enjoyed the company of myself in the past. It didn't take much to bring her onto the payroll, and the look in her eyes as she fastens her seductive gaze on me is one of longing that will never be returned.

Jefferson is already nervous. I can tell by the wild expression in his eye and the sweat beading on his brow. He holds out his hand, which I studiously ignore because grasping a sweaty palm before I eat is not good for my health.

Purity is completely overwhelmed, and I nudge her as Jefferson turns to her and stares in awe. I dive straight in with the introduction and say deeply, "Good evening, Jefferson, Gina. May I introduce my fiancée, Purity?"

Gina's eyes widen in shock and Jefferson stares as if he's witnessing a living miracle and yet he recovers quickly and says nervously, "Congratulations. I didn't know."

I shrug, guiding Purity into the chair beside me and draping my arm along the back of her chair.

"Nobody does. It was agreed earlier today."

"Agreed." Gina stares at Purity with a mixture of concern and envy.

Purity smiles and I love that her voice holds none of the nerves she has inside as she says pleasantly, "Yes. Killian asked me to marry him, and I accepted, of course."

She turns and smiles at me with so much adoration it catches me off guard a little.

"I am so happy. We are so happy; it's a dream come true."

I reach for her hand and raise it to my lips, kissing it softly while staring into her eyes the entire time, causing the desire to deepen in hers, leaving our guests in no doubt at all about our feelings for one another.

"I'm shocked." Gina says, breaking the spell. "I thought you were the eternal bachelor, Killian. You have surprised me."

I shrug and turn my attention back to my guests and note the bitter expression of jealously on Gina's face.

We are interrupted as the waiter arrives and pours us each a glass of the finest champagne that I pre-ordered and I sense Purity stiffen beside me as he fills her glass to the brim.

I nudge her leg with my knee and as I raise my glass, she follows my lead. "To a long and happy marriage." I say, touching her glass with mine and as our guests echo the toast, I love the way she takes a deep breath and then holds it as she attempts to enjoy the bubbles that pour down her throat.

I field the inconsequential conversation as we sample the food, preferring instead to watch Purity's reaction to cuisine she will never have experienced before.

Oysters dressed in champagne almost cause her to gag, yet she hides it perfectly behind the starched white napkin that protects her naivety from our guests. Her eyes water when she is faced with the rare steak before her, the meat barely touching the flame.

As she eats, I can tell she is struggling to swallow, and she shifts nervously in her seat as she tries to remain interested in the conversation.

Gina steals many glances her way and I can tell she is curious. However, Purity doesn't notice them, or doesn't care. She is more concerned about getting through the meal and, to her credit, she eats every last morsel on her plate, including the garnish.

Gina is mesmerized and says with respect, "You must have been hungry, Purity. Hasn't Killian been feeding you?"

Purity nods, setting her cutlery together on the plate in a show of good table manners, and smiles at Gina.

"He has, very well in fact, but it hasn't involved a lot of food."

Jefferson disguises a chuckle as Gina stares at her in shock and I don't know who is more surprised at this table as Purity turns to me and says with a wicked smile, "I've built up quite the appetite today and I have this man to thank for that."

She fixes me with a sexy smile, and I swear I am rock hard right now. Then she says politely, "If you will excuse me, I need to use the restroom."

She makes to stand, and, in a flash, I push back my seat and make to help her and hate that Gina is quicker as she says loudly, "Good idea. I'll come with you."

I can't even argue because I have never accompanied a woman to the rest room in my life–ever, but I want to now. I want to lock the door and bury myself deep inside this woman who ticks every box I ever owned, but I realize when I am beaten, so I drop a light kiss on her lips instead and whisper, "Don't be long."

She pushes me away and turns to Gina with a brilliant smile. "Shall we?"

I watch them go with a sense of helplessness that angers me. Why do I care if Purity uses the bathroom? It's what women do several times of an evening but as she walks away, I have an overwhelming urge to follow her.

Jefferson distracts my attention with a low, "I can see why you moved fast. She is adorable. Where did you meet?"

The fuck I'm going to discuss my private life with this weasel, so I sit and ignore the question completely and snap. "Let's get to business."

It has the desired effect, and his earlier unease returns as I fix him with a deepening scowl.

"You requested a meeting. I'm listening."

He shifts nervously in his seat, which angers me a little because it shows his weakness.

Jefferson Stevenson is a privileged frat boy who has been cushioned and funded his entire life by his father, Judge Stevenson. The best schools, the finest living and now a position in chambers, courtesy of his father's connections. The fuck I understand a man like him, let alone want to do business, but I am mindful of my instructions, and this is just one of the first of many meetings like this.

"I believe we could work together and forge a mutually beneficial arrangement."

He says in a low voice to hide our conversation from eager ears.

"How?" I shrug as I lift my glass and he says, leaning forward. "We both know our families has enjoyed a mutual connection over the years. Their time is ending and we, as the next generation, will be taking the baton. I will rise to become the most respected Judge in the country, just like my father and can offer you many, um, favors should the need arise."

"I repeat my question. Why?"

I fix him with a dark glare, causing him to wince visibly when I say dismissively.

"I have no reason for favors. I operate inside the law and make my own luck. I don't require your help because we both know nothing is for free in this life."

He licks his lip nervously and whispers, "The um, organization. It exists on favors to mutually benefit the members."

"My grandfather's organization." I say in a hard voice.

"Is that what you are talking about?"

He seems taken aback a little and nods, his eyes flicking around the restaurant nervously, reminding me why I will never trust any of my business with him.

I stare at him with a hard expression and say in a harsh whisper, "I have discovered your involvement with Mario Bachini didn't end well. I heard that he acted against the code of conduct we expect our members to adhere to and you assisted him in that. I also heard that you have used our fine organization for personal gain and bent the rules so far out of shape it brought unwelcome attention to our club, so why would I want to do business with a man like that?"

"It was Mario, acting on behalf of his father." He says quickly, shifting nervously in his seat.

"Ah, yes. Carlos Matasso. My uncle, if you like. That fool who believed he was bigger than the entire organization. He used it and abused his position and made my aunt's life a misery, and he was executed by an assassin for his sins."

I stare at him with obvious disgust. "My job, Mr. Stevenson, is to clean up the dirty trail your dealings have caused. We are not about underhanded arrangements and murdering innocent people for a sadistic kick. We are honorable and exist to do good, not evil, and your membership is seriously pending right now until you can prove you are worthy of your name on the members list."

"What do I have to do?" He is visibly shaking, and I say with steel in my voice. "You prove your allegiance. To me."

"You?"

I nod. "My grandfather is passing the job title to me and as his successor as the Supreme Dark Lord, it is my intention to clean up the member list. We are a charity, Jefferson. Do you know what that means?"

He looks uncomfortable.

"We give rather than take. We make good what others have made bad and we act for good rather than evil. If anybody threatens that, they suffer the consequences, which I don't need to spell out for you. There will be no allegiances and no favors granted until you prove to me that you are worthy of the title of a Dark Lord."

Jefferson appears so weak as he sits before me, cowering under the threat of losing his easy life and his future. Without the backing of The Dark Lords, he won't go far, and he needs us way more than we need him. However, I am aware The Dark Lords are striving for everything I said and the Vieris are the cancer that threatens their existence. That is why we will fight them back with their own weapon. Innocence. We will become the whitest light in their organization, beyond reproach, and turn their own guns against them.

Good is no match for evil and if I must cloak our retribution in charity, I will. With Purity by my side, we are about to become the power couple of the fucking country, and nobody will dare speak out against me. Then, when I have full control of our family's organization, I will systematically destroy every person in it who tried to take it from us. Beginning with Jefferson's father, Judge Stevenson.

I lean back and say as an aside. "Your father."

He appears worried. "What about him?"

"I understand he is acquiring money for favors. Turning a blind eye to criminal activity and handing out get out of jail free cards."

Jefferson pales as I lean in and whisper, "You can get me the information I need. If you compile the evidence, I will reconsider your membership. You will prove your allegiance to the cause and demonstrate you will help clean it up."

"But he's my father." Jefferson stutters in disbelief.

I shrug. "A title, nothing more. It's up to you. Assure your own future at the expense of his or watch everything he has worked so hard to build crash and burn. Encourage him to retire rather than face the rest of his days in prison. You take over his empire and your futures are guaranteed. He lives a comfortable retirement and you become everything you wanted to be. I don't see what the problem is."

Jefferson's hand shakes as he grasps his drink, and I watch the light in his eyes dim to darkness. Yes, Jefferson Stevenson is weak and was always going to do exactly as I wanted him to. Then again. They always do.

CHAPTER 21

PURITY

Gina walks beside me to the restroom, and I try so hard to walk as normally as possible. She is poised, elegant and everything I want to be and the last thing I want is her thinking I'm not. I owe it to Killian because this is what he wants. It's written in the contract—our marriage contract and I will not let him down.

As soon as we reach the sanctuary of the ladies' restroom, I excuse myself and head to a cubicle, hoping I don't embarrass myself.

Once the door locks, I turn and vomit into the bowl, thankful I made it in time.

"Are you ok in there?"

Gina's concerned voice tells me I'm not being discreet, and I say with a strangled gasp, "I'll be ok. I don't …"

I can't finish my sentence because a fresh wave of nausea hits me and most of what I ate joins the rest as I violently reject the rich food.

A gentle knock has me reaching for the toilet tissue and wiping my mouth clean. I wish like crazy I was alone because this is a disaster. I wanted to be a woman Killian would be proud of. Not someone who can't stomach the fine cuisine and alcohol that cost more than my father probably makes every month.

"Purity, unlock the door."

Gina says, slightly anxiously and with a heavy heart I do as she says, and her concerned expression causes the tears to well up in my eyes.

"Honey, what's wrong?"

"The food."

I place the lid down and sit on the toilet seat, hoping she doesn't notice me kick off the hated shoes. My feet are throbbing, and my stomach is raw, and I have never been more uncomfortable in my life. The diamond choker is strangling me, and I am struggling to breathe, courtesy of the tight-fitting corset thing Killian made me wear.

She shakes her head and whispers, "I've got you, honey. Take a few deep breaths and I'll fetch you some water."

I hear the tap run and am grateful when she heads back with an apologetic, "I'm sorry, this paper cup is all they have by the water cooler."

I drain it in one go, desperate for the cool liquid to calm my raging thirst.

She crouches down and takes my hand, saying softly, "Is everything ok, honey? You can tell me. I can help you."

For some reason, her kindness weakens me and causes the tears to spill down my flushed face.

"It's nothing. I'm not used to alcohol and that food. Well, I'm not used to that either."

"What are you used to?" She smiles and I shrug. "Plain country cooking and water. That's all I usually have."

"Then you met Killian."

She is being so nice, I sniff and raise a small smile.

"Yes. He is educating me on how to be socially acceptable."

Her eyes flash with anger as she says through gritted teeth, "I bet he is the bastard."

I'm surprised at the venom in her voice and say quickly, "You sound angry at him. Why?"

"Because he is manipulating you, Purity. It's what he does."

"I don't understand. He has been so kind to me. He is the first person who has since I came to Chicago."

"Tell me how you met."

Her sharp gaze stares right through me and I say with a shrug. "I applied for a job, and he gave me this one."

"What job?"

"His wife."

Her eyes widen and she glances over her shoulder and says quickly, "Listen, honey, whatever arrangement you have with Killian is best kept between the two of you. He won't like it if you tell everyone the nature of your relationship."

"Why not? We are getting married. Isn't that what marriage is, a business contract?"

"Is that what you think?" She appears horrified and I consider my own parent's marriage and everyone else's in Heaven and say in confusion. "It isn't what I think. It's what I know."

"Where did you say you were from?" Gina is staring at me as if I've fallen from space and I say miserably, "Heaven. Not the … well, you know, the town."

She holds up her hand and sighs heavily. "Now I understand."

"You've heard of it?" I'm shocked because nobody has ever heard of the town called Heaven, but she obviously has.

"Jefferson was talking about it yesterday. I overheard him on the phone and questioned him about it. He told me it was a place that lived by its own rules and was governed by a preacher. It doesn't sound the kind of place I want to visit, but it appears you grew up there and know no different."

For the first time since I arrived in Chicago, it's as if somebody actually understands me, and I smile gratefully.

"I ran away."

"Good for you."

Gina reaches for my hand and says softly, "Let's clean you up before Killian kicks the door open and comes for you."

It makes me giggle. "He wouldn't do that."

"You don't know him very well, do you?"

"Do you?" I enquire and note the slight flush to her face as she says quickly, "We have met before."

She busies herself by rummaging in her purse and she pulls out a brush and a stick of gum.

"Here, chew this. It will take away the bad taste in your mouth. You can brush your hair and I have some make-up to repair yours."

"Thank you. I really…"

She holds up her hand and appears a little sad. "Don't thank me, honey. It's what anyone with compassion would do. Anyway, tell me about your marriage. When is the happy day?"

"I couldn't tell you. Soon I think."

She sighs heavily and stares at my reflection in the mirror and says softly, "I wish you luck, Purity, but if I may offer you one word of advice."

"Please. I could use some." I turn, eager for any help at all, and she leans closer and, to my surprise, hugs me, whispering, "Just don't fall in love with him. Guard your heart above everything because that man is incapable of loving anyone."

"Love!" I'm astonished and pulling back, say with a slight shake of my head. "Since when did love enter the arrangement? A marriage is a business contract. Love doesn't even feature in that. I've known that my entire life, which is why I am happy my own was through my own negotiation and not my parents."

She appears a little stunned and her eyes fill with tears that she blinks quickly away as she whispers, "Forget I said it. Of course, you're right. Love has no place in your marriage to Killian. It's only business, after all."

She turns away and I resume brushing my hair, feeling a lot better now than I did when we first entered the room. I'm upset that I wasted the expensive food, but I couldn't keep it down. Wishing I could dispose of the heels as easily, with a sigh, I inch my feet back into them and wince as they crush my toes.

Then, with a final check on my reflection, I follow Gina back to the table.

CHAPTER 22

KILLIAN

As soon as I see them return, I can tell something has happened that sharpens my claws. If Gina has spoken out of turn, her employment contract will be terminated along with her life. I leave no loose ends and over familiarity is often a cross I must bear, but the warning expression in her eyes is directed at me, telling me she has heard something I should know.

I stand and pull out Purity's chair like a gentleman, noting that Jefferson remains seated while Gina deals with her own chair. He is subdued and obviously deep in thought, and I take his distraction to stare hard at Gina as I push in Purity's seat. She nods imperceptibly and I will undoubtedly have a full transcript of their conversation by the time I make the journey home.

Gina Di Angelo is one of my paid spies. A woman who stands high in society courtesy of her parentage. An heiress if you like who took a walk on the wild side—with me. She fell hard and deep and soon became a useful part of my organization, gathering information and passing it to me for more money than her daddy gave her each month. She loves the thrill, the danger and is driven by adrenalin, and it inevitably led her to my bed. We were good together until she wanted more. I cut ties and made it clear this was a business arrangement and nothing more and now, strangely, she is one of my most trusted employees.

However, I'm not one for sentiment and realize that everyone can be bought, so I keep her in her place and use her when the occasion dictates.

She has been 'dating' Jefferson Stevenson for three weeks already. They are the newest hot couple in town and big news. Her mission was clear. Discover his secrets and report back. I'm aware she can't stand him. It's evident in her eyes when he's not looking, however, to his face, she is deeply in love with him, which is why I would be sorry to lose such an accomplished spy.

Purity sips her water and I note she has slipped the shoes from her feet, causing me to frown. As I sit beside her, I tuck her hair behind her ear and whisper in a low voice, "Put those god-damned shoes back on and learn to walk like a lady. Do not let them conquer you. They are just fucking shoes."

She stiffens and yet maintains her cool facade and it angers me when she kicks them away a little further and says to Jefferson, "How long have you been together?"

I can't believe what I'm hearing and hate the amused twinkle in Gina's eye as she notices my displeasure.

Jefferson glances up as if he's forgotten where he is and says quickly, "Three weeks, give or take a few days."

He turns to Gina and smiles.

"We met at the Heath's summer barbeque. We've been inseparable ever since."

Gina smiles at him fondly, but I can tell how much she hates him when he obviously allows his hand to wander where it shouldn't among company.

The resignation in her eyes and the way she edges away tells me everything I need to know, and I say loudly, "Thank you, but we must go. The check has been taken care of; we must bid you goodnight."

Jefferson stands as I take Purity's hand and pull her from her seat and Saint steps behind me and Pax steps in front, signaling there will be no more conversation.

I guide Purity through the restaurant, sensing the stares of fascination as we pass and ignoring everyone who calls my name. I nod to Pax, and he presses a huge bundle of one hundred bills into the head waiter's hand.

We make it to the car in seconds and as soon as the door closes, and the car moves away, I say firmly, "What happened in the rest room?"

"Do I really need to spell it out?" She says with amusement, and I turn and fix her with a glare that causes her to sigh. "If you must know, I threw up that rich food. My body obviously hated it as much as my taste buds and I only just got there in time."

I stare at her in shock, and she says with a slight shake of her head. "Look, I'm sorry. I tried to like it, I really did, but that shell stuff was disgusting and as for the meat, it wasn't even cooked. I would have asked for my money back."

"It was steak tartare. Of course, it was hardly cooked."

I stare at her in disbelief, and she shivers with revulsion.

"I hated it."

"What do you like then?" I question her, hoping to call her bluff because I'm guessing Purity Sanders doesn't even know that herself.

"I want a Macburger."

"Excuse me."

I'm shocked and she says with excitement. "I saw an ad for it on television one day. Apparently, it's the best burger in the world and you should have seen the delight on the faces of the people who were eating it. I would give anything for one of those."

"Anything?" I raise my eyes and she grins.

"At least it looked cooked, and it came with lettuce, tomato and the secret sauce, whatever that is. I'm guessing it's what makes it the best burger in the world."

For some reason, all the tension leaves my body and I'm astonished at the deep chuckle that tells me I'm losing my sanity.

Tapping on the partition, I say to Saint. "Head for the drive-in on west street. Purity wants the best burger in the world."

Saint catches my eye and the twinkle in his tells me he has seen the ads too and as the partition closes, Purity says with excited pleasure. "Really. We can get one. Oh my God, this is amazing. I can't believe it. Thank you."

I stare at the delight on her face and the sparkle in her eyes and I have never seen anything so beautiful in my life. I want to gaze at her all night, and I'm even more astonished when she leans forward impulsively and presses a soft kiss on my lips.

"Thank you." She whispers and then says with a smile, "You are a man of your word. You really are educating me in the pleasures life has to offer. If you told me earlier I would be tasting the best burger in the world tonight, I wouldn't have believed you? I didn't even realize it was made here. I knew there was a reason Chicago beckoned me."

She giggles and I swear every part of me aches right now. She is so innocent. So happy about a fucking dead-beat burger when she has just thrown up the finest meal in Chicago.

I have never met a woman like Purity in my entire life and the more time I spend with her, the more I want. She is fast becoming the light of my day and the pleasure of my nights. The thought of her heading to the guest room tonight is so not going to happen. I want her with me, by my side, where I can touch her, hear her sweet voice and gaze upon her pretty face. She is everything I have been searching for and I can't believe my luck.

The neon sign appears before us, and Purity grips my hand hard. "There it is. Oh my god, we are really doing this."

"Purity."

I attempt to put this into perspective.

"Macburger is a chain of fast-food outlets and their statement that..."

I note her trusting eyes and the pleasure on her face and strangely I can't bring myself to dismiss her excitement with the cold hard facts. So, I just exhale sharply and say with resignation, "Tell them what you want."

"Tell who?"

She is confused and then as I press the window down, she stares in shock at the machine, waiting to take her order.

As the voice asks what she wants, she hesitates and I groan and say roughly, "One Macburger meal with fries and coke. Actually, make that one of everything on the menu."

As the voice repeats my order back to me, I curse my generosity, knowing how bad for her health this feast will be. However, the gratitude on her face mixed with adoration makes me feel extremely good about myself for once and as the window closes and we move to the next one where Saint pays the check, she grasps my face in both of her hands and whispers, "You are a good man, Killian. Thank you."

Then, she kisses me so softly, it throws me a little because I don't experience moments as pure as this one—ever and for some reason, I like it.

We collect the order at the third window, and I reach into the bag and hand Purity her treasured Macburger and watch with amusement as she holds it in her hand as if she has found the Holy Grail. Her eyes are lit with pleasure and she unwraps it as if it's Christmas day and stares in wonder at the cheap food.

She takes a sniff and groans and I swear I could fucking come hard right now as she takes a tentative bite and moans softly as she chews the food as if it's the best thing she has ever tasted. I could watch her all night and as the car moves away, I tap on the partition and say gruffly. "Pull over. There's enough here for the whole line. Help us out."

* * *

FIVE MINUTES LATER, we must be a curious sight. Three men dressed in black, sitting on a grassy bank by the side of the road, with an angel in our midst. She shines like the brightest star as she sits on my jacket and as we finish off the food, she keeps us amused as she samples a little of everything, squealing with delight when she finds something she likes.

My men are as fascinated by her as I am. We are not used to such childlike behavior. Not in our world. The women are sultry, sexy, and conniving. Not like her. There is no one like her.

Even my men are comfortable around her, and we listen to her excited chatter as she tells us about life in that god awful town she came from. She doesn't know it, but every single fucking word is committed to my memory because as soon as I get the chance, I will ruin her parents' lives because of the way they have treated her.

She thinks I'm interested in hearing about life in Heaven. What she doesn't realize is I am gathering much-needed information. Yes, Elijah Sanders will soon discover that nobody messes with my wife, and he will regret the day he allowed her to escape.

He will regret the day she found me.

CHAPTER 23

PURITY

I am drunk with happiness. Killian is my dream man. He is trying so hard to make me happy and I feel bad that I wasn't grateful for the expensive meal he provided tonight. He is attentive and kind and it's as if I can tell him anything. I can't believe how lucky I got when he saved me from Miss. Sinclair and that horrible place she took me to. I can't dwell on what happened there. It's too painful, but I know the most important thing in my life right now is making Killian Vieri happy.

We finish up and as Saint deals with the trash, we head back to the car, and I snuggle up beside Killian and say sleepily. "That was the best evening I have ever had. Thank you."

He pulls me closer and twists his fingers in my hair. It feels so nice and as the car pulls away from the curb, my eyes are heavy. As I drift off to sleep, it's in the knowledge I am the happiest woman alive and all because of one man. My soon to be husband.

The next thing I know, the car stops, and he whispers, "We're home, Bella."

I blink as he takes my hand and helps me from the car. As my feet hit the concrete, I stumble on those god-damned heels and, to my surprise, he sweeps me into his arms and I cling to his neck, loving how safe I am in his strong arms. He presses his lips to my hair, and he smells so good. So intoxicating and as he carries me up to bed, I don't even register the location until he lays me gently on his bed and whispers, "Allow me to assist you."

He unzips my dress and eases it down gently, and I sigh as his hands flutter against my skin. His low groan makes me open my eyes and smile at him as he openly stares at my body dressed in the scraps of fabric he calls lingerie.

"So beautiful. My Bella."

He whispers as he dips his head and plants soft kisses on my increasingly heated skin.

It causes me to sigh with pleasure and as he slowly undresses, I stare at his body with a deep desire for more of it.

The bed dips as he joins me and he leans down and kisses my heaving breast, lowering the corset thing so they spill over the top. He sucks on them in turn, and I moan his name, loving how good he makes me feel.

My back arches as he peels down my panties, or what passes for that, and his strong hands force my legs apart so he can bury his face deep between my thighs.

I love the pleasure he brings to my body and gasp as he sucks my clit, causing me to cry out his name and the rush of wet heat tells me he is everything I want.

He wastes no time in moving up my body and pushing his cock against my pussy, demanding entrance which I am only too happy to give willingly. As he slides home, I stare deep into his eyes and my breath hitches at the desire I see reflecting at me.

His hands push against my neck, pinning me to the bed,

and I should be very afraid right now because his eyes are as black as the night sky.

As he moves inside me, I savor every minute of it and as he thrusts faster, harder with more power, it makes me cry out. It's as if a wild animal is tearing me apart as he stretches my body to its limit, his hand closed around my neck, making it difficult to breathe.

It's almost as if he is punishing me for something and as he roars into the darkness, my cries join his as I come so hard my entire body shudders under his hand. I lose control as he explodes inside me and then he shocks me by gripping my neck even harder and growls, "Never leave me, Purity. You belong to me now."

My eyes are wide, and the tears aren't far away because he is hurting me. All I can do is implore him with my eyes and attempt to nod because, of course, I won't leave him. Our marriage contract will forbid it. Until death do us part. I know the script.

His hold relaxes, and he dips his face to my neck and kisses where his fingers once held me so tightly, and then he pulls away and says roughly, "Come. We need to clean up and grab some sleep. Tomorrow will be a long one."

"Why, what's happening?" I clamber after him as he strides to the bathroom, and he says over his shoulder.

"We leave for Italy. To be married."

"Oh." As I follow him, it's with a huge smile on my face because I'm getting married. Tomorrow. I can't believe it. It's really happening and for the first time in my life, I will be someone other than Purity Sanders. I will be his wife. A Vieri and there is nobody who is happier about that than me.

* * *

PURE EVIL

SLEEPING with Killian is an unexpected delight and I love that he turns me away from him and wraps his muscular body around mine. I drift off to sleep inside those insane arms and I love the scratch of his jaw on my neck, reminding me I'm not on my own anymore. I never will be again because we are getting married.

I wake with a smile on my face as he gently nuzzles into my neck and whispers huskily, "Wake up, Bella."

I sigh with pleasure as his cock presses hard against my back, reminding how much he desires me.

I jump as he enters me from behind, slowly, stretching my body to its limit, reminding me he controls it now which I am more than happy about. He grasps my hair in his fist and pushes in deep, spinning me around so I am facing the pillow. It's different at this angle, and as he lifts my ass with one hand under me, my face slides against the silk fabric as he dominates my body. It's a little uncomfortable but so sexy because I can't see him—only feel him.

He whispers in my ear, "Tonight we will fuck as husband and wife and then your education really begins."

It causes my body to melt inside because what can be more pleasurable than this? He is so skilled at playing my body, I don't believe anything can match it and for some reason his words turn me on, and I scream into the pillow as my body clenches around his cock.

His deep groan makes me smile as he comes so hard inside me it stuns me a little. However, before my own orgasm can join his, he pulls out and spins me around, the lust heavy in his eyes.

"Follow me."

My body screams at him to finish the job, but with a wicked grin he pulls me after him to the shower and as he turns on the jets, he says almost conversationally. "You will get your reward later. The next orgasm will be as my wife. I want you desperate for me when we consummate our marriage."

He pulls me into the shower after him and as he soaps my body, I don't believe I have ever been so happy. Then he surprises me by saying firmly, "Your turn."

He squeezes some soap onto my outstretched hands and as I tentatively rub the soap over his shoulders, I love the hard muscles that flex under my hands. He feels so good, and I surprise myself by pressing light kisses on his chest as I continue to massage his skin. Feeling bolder, I move down his body, rubbing and kissing, loving how he stills and groans at my touch. He likes it. I am pleasing him.

I reach his cock and hesitate, and he growls, "Touch it."

I'm a little afraid, but as my fingers close around the hard shaft, I am delighted at how soft it is. Then he shocks me by saying roughly, "Get on your knees and take it in your mouth."

I glance up at him and he smiles with encouragement and, remembering everything he has done for me, I smile bravely and drop to my knees before him.

He rests his hand on my head as I slide him into my mouth, his rigid cock filling it completely. He moves slowly, groaning with pleasure as I suck him, my eyes watering as he hits the back of my throat. It's uncomfortable on my knees and a strange experience as he thrusts harder into my mouth, grasping my hair with his hands, using my mouth for his own pleasure. I wonder if it will ever end until from out of nowhere, he fills my mouth with hot, salty cum and I gag as he growls, "Swallow it."

My eyes water as I attempt to do as he asks, gagging as the salty liquid chokes me a little. It drips from the sides of my mouth, and I wonder if it will ever end as he continues to spurt down my throat while holding my head in place.

Finally, he finishes and pulls me up to face him and the

heavy desire in his eyes makes everything better again because obviously I did something to please him—a lot and he whispers, "You will get used to that."

I nod as he leans down and kisses me slowly and softly and I melt against his strong body, loving how his arms wrap around me and the water cleanses the burn that reminds me he was inside it. He pulls back and lifts my chin to face him and says huskily, "You will make the best wife, Purity. I am a lucky man."

He stares at me with an intensity that shocks me a little as I smile happily at him, and then he breaks the spell and turns off the shower, saying quickly, "We should dry off and dress. There is an outfit for traveling waiting in your room. I have instructed my sister Serena to take care of the rest of your needs and you will find them waiting when we arrive."

"Your sister." My eyes shine because I have never met a family with siblings before and I really hope she likes me, and we can become friends.

"Yes. I have a brother too. You will meet them both at the wedding."

I follow him across the room, naked, and as he opens the door, I say nervously, "Maybe I should wrap my body in a towel incase anybody sees me."

He shakes his head and says almost angrily, "Who the fuck cares? This is my house, and they know you are mine. If I want you naked the entire time, I will make it happen. I will deem what's best for you, Purity, and I like to see your fine body knowing it is mine."

"Oh." I'm a little taken aback at that and then from out of nowhere, I say angrily, "Excuse me, Killian, but my body is mine, actually. You don't own me, nobody does."

He turns slowly and stares at me in surprise as I plant my feet on the carpet with my hands on my hips and say stubbornly, "May I remind you this marriage contract is a business one? A mutually beneficial arrangement that you are paying me for. If this is what it involves, I may pass because I ran from one life of imprisonment and I can do it again."

I think I've gone too far when a thunderous expression consumes his face and he stares at me with pure rage and I'm shocked when he moves past me and drags the fur throw off the bed, tossing it at me and growling, "Here. Cover yourself if you must. Now go to your room and change and meet me downstairs in thirty minutes."

He stands by the open door and, feeling as if I've scored a victory somehow, I move past him, gripping the throw around my body, refusing to look at him as I pass. As the door slams shut behind me, I discover I'm shaking because something is telling me I just made a huge mistake when I answered him back.

CHAPTER 24

KILLIAN

Nobody ever answers me back. I am enraged. Then again, Purity isn't like anyone I've ever met and I kind of respect that about her. However, it wasn't her request to cover up that enraged me. It was informing me she would leave that caused the blood to boil and the rage to filter through my veins like a fire out of control. Like fuck will she leave me. Over my dead body and I pace my room like a caged animal as I try to get my anger under control.

Nobody leaves me by choice—ever. Definitely not a woman like her. One I want. One who is perfect for me. I need to regain control because this could end very badly for her if I believed for one second she will betray me.

I won't allow it. I will lock her in her room and throw away the key if she even hints at leaving me again and as I dress, my mind works hard to formulate a plan where she will have no choice but to stay.

The fact I've fucked her with no protection should seal her fate. If she's not pregnant already, she soon will be. She hasn't even considered birth control. Why would she? It was probably never discussed and probably forbidden in that crazy town she ran from.

I sense the rage seeping away as I picture her swollen with my child. The final nail in her coffin because I know she will never take a child from its father. I understand her already and love her fierce sense of right from wrong. She will consider it her duty to be the perfect mother and so if I must make her pregnant to keep her, I will.

I finally calm down and dress in a casual outfit of black chinos and a black button-down polo shirt. The brown leather belt is my only concession to color. I grab a short jacket to hide my gun that is strapped against my shoulder and as I leave the room, I promise things will be very different when I return. I won't be alone anymore. I will have a wife and soon a family. My life begins today, and I will make it everything I ever wanted.

I am quite upbeat when I meet Saint in the dining room and note the coffee already waiting at my place setting.

James hovers nearby to fetch what I desire, and I nod at Saint, who takes a seat beside me.

"Anything to report?" I ask, and he nods.

"The priest will be at the house at three pm. Your family is expecting us, and everything has been arranged."

"Perfect."

I reach for my phone and note the message waiting from Gina and press to listen. It's a recording of her conversation with Purity, reminding me that Gina never passes an opportunity by for information, no matter how trivial it may be.

When I hear Purity's sweet voice, it makes me smile and yet by the time the conversation ends, I am angry again. I shouldn't be. She has stated fact, but I don't want anyone else thinking she is anything but madly in love with me. The fact I don't love her and probably never will won't matter. It doesn't sit well with me knowing she is playing me at my own game.

"Problem?" Saint raises his eyes and I shake my head. "Nothing that can't be solved."

I reach for my coffee as Purity enters the room and I swear every part of my body responds to her.

She is dressed in a black pant suit, her hair soft and flowing around her shoulders in direct contrast to the dark fabric encasing her body. Her face is fresh and free from make-up, and she smells amazing. Like a breath of fresh air that I need to inhale to rid my head of the disturbing thoughts swirling around it. She is so innocent, so pure, and yet I want to tear it apart and watch her burn.

She smiles sweetly at James and Saint and says softly, "Good morning. What a pleasant one it is."

They both nod and return her greeting and as she takes her seat beside me, she smiles like a sweet angel and says, "You look nice."

Saint coughs and then pushes his chair back and says quickly, "I'll prepare for our departure."

James steps forward quickly and asks what she would like for breakfast and her eyes widen. "I have a choice?"

She turns to me for guidance, and I say, "Fruit and yogurt to begin, followed by two poached eggs medium on sourdough."

James nods and pours her a coffee before he leaves to deal with her order.

"I can't believe you live like this," she says, her eyes wide as she gazes around her. "Back in Heaven, we ate oats for breakfast with a dash of honey on weekends. You really are living the dream, Killian."

"Tell me about your life there." I say with sudden curiosity.

"There's not much to tell, really. Every family was allowed

one child. They had to teach them the bible. It was forbidden to talk during meals unless the men believed it was educational to recite bible passages. Then they would head to work and the children to school, returning to help with their chores and spend the evening doing bible studies."

"You have got to be kidding me?" I'm appalled, and she nods, not really understanding how wrong it was.

"Marriage was arranged when the woman turned nineteen. The day after she left school. It was a carefully chosen path, and the husband was agreed between the father under the reverend's direction. Then the woman becomes the man's property and bears him a child and cares for the home and family. She is not allowed to work and must bend to her husband's will in every way."

Maybe it's not so bad after all. It's not much different to my plan for her, although luxury living will play an important role in her life. I expect the best and my wife must *be* the best. Once again, I congratulate myself on finding Purity. The hard work has already been done and she will not expect much in return.

Perfect.

Then she ruins my carefully laid out plan by saying with a deep sigh. "I always knew I didn't want that life. I wanted more. I sensed there was more and when Miss. Sinclair came to Heaven, I saw a woman I wanted to be more than anything."

"Tell me about that meeting."

I'm interested and she says with excitement, "I returned from school, and I saw a huge white car parked outside our house."

"Don't you mean black?"

She shakes her head. "No, it was definitely white. I decided in that moment I wanted a white car one day. Anyway, Miss. Sinclair was leaning against it, and she looked unreal. She was the most beautiful woman I had ever seen, so chic and elegant, and her clothes were fashionable. Her hairstyle was sophisticated, and she stood on high heels that made her legs look incredible."

She laughs out loud. "Beauty is cruel. I see that now because it must take a lifetime of education to walk properly on them."

I love how her eyes sparkle as she casts her mind back, and she takes a sip of coffee and continues.

"She saw me approaching and ground her cigarette into the dust and smiled. I was curious, and she came over and acted so kind. She told me I was pretty and asked for my name. She said she loved it and if I ever wanted to leave Heaven, she would help find me a job. Then she gave me her card, but before I could say anything, a man came out of our house and called her name, quite sharply I might add."

What the fuck?

I say casually, "This man, who was he?"

She shrugs. "I don't know. He was just a man in a white suit. I remember thinking he was nowhere near as sophisticated as Miss. Sinclair. He appeared angry about something and before I knew it, they left. As I crept into the house, I heard my father on the telephone speaking to someone and he sounded angry."

"What did he say?"

"Something about the wrong man and he would never do business with the monkey again. It was the organ grinder or nothing."

She rolls her eyes. "It was a strange conversation that stopped the minute my mom caught me and told me loudly to go to my room and change for supper. You know, it was a curious encounter, but I had listened to similar conversations over the years. Many strangers stopped by our house on their way through, mainly men in expensive cars but never a woman. My father would *never* do business with a woman. It just wasn't acceptable, which is probably why Miss. Sinclair waited outside."

James reappears with her breakfast, and she falls on it with a ravenous appetite, leaving me to reflect on our conversation.

I remember the trip. Not long after Gabriella started working for me, she told me about a producer deep in the middle of nowhere we could do business with.

They had fields of opium of good value, and we could make a killing with none of the usual risks involved in importing the stuff over the borders. I sent her there to negotiate a contract I didn't have the time to do myself, so who the fuck is this man and since when did we travel in white cars?

Something is very wrong here and I will discover what the hell Gabriella has been playing at while my attention was elsewhere.

CHAPTER 25

KILLIAN

She is beyond excited. After breakfast we drove to the airport, but it isn't any kind of airport because there is only one jet waiting, and it's painted in black with a gold hawk on the tail.

I have been brooding since I slammed the door on her earlier and despite her attempts at conversation over breakfast, I haven't said much at all.

I grasp her hand and pull her after me and as we head up the steps, she blinks in wonder when we head inside.

I'm guessing she's never seen anything like this in her life as she gazes in wonder at the chrome tables with black leather seats atop a cream luxurious carpet. There are couches and a dining table with cream leather chairs set around it. Blinds hide the windows and there is even a bar set at one end. A curtain leads through an arch, which is where I head to a corridor with several doors leading off it. She gasps when I push her into the furthest one.

"Wow! Is this…?"

"My bedroom. Yes, it is."

She stares at the huge king-sized bed covered in black

and gold silk. Mirrors are everywhere making it appear the room is treble its size, and she peers in astonishment at the full-sized bathroom that leads off it.

"I can't believe this is real," she says in wonder as I sit on the edge of the bed and stare at her with darkening eyes.

"Our contract."

"What about it?"

She is still in awe of her surroundings and appears to only have half an ear on the conversation.

"I want to run over a few details before we go any further."

"Okay." She smiles and makes toward me, and I hold up my hand and say firmly, "Stay where you are."

She falters and I say roughly, "You believe I don't own you. That you have choices. That you can leave."

"Well, don't I?"

I shrug. "It's just business and sometimes business changes. I know that."

She appears confused by our conversation and I exhale sharply and say in a slower voice. "Purity. I asked you to trust me; several times, in fact. For this marriage to work, I need your unquestioning trust. You see…" I gesture around the room and say darkly, "I am a very wealthy man and with that wealth comes many enemies."

"Enemies!" Her eyes are wide, and I nod, loving how uncertain she is right now. I remove my jacket and her eyes zone in on the gun and, removing it from the holster, I hold it reverently in my hand.

"I have protection. Both in bodyguard form and steel. There are many people who want to remove me from life and as my wife, you will be a target for them."

"I will?" She bites her lip nervously and I say roughly, "If you believe walking away from me is the better option, think again. My enemies would easily find you and deliver you back to me in a coffin."

The tears spring into her eyes and she looks so worried it amuses me.

"That is why you need to trust that I know what I am doing. Protecting you from those enemies and keeping you from harm. To protect and care for you and all I require in return is your company. To be the best wife a man could ask for and to follow my lead without question. I guarantee your safety and you take care of my physical needs. However–"

I shake my head in disgust. "Our marriage will be nothing like your parents' one. I will treat you like a queen and give you the world. We will travel in luxury, and I will buy you whatever you desire. I will keep you safe and in comfort, and yet if you walk away, I cannot guarantee your safety."

I appear to have struck the fear of God in her and her lip trembles as she whispers, "I'm sorry, Killian. I didn't know."

A rush of power floods through me as my world rights itself and I pat the space beside me and say darkly, "Then allow me to demonstrate how good this partnership will be."

She nods and sits beside me nervously, and I experience a rush of power as I grasp her hair in one hand and pull her head sharply toward me. Her lip quivers as the pain intensifies, which turns me on so much, I pull a little harder.

"Ow." She whispers as the tears glisten in her eyes, and I push the straps off her shoulders and caress her right breast with a soft touch.

She instantly groans and I whisper against her lips, "Do you want me, Purity?"

"Of course." she whispers huskily, and I say darkly, "Will you do anything I ask?"

"Anything." Her breath quickens, and a huge weight shifts as she comes right back to me.

The engines start and her eyes appear stricken, and I say

in a low voice, "There is no way back now."

Her breath races as her eyes darken with desire and I say roughly, "Strip for me."

I release her and she stands nervously before me and, to her credit, removes her jumpsuit, revealing the silk underwear I had delivered in the package. It heats my blood as I view her trembling body, her face flaming as she waits for instruction.

I point to the floor and grunt, "Kneel."

She doesn't question me, and I bark, "Unzip my pants and take me in your mouth."

She follows my instruction without question and as I plunder her mouth with my own pleasure in mind, I hold on tightly to her hair, pounding into her with no regard for her comfort. It turns me on. Domination, power and having a woman at my mercy. I *want* her at my mercy and not contemplating a life without me in it.

With every thrust, I seal her fate. She is chained to me until I say otherwise. A perfect angel to ruin at my pleasure and she will thank me.

As I cum hard, she struggles to deal with it, and I love knowing she is kneeling at my feet. It's what I love. Domination. I have never wanted love. It's a wasted emotion that achieves nothing. This is what powers my soul and as I pull out, I stare down at her flushed cheeks with a sense of pride that she has never known another man.

She is all mine, and she always will be.

* * *

WHILE I CLEAN UP, I instruct her to lie on the bed and wait for me. I take my time knowing we have several hours of pleasure to enjoy before we reach our destination. Grasping the bottle of champagne from the ice bucket, I pop the cork and head back into the bedroom, noting how still she lies as if afraid to move.

I take the bottle to the bed and, pulling her head up with one hand, I place the bottle to her lips and say huskily, "Drink it."

"I…" She shakes her head and I growl, "I said drink it."

Her mouth closes around the bottle and as I tip the sparking liquid into it, she gags but attempts to swallow.

"Try again. Control your movements." I say huskily and she nods, trying desperately to master the art of drinking from a bottle.

After a while, she achieves what I wanted and I take a long drag myself and say, "It's all about control. It's more pleasant when you take your time and allow yourself to adjust to it. It's the same with oral sex. Do it at a pace that suits you. Get used to it, accommodate it, and it will be a more pleasurable experience."

She nods, her eyes wide with interest, and I love how desperate she is to be educated. I push her gently back on the bed and whisper, "Open your legs."

Her face flames, but she does as I say, and I pour the champagne on her breasts, watching it spill and roll down her body.

She groans and I grasp the bottle and hold it to her pussy and her eyes widen as I whisper, "Trust me, Bella."

As I insert the bottle, she cries out as the cool liquid spills inside her and as she bites her lip, she bears down on the bottle.

"Does that feel good, Bella?" I whisper against her neck, and she groans. "So good, Killian. So fucking good."

It makes me chuckle softly and then, as I remove the bottle, I replace it with my tongue and lap up the liquid that mixes with her scent.

"What about now?" I say as I pull away and her eyes roll

back in her head as she groans, "So good."

I part her slick walls and suck on her clit, causing her to come so hard she screams my name.

As she lies beneath me, completely at my mercy, I experience a rush of power that never gets old. The difference with her is she's so innocent. Touched only by my hand and she will be my wife. There will never be another man anywhere near my beauty, and any talk of leaving me will not be tolerated. It's like a drug to me and as my cock hardens, I decide to add to the chances of planting my seed inside her, chaining her to me forever, whether she likes it or not.

With one feral groan, I thrust inside and, gripping her hands in mine, I hold them above her head and push in hard, deep and rough. She cries out as I show her who she's dealing with, and I love the way she stares me straight in the eye and I note the excitement in her expression.

I have met my match in Purity. I knew that the minute she wrote me the note and walked away. This time tomorrow we will be husband and wife and I will have a lifetime to play with her.

I cum hard inside her and love how her own orgasm rocks mine and as we come down from our high, I hold her in my arms and cling on tightly. I don't know why, but I like holding her. It's unusual for me because I never hold a woman after sex. I send them on their way and carry on with business. Even when I've fucked women on my plane, it was never with the intention of them getting comfortable. They were sent back to their seat while I enjoyed my own space. Not Purity. I need her with me, which surprises me.

As we lie with her head on my chest, I stare at the ceiling and stroke her back, loving the intimacy of having someone to hold. I drop a light kiss on the top of her head and feel a surge of affection for her. At least that's what I think it is because it can't be anything else.

CHAPTER 26

PURITY

For some reason, I am happy. Something is telling me I shouldn't be. This is not what I wanted when I came to Chicago. I came here for independence. To break free from imprisonment and allowing others to rule my life. I just swapped one owner for another, and yet there are no men like Killian Vieri in Heaven. If there are, I've never met them. He is so sexy. Just one look is all it takes to bring me under his spell. He speaks to my soul and yet the words he uses aren't necessarily ones I want to hear. He wants to own me. To control me and to keep me. I should have said no. Should have.

The trouble is, I want to be here more than I don't. This life is intoxicating, that's for sure. The material wealth he enjoys is captivating, tempting, and too much to comprehend. However, it's not his wealth I love. I've never had any, so why do I need it now? I suppose what attracts me the most is having someone on my side for once.

He saved me.

He sent his men to rescue me and has given me everything.

He wants me.

Nobody has ever wanted me before. I see it in his eyes when he looks in my direction. There's a deep yearning for companionship. I recognize it because I feel it too. Two lost souls searching for that someone who makes living worthwhile.

"I will love being married to you." I say with a light kiss on his chest, and he stills, his fingers freezing in mid-stroke on my back.

I say lightly, "I've never been close to anyone before, unless you count my best friend, Faith. Oh, and Jed Turner who taught me how to fight."

"To fight." He sounds amused, and I giggle softly.

"Yes. We used to meet in Hunter's meadow, and he would teach me. I'm not sure how it started. I think he punched me once and was surprised when I retaliated."

"He punched you." His voice lowers to an ominous growl. "What was his name again?"

I say dreamily. "We became friends, of sorts. He respected my bravery and took it upon himself to teach me to defend myself."

"How old were you?"

"Six years old. Over the years, we enjoyed a hidden friendship because it was forbidden to mix with the other sex in Heaven. To mix with anyone really, but I had Faith, and I had Jed."

He resumes stroking my back and I think about Jed fondly.

"You know, he left Heaven when he was sixteen years old."

"Where did he go?"

"I don't know. He was never spoken of again, but I missed him. I wish I knew if he was okay. Maybe that's what gave me the courage to run myself."

"How did you make that happen?" He says softly and I grin. "My best friend, Faith, met a biker called Jonny. He came from Heaven and escaped like Jed. Anyway, he came back and they, well, hit it off and she became pregnant."

"That must have caused quite a scene."

He chuckles softly and I nod. "It's a very long story, but the result was he came for her, and I helped them escape. Subsequently, I was given a ride by one of the bikers and he gave me money and a phone and told me to call him if I needed help."

He tenses again and stops stroking my back and jealousy laces his voice as he growls, "What biker? What happened?"

"I told you. He gave me a ride out of town and took me to the airport and paid for my ticket here. I still have his phone and just before I came to join you at breakfast, he called me."

Killian sits up and twists my face to his and says in a rough voice, "What did you tell him?"

Once again, I witness the panic in his eyes, but this time I'm prepared for it and I smile, "I told him I didn't need his help. That I was dealing with it."

"Dealing with what?" He says through gritted teeth, and I lean closer and touch my lips to his.

"Dealing with life. I am making my own way and I don't admit defeat easily. I'm happy with my choices and wouldn't change a thing. However…"

He stares at me hard as I grin. "It's always good to have options, don't you think?"

I'm not sure why I thought it would be fun to poke the bear, but the scowl on his face chases away our easy conversation as he hisses, "Options. The only options available to you are the ones I give you. Do you understand?"

I should be angry, incensed, even. I should stop this now before we go in any deeper, but his words do something to my heart instead. They make me feel wanted, and that's a powerful emotion to offer a girl who has never felt wanted in her life and as a result, the tears spill from my eyes and I whisper, "Thank you for wanting me, Killian."

His eyes flash as he pulls my lips to his and kisses me so hard, I can't breathe. It's as if he is starving and I am his last meal and as our tongues clash and our breath joins us, I really believe I have everything I want holding me so possessively in his arms.

I am fast realizing he is a possessive man. Jealous and controlling, but for some reason I like it. It makes me secure and feel as if I can ask him anything and after another hour of him showing just how much he likes to control my body, we are lying together once again, my head on his chest while he plays with my hair, something I am fast realizing he loves to do.

"Tell me about your family, Killian. Will they be at our wedding?"

"Most of them. The important ones, anyway."

"Your parents?" I am intrigued by this man and want to know everything about him.

"No."

"Why not?" I say sleepily, loving how good his fingers in my hair make me feel.

"My father has been banned from the island and my mother lives in Australia."

"How come?" It all sounds very unusual because surely his mother and father live together.

He sighs and shifts up a little, his back against the padded headboard and he says bitterly. "My father turned his back on our family when he wanted out of the business. It's everything to a Vieri. It's what makes the blood flow in our veins. He wanted no part of it and is indifferent to the very machine that made us who we are today."

"But surely family is more important than business?"

PURE EVIL

He stills, and I think I said the wrong thing when he growls ominously. "You will soon learn that business *is* family to a Vieri. Everything we do is with business in mind. Surely you have understood that already."

"I guess." He reminds me of our own arrangement and I kind of get it.

"Tell me about your mother. Why does she live so far away?"

"Because she left my father and went to live in Australia to get as far away from him as possible."

"And you. She left you." I am horrified, and Killian shrugs as if it's of no consequence. "She left all her children because she had no choice. We are Vieris and belong with our family. She understood that."

"Weren't you upset?"

"Were you when you ran away from your own parents?"

"You're answering a question with a question again, but I'll allow it this time because it proves a valid point."

I turn to face him and grin impudently, and he surprises me by chuckling softly.

"You're a surprising woman, Purity."

"In a good way, I hope." I grin and he cups my face in his hands and whispers, "You are a rare, exquisite creature. A unicorn, in fact. So trusting with the mind of a razor. I like that. I like that you question everything with no emotion. They are qualities I admire and rarely see in a woman."

"Have you, shall we say, 'met' many women?"

He nods. "Of course."

His answer isn't surprising, but I don't like it and he apparently approves of the way my eyes lower and my face falls because he pulls my lips to his and whispers, "But none I want to keep until now."

As he kisses me softly, my entire body blooms. That's how it feels, at least. It comes alive under his touch, and I surprise myself by kissing him back so deeply it's as if only he can keep me alive.

His hand wraps around the back of my head and he bites my bottom lip, sucking my lower lip into his mouth and causing me to groan out loud. Something feels different. There's more intimacy than before and I put it down to the fact he opened a little piece of his soul and allowed me to glimpse inside. He has revealed there is a human inside the machine after all, and I wonder about that.

He is the first man I have ever spoken to about anything, really. The first real conversation about emotions and the first man I have ever kissed. He is all my firsts wrapped into an intoxicating package and yet I have hardly scratched the surface because there are a lot more secrets to unravel hidden inside Killian Vieri.

CHAPTER 27

KILLIAN

One hour before landing, I shake Purity awake, loving how exhausted she was when she finally fell asleep in my arms. I listened to her gentle breathing as I went over my plan. We have a long, hard road to travel, and I wonder if she is up to it. Purity isn't used to walking, but I will be beside her every step of the way and I'm guessing she will stumble, just like the heels I have insisted she wear to practice. I will not let her fail, and I wonder what my grandparents will make of her when we show up.

We shower and dress and make our way into the cabin where there is a meal laid out waiting. Most of my men are in a different part of the aircraft, and the attendant is discreet and remains hidden in the galley. I prefer my solitude on flights, usually taking the opportunity to sleep and contemplate business. I have never entertained a woman for longer than a quick fuck before and then sent her back to the others. Gabriella mainly because she traveled with me as my assistant. It reminds me to ask Saint about her movements since I fired her.

But that can wait because I am hungry and I'm guessing

Purity is too and as we sit facing one another, I love the freshly fucked face, staring back at me as if I am fucking God himself.

It empowers me. Nobody has ever looked at me as if I am a king. They fear me, desire me, want me even, but there is always a hint of fear hiding behind their eyes. They never question and never speak out of turn, which is why it's refreshing to spend time with somebody who does.

Purity gazes out of the window as she chews a mouthful of the finest beef.

"This view is incredible." She says in a wistful voice and as I gaze at her uninterrupted, I find myself agreeing. "It is."

"The clouds are so beautiful, aren't they? Almost as if I could lie on them as the most comfortable bed."

"I wouldn't advise it." I say with amusement, and she giggles as she turns those astonishing eyes toward me.

"So, tell me about your sister. Will she be there?"

"Of course. My brother too."

"What are their names?"

"Serena and Shade."

"I like their names."

She has so much honesty, her expression is irresistible. I want to hold her in my arms so badly, which shocks me a little. In fact, I am struggling not to touch her every hour of the day and I put it down to my basic desire to ruin her soul.

I am intoxicated by her. Fascinated by a woman who is so pure and untainted. Knowing that I have been the only man to touch her, to explore the places nobody has ever been, feeds my need for power and domination.

There is so much I want to do to her and when she is my wife, I will bring her firmly in line. She will experience the full force of my obsession with her while I tear her apart for my own pleasure. Like the small boy who was destructive and ruined things. My sister's dolls, a freshly bloomed flower and any toy of my brother's. I did it because I loved the power it gave me and when I grew up, I played with real life dolls. Loving how they did everything I told them to and yet adored every minute of it, begged me for more, in fact. It makes me hard just thinking of what I will do to her and as she smiles at me as she eats, I just fucking can't help myself.

"Come here."

She blinks in surprise. "I am here."

"No."

I stand and in one swift move, I sweep the contents of the table to the floor, causing her to yell, "What are you doing?"

She makes to retrieve the dishes from the floor, and I say in a deep voice, "I said, come here."

She peers up at me nervously and says with a quiver in her voice, "Have I done something to upset you?"

"On the contrary, Purity. I want to show you something amazing. An experience you will never forget."

"Oh." Her eyes widen and I tug her up to face me and whisper, "This is about trust again. Do you trust me, Purity?"

"Of course." Her eyes are so innocent, and I know she doesn't lie and the power surges through my body as I turn her to face the window, pushing her face down on the table and ripping off her clothes.

"What—"

"Shh. I whisper, my voice dressed in desire. This will be a memory you will always treasure if you do as I say."

She relaxes and I kick her legs apart, loving her fine ass as it bends before me so temptingly.

"I unzip my pants but don't remove them and palm my throbbing cock as I position it against her tempting ass.

"Palms on the table, Purity." I command and she does as I say, her breath labored as her excitement takes over.

I reach down and tease her clit, loving how wet she is already, and I smear her wet heat from back to front, causing her to groan and then as I position my cock against her ass, I whisper, "Look out on those clouds, Purity. Gaze at the beauty before you. Know we are flying high and are free. Nothing can touch us here. Nobody can see us. We are invincible and up here — we are free."

She gasps as she whispers, "It's so beautiful, Killian."

"You are beautiful, Bella. My beautiful wife and I will give you the world." She groans as I ease my cock into her tempting ass and gasps, "What's happening?"

"I'm claiming every part of you, Bella. This is what happens when a man is besotted by a woman. He must own every inch of her body, and I will own yours."

She shifts back a little and I swear something explodes inside me.

I never imagined there was a woman alive who could hold my interest for longer than it took to fuck her out of my system.

I never understood what nonna meant when she told me to open my heart and let someone in.

I dismissed her when she told me life was better shared, but right now, staring out of the window at the sun lighting the clouds with majestic beauty, I believe in all of that because of the woman I am marrying. I wasn't kidding when I said I was besotted. I am. She is the only woman who has ever held that honor and as I push inside her ass, it's a move that causes her to cry out, "Oh my God, Killian, why is that so good?"

I lean forward and grip her chin hard and force her to stare at the clouds as I fuck her ass. I am claiming every part of her because she is mine and always will be and there will be no part of her body that doesn't enjoy my touch. Even this and as I move slowly and carefully, I watch her tears splash on my fingers as I hold her face and I whisper huskily, "Am I hurting you, Bella?"

"A little, but that's not why I'm crying."

Her voice is high and breathless, and she feels so fragile in my arms. As if she could break at any moment and she whispers, "I am crying with happiness."

I lighten my hold and kiss the back of her neck softly and reaching down, play with her clit, causing her to tremble against me. There are so many emotions surrounding our hearts right now and as she pushes back onto me, I swear something heated explodes in my chest. I have never experienced anything like this before as I fuck my wife facing the heavens. It is just too good, too addictive and as she tenses and her body squeezes my cock, I can't hold on as I explode inside her ass, both of us reaching our orgasm at exactly the same time.

I pull out as Purity lies on the table, exhausted and unable to move, it seems.

I reach for the napkin and clean myself up before zipping my pants and pulling her into my arms. She is so weak, like a wounded animal with no fight left in it, and I swing her into my arms and carry her back to the bedroom. She snuggles against my chest and whispers, "You were right. That was a memory I will cherish forever."

There is a dull ache where I believe my heart lives inside me. Something that is growing that is becoming hard to ignore. Every word she speaks I listen to in wonder and every smile she directs my way fills my chest with something I can't quite place.

She is so fragile, so weak in many ways, but strong where it counts and if I thought fucking her all the way to Italy would calm my fascination for her, I was wrong.

If anything, it has only intensified.

CHAPTER 28

KILLIAN

As she sits beside me in the back of another black car, I can tell she is excited. Probably because the scenery is very different here. A beautiful landscape with different looking trees to what she's used to. The houses and buildings are old and slightly crumbling and the sea that sparkles beside the road we travel on makes my eyes shine.

"Look. I can see the ocean. I can't believe it." She says with an awed gasp.

I shrug. "It's an ocean. Nothing special."

"Nothing special. It's paradise."

"Have you never seen the ocean before, Purity?"

"Not in reality. Just in books and what we learned about it in class."

Her eyes are the match of the blue lagoon outside and I have a strange anger that she has been denied the experience.

"You will soon become acquainted with the ocean, Bella. My family's island is in the middle of it."

"How will we get there?"

She smiles with the enthusiasm of a child and there's a

knot in my stomach when I realize she was one not that long ago.

"Our boat. We use it to travel to the mainland. It will be waiting for us."

"A boat." Her eyes are wide and shining with disbelief. "You have a boat too. You are so lucky."

"You make your own luck in life, Purity. You made yours. Surely you can tell how it works."

She cocks her head to one side, which is so adorable I am ready to pounce once again, and she says with a small giggle. "You're right. I did change my own direction. The lucky part was finding you."

She turns away and my heart beats faster because if she only realized how *unlucky* she was to find me. I'm not her happy ending, not even close. She may be excited now, but what happens when I am bored playing with her? She will be relegated to living as my wife in name only while I get my kicks with other women. Isn't that what happens? It did in my father's case.

A lifetime is too long to dedicate it to one woman. But I will never give her the same opportunity. She will only belong to me. I will make sure of it.

The cars spill into the marina, and I notice the family boat waiting. It's the biggest boat in the dock and stands majestically, putting every other boat in the shade. The staff are dressed in white and are waiting to help us board. Everything will be as instructed, and I have no reason to doubt it will be anything other than perfect.

We stop by the navy-blue carpet leading up the steps to board and Purity says with excitement, "I really am living the dream. Who knew people lived like this?"

I catch the surprise on the face of the skipper, and he nods respectfully as she flashes him a brilliant smile, causing the beast within me to growl. "Come."

I grab her hand and head inside the cabin, away from the stares of the crew and away from my men. Purity has the ability to make every person in the room want to be around her. She is natural and unaffected with a childlike enthusiasm for life. It's adorable but angers me too. She is desirable in so many ways and I hate that one day she may wake up and realize I'm not so great after all.

Just imagining her looking at me with anything but adoration leaves a chill in my heart. The trouble is, I'm not sure what I must do to keep that expression in her eyes other than fucking her senseless and buying her expensive things.

Purity insists on a tour of the boat and ordinarily I would instruct one of the crew members to do the honors. But not with her. Never with her and I take my time and show her around myself. Her addictive exuberance for every inch of it lifts my spirit. It's contagious and I find myself chuckling on the odd occasion as she makes an observation that causes me to laugh.

We finish up on the forward deck and as we speed through the waves, she turns to me and the delight in her eyes makes me swallow hard. "I love the ocean." She says, turning her face to the breeze and closing her eyes.

There's a dull ache in my heart as I watch her enjoying the simple pleasures when we are surrounded by wealth. She is interested in it but not bothered by it. I am fast realizing that Purity is a rare treasure. Unlike any other woman I have ever met and for a man who covets rare beauty, she is becoming more important to me than I thought possible.

I need to touch her. To hold her and to be around her. Every minute that passes reveals another part of her that I like, and discovering Purity is like seeing life for the first time. Through fresh eyes that see the wonder in it, not the pure evil that I am used to.

I reach out and pull the hair away from the nape of her

neck and kiss her softly, inhaling the fresh scent of innocence that is fast becoming my favorite one. My arms wrap around her from behind as she stares out to sea, and she feels so good in them. As if she belongs there and she snuggles back against me with a soft, "I am so happy, Killian."

I squeeze her a little tighter, loving this stolen moment where nothing else matters but holding her. A woman who walked into my life with her eyes open and with none of the preconceptions many others have. She knew nothing about me. She still doesn't and I'm astonished to discover I hope it stays that way. If she realized what I was capable of. What the beast that lives inside me is capable of, she would regard me with a different expression on her face.

Perhaps it's better she faces the ocean so she can't see the evil holding her so tenderly in his arms. A man who doesn't deserve to hold an angel like her. Who deserves for this happiness to be taken from him because he never earned the right to claim it.

I took it and made her mine and never gave her a choice. I manipulated her to my advantage, something I've always done with every business transaction I have ever made. The trouble is, I don't view Purity as a business deal anymore. I see her as my world and that is a huge problem that I don't know what the fuck to do about.

CHAPTER 29

PURITY

My heart is full. Somehow, everything has aligned, and I am where I dreamed I would be. I will be getting married today to a man I chose. Not my parents.

A man who makes my heart skip a beat and intrigues me. A powerful man who will keep me safe and show me everything I ever dreamed of. He will make a good father for my children, and I will be the perfect wife. This is what I always wanted. Him.

* * *

We reach the island and I stare in surprise at the size of it. I don't know what I expected, but it wasn't anything on this scale. I suppose I thought it would be small, but I can't make out the end of this one.

As we stare at the approaching shore, a speedboat heads our way and as it pulls aside, I watch men dressed in black circle it before heading to the front to guide us in.

"Who are they?" I ask, as I stand wrapped in Killian's arms, as I have done for the entire time we've been on this boat. We haven't moved from our position, which suited me fine. I love it when he holds me. It makes me feel safe. As if he is looking out for me and I don't question it at all. This is what he likes.

At first it surprised me because in my entire life I have never seen my father hold my mother. They never touch and yet now I've experienced it, I'm a little sad for them. This is an unexpected perk of a relationship I never considered, and I like it. In fact, I like everything about my relationship with Killian and hope I don't do anything wrong. Perhaps I should have studied the contract a little closer. It must be written in there somewhere about what I'm expected to do. It's playing on my mind, so I turn and whisper, "Did you bring a copy of the contract with you? I would like to check up on a few things."

"What things?" He tenses and I say lightly.

"My role, I suppose. What you expect of me because I don't want to disappoint you by missing out on doing something you expect."

For some reason my words anger him, and he drops his arms and turns away with an abrupt, "You don't need to be told what to do, Purity. There is no bullet point list to follow. You figure things out as you go along and just for the record, you are doing everything perfectly. Trust me and follow my lead, and you will be fine."

"Thank God." I exhale a sigh of relief and say with a smile. "I'd hate to do something wrong. I'm loving it so far."

"It's time to go."

He turns away and my heart lurches because what did I say? He appears angry about something, and I think back on our conversation. I follow him, cursing the high shoes he insists on me wearing and I wonder if it's that. The way I am so clumsy on them. I can't think of anything else because I've done everything he asks.

If anything, I'm a little annoyed at his constant mood swings. What was wrong with asking to be better at my job? The man's an enigma, that's for sure.

With a sigh, I follow him, loving my experience of boating, or whatever they call it. I love the faint taste of salt on my lips, the wind in my hair and the sun on my face. I love the sense of freedom out here and the way the birds follow the boat. They are magnificent and their cries are like music accompanying us.

When I picture the dusty town I grew up in, I wonder why nobody ever leaves. Few manage to make the journey past the mountain ranges, and I'm convinced if they discovered how amazing life was on the other side, they would be packing up in their droves. When I remember the wicked reverend who ruled over it, I shiver knowing I had a lucky escape. What he did to my friend Faith was wicked and evil, and I am so glad Killian is nothing like that.

We park up on the edge of a wooden road of sorts. I overheard one of the crew call it a pontoon and I wonder about this language I have never heard. No wonder Killian is angry with me. I am so uneducated it must annoy him. I must do better, so he doesn't regret my position and so, with a deep resolve, I follow him closely as we exit the boat.

He strides in front of me, and I stumble constantly as I attempt to keep up with him. Saint is behind me and many times I almost trip him up as I catch my heel in the wooden boards and yet he never reaches out to help me.

We come to a smooth surface of what appears to be marble and I'm a little flushed as we head toward the most beautiful building I have ever seen. It actually shines as it looks out to sea. A beautiful white palace of majestic grandeur surrounded by colorful flowers and gently swaying trees.

I notice two people waiting and as we get a little closer, I see an older man and woman holding hands as they watch us. As we draw nearer, the woman steps forward and says with delight, "Killian. It's good to see you."

I watch in fascination as he kisses her three times and then pulls her into his arms and I witness the happiness on her face as she hugs him back. Then she pulls away, and the man steps forward and does the same and it confuses me. This must be how you greet people on this island. Touching was forbidden in Heaven unless your husband allowed it, which he never did to my knowledge, unless it was to shake the reverend's hand. This is different and as their attention turns to me, I feel their curiosity burning through my soul.

There is something incredibly powerful about these people. The air surrounding them is laced with power.

The woman steps forward and peers at me with curiosity and then smiles, causing me to sigh with relief.

"You are beautiful, Purity."

I blink in surprise. "You know my name."

I'm astonished and she laughs softly, "I know everything, my dear. You will soon realize that."

She turns to Killian, and I note the approval in her eyes as she says in a voice that offers no disagreement. "We will leave you now. The next time you will see your bride is at the altar."

Before I can say anything, she takes my hand and pulls me after her and the brooding stare of the man I'm to marry follows me as I attempt to keep up with her.

* * *

As we enter the house, I stare in amazement at the most beautiful room I have ever seen. I'm surprised because it's filled with plants, art hanging on the walls, and deep couches laden with cushions. The sun streams in through the open doors, its warm fingers touching every corner of the room, filling it with welcome.

"You have a lovely home, Mrs. Vieri."

I take an educated guess on her name, and she turns and smiles. "Call me Nonna."

"Okay."

I return her warm smile and she says with interest. "I can see why my grandson chose you. You are everything he was searching for."

"Searching for?"

I'm confused, and she nods. "He was looking for a wife who he could mold into his perfect woman." She shakes her head as if a little disappointed by that, and then she stops and stares at me hard. "Don't make it so easy for him, Purity."

"Why not?" I'm confused, and a little surprised and she replies with an infectious twinkle in her eye.

"Because men like my grandson — like all the Vieri men – relish a challenge. If you make it too easy, it strips away the fun. Make him work hard for your heart and you will keep it forever."

"His heart?"

I don't understand and she sighs a little and then surprises me by saying, "Do you love him, Purity?"

"Love." I blink and consider her words before replying. "I don't know what love is, Mrs. um, Nonna and I don't understand what it has to do with marriage."

Her face falls and I wonder if I've said something wrong, which worries me. Then she says with a deep breath. "I see."

She seems a little sad and I say nervously, "Have I said something wrong?"

She shakes her head. "No. If anything, it tells me what I suspected all along. Come. We don't have long."

As I follow her up a huge white staircase, I think back on our conversation and struggle to understand what placed that disappointment in her eyes. I really hope it wasn't something I said because more than anything, I want to make Killian proud of me, not disappointed that somehow I didn't measure up.

CHAPTER 30

KILLIAN

My grandfather appears thoughtful as we sit facing one another in his den, the sun streaming through the window, unlike the previous time we were here.

I have done everything he asked of me and as he makes certain everything is to his liking, he pours me a glass of whiskey and, handing it to me, says in his deep voice. "To your marriage. May it bring you everything you want."

"To my marriage." I raise my glass and savor the bite of the amber liquid as it slides home.

He sets his glass down and says thoughtfully, "Can you trust the girl?"

"Of course."

"I have investigated her family. That's a strange town she comes from."

He appears thoughtful and I must agree with him.

"Heaven is an anomaly in our great country. However, it's precisely that which makes it of interest to our organization."

He nods, staring at me through sharp, deadly eyes.

"Her father, Elijah Sanders."

"What of him?"

I am interested to see what my grandfather's point is.

"We have heard of him. He runs an opium operation."

"That was checked out and found to be wrong for our organization. We used it in the past but reports weren't good so I sent someone to investigate."

"Who did you send?" He is alert and is obviously hiding something from me and my thoughts turn to Gabriella and the mysterious man in the white suit.

A shiver passes down my spine as I sense he is about to remind me why we leave nothing to chance, and I realize I made a terrible mistake in trusting that woman.

"Gabriella."

A flash of irritation passes across his face and my heart sinks, knowing I fucked up.

"What did she tell you?"

"That the opium wasn't up to standard and wouldn't pass the most basic test if we tried to sell it on."

Before he can speak, I say with a growl, "I have information that I need checked out."

"I'm listening." He raises the glass to his lips, and I lean forward, staring at him with a dark frown.

"Purity remembered meeting Gabriella that day. She was on her way home from school and saw Gabriella leaning against a white car."

He says nothing and merely swirls the liquid around his glass as I continue.

"She handed Purity her business card and told her if she ever needed a job to come and find her. She did."

He nods. "Not unexpected. Gabriella never passed an opportunity by to make money."

"That isn't what's bothering me."

His eyes gleam as I speak. "She wasn't alone. Purity told me a man in a white suit came out from the house and ordered her to leave. He appeared angry and as they drove off, Purity entered the house and heard her father on the phone. He was angry and said he wouldn't do business with the monkey. They needed to send the organ grinder. Then her mom appeared, and she heard no more."

My grandfather leans back and there is no expression on his face telling me his thoughts. There never has been and I wonder if he's angry, disappointed, or even happy at what I told him.

The seconds pass as he stares at me long and hard, and I know better than to interrupt him. Then he surprises me by pulling out his desk drawer, retrieving a leather-bound folder and opening it before him.

He pushes a large photograph toward me, and I stare in shock at the scene I just described moments ago.

However, it's not the scene itself that angers me and tugs the bottom out of my world. It's the face of the man leaving Purity's family home.

"Did you know about this?" I say in confusion, and he sighs heavily.

"No."

"The photographs?" I study the set he gives me and for some reason, it's the face of the pretty girl in the school uniform that affects me more. I stare at her angelic trusting face as she hovers close to Gabriella, the card in her hand before she hides it away.

My heart beats so fast as I stare at a vision and, for some reason, knowing what I have already done to destroy her, doesn't make me feel good about myself. It's a snapshot in time of the beginning of Purity's road to damnation and it's choking me, dragging me into that dark place I can never escape. Then I'm reminded of the shady world we live in as I glance at the other two people in the photograph.

"What does this mean?" I stare at my grandfather, and he shrugs.

"It means you have a lot to learn, Killian, before you deserve the title of Don Vieri."

He appears angry and yet that anger is replaced by an expression of pleasure when the door opens and my sister walks inside with no invitation.

"Grandfather." She addresses him first and heads to his side, throwing her arms around him and kissing him eagerly, several times on both cheeks, causing him to laugh fondly.

"My beautiful princess." He says with pleasure and immediately the dark moment is lit by brilliant light.

She turns to me and grins. "The bridegroom that I never thought would see the day."

She cocks her head to one side. "I must meet this paragon of virtue who has met your high standards."

She heads toward me and kisses me three times and then stands back and sighs heavily.

"You always look so angry, brother. Even on your wedding day."

I catch my grandfather's expression and know this conversation will not be revisited. It is up to me to deal with the problem and yet I have many questions that need answering.

But not now. Not with Serena in earshot and she studies me hard and then whispers, "She's a lucky girl."

"If you say so." I shrug, causing her to roll her eyes.

"One day, Kill, you will let someone inside that cold heart of yours. Hopefully, when she becomes family, you will offer Purity the same respect you give to us."

I grin because Serena always can lift my mood.

"Keep dreaming, princess."

She shakes her head and then blows us both a kiss as she

heads to the door. "I'm going to seek out this wonder woman and discover if she is as mentally disturbed as I think she is."

Her laughter follows her, and I have a growing sense of unease that I'm doing the wrong thing. Not for me. For Purity because, as I glance down at the angelic face in the photograph, I feel like the big bad wolf who is about to gobble Red Riding Hood up.

I am brought back to business as my grandfather retrieves the photographs and places them back into the leather folder, sliding it my way with a sad expression in his eye.

"Do what you must, but you *will* do it, Killian."

His eyes are as dark as the blackest sky and hold an approaching storm that would have many men running for shelter.

Not me. I must stand in the eye of it and conquer it if I am ever going to deserve the title of Don Vieri, supreme ruler of The Dark Lords.

CHAPTER 31

PURITY

Nonna shows me to a beautiful bedroom decorated in pale blue silk with pretty flowers woven into the paper on the walls. The palest blue silk curtains are fluttering at the open window and the view alone is breath-taking.

"You will prepare for your wedding. I arranged everything." She says with a slight twinkle in her eye.

"I am very grateful ma... I mean, Nonna." I say, suddenly a little nervous and she says with a hint of concern. "You are happy about the wedding?"

"Of course. I wouldn't be here if I wasn't."

Before she can respond, the door opens and I stare in delight as a pretty girl bounds into the room, causing nonna's smile to almost break its boundaries.

"Serena. Princess." They hug one another with so much fondness it surprises me. I've never seen such a public display of affection before, and I like it. It reminds me how little of it I had in my life until Killian entered it.

The woman turns and before I can react, I am pulled into her arms and she whispers, "You are so pretty, Purity.

Welcome to the family. Finally, another female to balance the odds."

She pulls back and smiles so sweetly it's infectious and my eyes shine as she whispers, "You will make a beautiful bride."

"Thank you."

I don't know what else to say, which doesn't matter because she appears happy to speak for all of us.

"So, where are we?" She peers around the room with a critical expression.

"How long do we have?"

"Four hours." Nonna says with a soft voice.

"Then we must eat." Serena says with determination and nonna nods in agreement.

"I arranged a meal to be served downstairs. Killian will remain in the main house, and we will assist Purity here in the guest wing."

Serena nods. "Good. I'm so hungry. We should head there now."

Nonna moves to the door, and I'm surprised when Serena links her arm in mine. "This is going to be an amazing wedding. Small but amazing."

We head to another gorgeous room with views over stunning gardens and I note the table is laden with tempting dishes of food.

It's all a little surreal as I take a seat in a cream velvet-covered chair and a man appears from nowhere and fills my glass with champagne. My heart sinks as I sense another meal I am going to hate.

Nonna takes a seat at the head of the table and Serena sits opposite me, draining her glass, causing her grandmother to say with disapproval. "Serena. Moderation please."

I try not to giggle at the mischievous wink she throws me before her glass is filled once again and she helps herself to some salad in the middle of the table, encouraging me to do the same.

"So, tell me about you and Kill. I must say, I can't even imagine him being married. I almost pity you."

She chuckles softly and nonna says rather sharply, "It appears that Killian has found his perfect match."

"Really." Serena's eyes are wide. "Are you saying the unthinkable has happened, and he is actually marrying someone he loves?"

I stare at her in surprise and shake my head vehemently.

"I think you've misunderstood. We are not in love, Serena. We are going to be married and will be husband and wife under the terms of the marriage contract I signed."

The food stops halfway to Serena's mouth and then she sets down the fork and glances at her grandmother, who nods with a sad gleam in her eye.

For a moment no word is spoken, and I feel bad that I've ruined the easy atmosphere.

Nonna interrupts, saying kindly, "Purity comes from a town called Heaven where marriages are arranged and entered into as a contract. There is no love involved, just duty."

Serena stares at me with a mixture of pity and disbelief and I wonder what I've said wrong.

"So, you're *not* in love with Killian?"

She appears disappointed about that, and I shrug. "I don't know what love is, but I do know it has no place in the marriage contract I signed. We get on though. I like him. I respect him and I want to make him happy."

"Why?"

She appears confused and I smile. "Because he makes me happy. He cares for me, and I feel safe with him. He rescued me from a terrible place and promised to show me the world. I will be the perfect wife and he will educate me in life."

Serena shares a look with her grandmother, and I don't like what I see. She just nods and says a little sadly. "I understand now. Forgive me, Purity, Nonna's right. You are both perfect for one another."

We carry on eating and I absolutely love the food and say politely, "Nonna. The food is incredible. I have never tasted anything quite so amazing. You know…" I laugh nervously. "I was worried it may be more of that shell stuff Killian likes and meat that hasn't been cooked. I'm so happy it's not. In fact, I could eat everything before me. It is that good."

I note the approval in nonna's eyes and Serena bursts out laughing. "You just earned nonna's undying love. She loves women who eat and appreciate what's before them."

"I do." Nonna smiles. "Good home cooking is the best there is."

"Will you teach me?" I say with enthusiasm, and she smiles, the twinkle returning to her eyes.

"It will be my pleasure."

I'm at ease with the two women who are closest to Killian, and I am very happy about that. They've made me so welcome, and I pinch myself that things worked out so well for me.

As soon as we finish, Serena says suddenly. "I have a plan to waste a couple of hours. It won't take long to get you ready, so why don't we relax for a bit?"

Nonna says carefully, "What are you thinking?"

She appears interested and Serena grins, throwing her grandmother a look that I can't quite place.

"A movie."

"Wow. That sounds so good." I say with happy delight because any movies I've ever seen were a few short moments snatched watching when I should be somewhere else entirely.

"Then I'll leave you to it while I make certain everything is in place."

Nonna smiles and leaves the room and Serena once again links her arm in mine.

"Come, there is a cinema room at the top of the house. We can make ourselves comfortable and chill for a bit."

I follow her upstairs and once again can't believe my luck and I really do consider I'm the luckiest girl in the world right now and nobody can persuade me otherwise.

CHAPTER 32

KILLIAN

Time passes so quickly I'm surprised when nonna heads into my room and says with amusement. "It's time. You have one hour."

Saint makes to tidy away the folder we've pored over for hours and come to a very disturbing conclusion of what must be done. The facts are too horrific to ignore and it's with a heavy heart I nod and say wearily, "Of course. The plan still stands. As soon as I'm married, we will head back to Chicago and deal with this latest information."

Saint nods and leaves with the folder tucked under his arm and as I stand, nonna says with concern. "I want you to be happy."

"I am happy, Nonna."

She raises her eyes with concern.

"Are you sure about that?"

"Of course." I really don't have time for this and then she says sadly, "I want you to love, Killian. To know what it's like to experience the most powerful emotion God can bestow on you. Not this. Not this business arrangement that will destroy an innocent girl's life."

"Love." I say the word with derision. "I will not be held back by love. Love ruins everything. I've seen it for myself. My own parents loved, at least one of them did, and look where that got her. She tore a family apart because of love, not duty, and he allowed it to happen. I have no intention of allowing love to even enter my heart all the time I am fighting a war."

I make to leave, and she rests her small hand on my arm and says sadly, "Then I pray you don't find love, my son. I pray you don't wake up one day and realize that you lost out on something that could have made you more powerful than you ever dreamed of. If that happens, you will be destroyed and it will tear my own heart open and leave it bleeding out because if you never find love, Killian, you haven't lived at all."

I take a deep breath because talk of emotions isn't something I understand. I understand business. Nothing else. I desire, I covet, and I enjoy a woman's company, but the moment I think I can't live without another, is the moment I've failed.

Once I've kissed nonna on both cheeks, I leave her behind because the most important thing right now is to dress for my wedding and marry my bride. Then we can return to Chicago, and I can sort this shit out that my grandfather has so kindly dumped in my lap.

* * *

I SHOWER, I shave, and I dress in the handmade tailored black suit and white shirt. My shoes gleam and the gold Rolex on my wrist tells me I am running out of time as a single man. I never expected my wedding to be so soon. Here, with only my family and guards as witnesses. I never imagined marrying a woman like Purity either and as I think of her, my heart races. She is so perfect. Like an angel, and just the thought of owning such a rare beauty makes everything right with my world.

A tap on the door causes me to say gruffly, "Enter."

I grin at the man who does, and he says with an amused drawl, "I could not miss this."

"Good to see you, brother." I reach out and hug him hard and as he pulls back, he grins with a wicked gleam in his eye. "Rather you than me, Kill."

"It will happen. Make the most of your freedom while you can." I reply, casually adjusting my tie and staring at the face on my watch.

"We should go. Nonna will not tolerate it if we're late."

He nods and falls into step beside me.

"How are your plans progressing?" He says in an urgent whisper.

"As agreed, I will soon take a wife who will shine by my side and reflect the heat off me. We will become powerful, donating millions to charity and building the business into a billion dollar one. Beyond reproach and America's heroes, all the time we tear down our enemies before they even see it coming."

"And your wife. Will she pass the test?"

"Of course. Her training has already begun. She will trust me implicitly and do whatever I say. She is unwise in the ways of our world and won't understand what is happening."

"I hope it works out for you, brother."

I nod, not really contemplating anything other than my own success.

"What about you? How are things progressing?"

I know my brother was given his own instructions, and he sighs heavily. "Usual shit. Take out our enemies and make sure our business has no leaks."

Where I will run the acceptable face of our business,

Shade will run the unacceptable one, reporting to me as his don. We will work together as a family and everything we do will be for that family's success.

Aside from Saint and Serena, Shade is the only person I trust with my life. Brothers by birth, friends by choice. My siblings are close to me because they are of the same blood. The same mind and the same ambition. We will rule the Dark Lords as a family and extinguish those who are trying to bring us down.

Business as usual in the Vieri household.

We head out into the garden, and I smirk when I see the lengths nonna has gone to make this a proper wedding. A flower decorated arch is set on the edge of the terrace overlooking the beach below. The sea sparkles behind it and the waves lap gently to shore.

White seats are set on either side of it, decorated with flowers and ribbons. A red carpet leads me to stand under the arch where the local priest to the mainland is waiting, dressed in full regalia.

The staff and guards make up the guest list and a local photographer is waiting to record the happy occasion. Everything is perfect and as my brother stands beside me and my grandfather and nonna take their seats, the music begins courtesy of a recording playing through the speaker. This will be our wedding, but the celebration will be a far grander event.

When we return to Chicago, I hired the finest hotel in town and invited anyone of power and influence. It will be the biggest celebration Chicago has ever seen where I will launch us high into society. This is the beginning of an astonishing rise to power that nothing can get in the way of happening.

Now I just need my bride.

CHAPTER 33

PURITY

The woman staring at her reflection is nothing like me. I lost her somewhere between stepping into this house and pulling on this veil. My heart is fluttering, my stomach churning, and I am struggling to breathe. I thought I had it all figured out. Now I'm not so sure.

That movie.

I have never seen anything like it. It opened up a world to me that I never knew existed. In some ways, it was my world. In others, it was far removed from it. I felt an empathy with the woman in it, but unlike her, I don't imagine my story will have the same ending.

"You look so beautiful, Purity."

Serena's eyes are sparkling with happy tears, and I whisper, "Thank you. I couldn't have done this without you."

I'm not lying either. She is a miracle worker because the face she painted like a masterpiece is surely not my own.

I am beautiful.

I could stare at her art all day long and it brings tears to my eyes when I see the woman I wanted to be so badly staring right back at me.

My hair has been lifted from my shoulders and piled intricately on top of my head, a diamond tiara securing it in place. The diamond choker rests against my throat, which is the only jewelry I wear. White satin heels are strangely comfortable and the fancy lingerie I'm wearing is luxurious to the touch. I even smell amazing, courtesy of the expensive bottle of scent Serena almost emptied on to my skin.

We make our ways downstairs and out into the brilliant sunshine and it's as if I'm having an out-of-body experience. This is my wedding day. It's here now and as one of the guards thrusts a bouquet at me, I smile my thanks with a trembling lip.

Serena walks in front, a vision in scarlet that contrasts with her jet-black hair. Snow White and Rose Red were her words, causing her to tell me of two sisters in a fairy story. I realize that as a result of marrying Killian, I am gaining an instant family, which once again reminds me of how lucky I am.

They are so kind, so gentle and yet… That movie has shaken me and what I wanted is fading away as a memory and being replaced with something else entirely.

The music serenades me as I walk down the red carpet and I stare at the ocean twinkling in the distance.

I don't register the guests. They are strangers and yet I have no desire to see any faces from my past. My own family, even. They are now of no concern to me but—that movie is playing on repeat inside my mind.

Then I see him when Serena steps to one side and my heart flutters and my breath hitches because of him. His dark, devilish looks and his heated gaze draw me to his side as if I no longer have control of my body. I notice a man standing beside him who is the image of him and realize it must be his brother – I think his name is Shade. They are an interesting family for sure and I'm uncertain if I should be here at all.

As I draw near, Serena accepts the flowers from me and takes a seat beside her grandmother, and as Killian steps forward, he reaches for my hand.

The approval in his eyes makes me weak with longing because he is everything I want in life, but that movie has conflicted my thoughts.

We turn as the priest begins to speak and as Killian rubs his thumb over my hand, I struggle to breathe. I listen to the words but don't really register them at all because my mind is filled with images of a very different outcome to life.

I am told to repeat the words the priest says first, and I do so with a soft, faltering voice. Then he says the words that make me freeze.

"Do you promise to love, honor and obey?"

I falter and he repeats the words and I stare into Killian's eyes with a stricken expression. He says them again and I open my mouth, but nothing comes out and Killian leans forward and whispers, "Is something wrong? Just breathe, Purity, this will be over soon."

"But…" The tears fill my eyes as my voice deserts me and Killian appears angry as he whispers, "Just say the goddamned words, Purity."

"I can't." A lone tear spills down my cheek as I whisper, "I can't lie."

He appears confused and holds up his hand to stop the priest and pulls me away to the side, out of earshot of the waiting audience.

He stares into my eyes with a deepening anger. "What would you be lying about?"

He appears confused and I say with a sob. "I can honor and obey, but how can I say I will love you, Killian?"

"What?" He appears stunned and I say miserably.

PURE EVIL

"Gina told me not to fall in love with you. I didn't understand what that meant and then nonna asked me if I loved you. I told her no and said the same thing to Serena. I don't love you, Killian. Not like the woman in the movie. Not like them. Our marriage contract would be over before it began."

He stares at me as if I'm speaking in riddles and I notice something shift in his eyes. It's almost unbearable to watch as he shuts down before me. He appears to take a deep breath before he whispers, "What that means is you will love, honor and obey me during our marriage. You will learn to love me under the protection of the contract. It will grow in time, even if it's not there in the beginning."

"What if it doesn't—grow, I mean?"

"Then the marriage contract is broken and terminated." He says abruptly.

"So, I must learn to love you to keep you. Is that what you're saying?" I blink away the tears and he nods, a sad smile on his face.

"Yes, Purity. You may not love me now, but it's my duty to make you fall in love with me. It's up to you whether I'm successful or not."

For some reason, I feel a little foolish that I even questioned him. Of course he's right. Our love will grow. It will be like in the movie. At the beginning, it was a contract. A business deal that suited them both. Then, as they learned more about one another, it grew into something magical. Love.

I never knew I wanted it until I saw it happening right before my eyes and it's with a lighter heart that I blink away the tears and smile.

"Then I will learn to love you, Killian, because I can't bear the thought of losing you."

He stares at me for a split second with unguarded emotion on his face, then, without another word, he closes his eyes and pulls me close against his chest. His heart beats against my cheek as he whispers, "Come. We have a wedding to attend."

As we walk back to take our place before the priest, this time I have no doubts. I am doing the right thing and I will fall in love with my husband. Just like the movie.

I know it.

CHAPTER 34

KILLIAN

When Purity walked toward me, she was a vision. An angel walking into hell willingly and I couldn't tear my eyes from her. So beautiful, so elegant and so pure, as her name suggests. The perfect woman to be my wife and I was happy for once in my life.

Then she ruined everything with her hesitation and when she told me why, I was incensed. Damn Serena for meddling in my business because I know my sister and that movie was well timed. She has always been a hopeless romantic and obviously decided to teach Purity her own lesson and I will deal with her later because she nearly ruined everything.

Now, as the priest declares us husband and wife, it's as if the sun comes out from behind the clouds and everything is good again.

"You may now kiss your bride."

The delighted smile on her face is enthralling, but knowing her heart is empty of love strangely upsets me.

'I don't love you, Killian.'

Why did those words hurt me so much?

I should be happy about that, but I'm not. I felt rejected,

and I didn't like it. The fact I don't love her doesn't come into it. She *should* love me already. I've given her no reason not to.

I step forward and, taking her face in both hands, I stare into her eyes and drown in perfection. There is nothing I don't like about this woman. I crave her, am addicted to her and as far as I'm concerned, this wedding is getting in the way of what I would prefer to be doing—with her.

She smiles into my eyes with a happiness that tells me she has settled her mind and as I crush my lips to hers, it's as if I've come home. Like I needed the air she provides me to breathe and for a second back there I was afraid she was backing out of our deal. Not that she could. She doesn't realize that yet. We would marry whether she liked it or not. It's more convenient if she is willing.

As I taste my wife's lips, it sends a surge of power through my soul, knowing that I have got what I want and now she will be chained by my side for eternity.

I won. She's mine and I got what I wanted. So why is there still a prickling unease that she is still out of reach?

* * *

WE GO through the motions of celebrating our marriage. I can't tear my eyes away from the diamond sparkling above the solid gold wedding band. My own ring is unnatural on my finger, but I have a sense of pride when I look at it. We are man and wife. A married couple and I no longer have any use for the women who indulged my perversions. I will train Purity to be my everything and if it takes me my entire life, I will make her fall in love with me.

The thought of her leaving me caused a strange pain in my chest. I will *not* tolerate it. She is my perfect woman. She has to stay.

I can't believe she even thinks she has that option. Not now. Not ever. Over my dead body.

Nonna has transformed the island into a magical vista for our eyes. Fairy lights dance in the breeze in time to the music provided by the local band brought over from the mainland. We have encouraged our staff to join in to swell the numbers and there is much laughter as we enjoy a less formal wedding than the celebration I have planned in Chicago.

I pull Purity into my arms to dance under the moonlit sky and as her arms fold around me, she lays her cheek on my chest. "I am so happy to be your wife, Killian."

My chest hurts as if the life is being squeezed from it as I hold my gentle angel in my arms, as if she may break at any moment. There is something so incredibly powerful about this woman, and I have yet to understand what it is. I crave her. She's an addiction that only increases the longer I spend with her. I can't tear my eyes away from her when she's in the room and the thought of her anywhere but in my arms is too hard to bear.

I could dance with her all night and then Serena ruins it by cutting in and I reluctantly surrender Purity into my brother's arms.

It fills me with a strange jealously when she laughs at something he says and following my eyes, Serena teases, "You love her."

"You've had too much to drink."

I dismiss her words with the contempt they deserve.

She throws her head back and laughs softly and follows my gaze that is locked on my wife, giggling at something my nearly dead brother is saying to her.

"I'm not surprised."

Serena just won't give it up.

"She is a beautiful spirit, inside and out. Unspoilt and

genuine. Nothing like the mannequins you usually have hanging on your arm."

"She's a business decision. Nothing more."

Serena hisses, "Wake the fuck up, Kill and stare at the treasure you've got in your hand. Don't be a bastard and treat her like you do all the rest. She is the best thing that has ever happened to you and even if you won't admit that, I can see it. Nonna can see it, and even Grandpa can see it. Shade is doubtful, but then he's as big an asshole as you are."

It makes me smile because Serena has spent a lifetime calling us out on our failings and I'm almost amused they have been analyzing the situation.

However, I brush her words aside and stare once again at my beautiful wife and say with a sense of pride. "I am happy with her. Will that satisfy your romantic foolery?"

"It's a start, I suppose."

Serena lowers her voice. "Have you seen Benito since he was banished?"

The fact we call our parents by their first names tells me we don't consider them worthy of their true titles.

"No. Why would I?" I shrug as we move around the dancefloor in a way that has my eyes permanently trained on my bride and brother.

"Me neither and Shade says he wouldn't care if he never saw him again. A little harsh, but I kind of understand why."

She sighs and whispers, "I'm going to Australia next month to visit mom. Grandfather and nonna gave me their blessing and said I could only go for three weeks."

"Why do you even want to?" I shrug, not really understanding her reason, and she says crossly, "Because a girl needs her mom, Killian. Nonna is amazing, but I kind of miss mom."

"She has no right being missed by you. She never considered that when she ran off with Stoner."

"I know, well… but…" I look down at her because Serena never falters. She always has too much to say for that and she blinks away the tears and says brightly, "I'm just being silly."

She takes a deep breath and smiles sadly. "It's, well, sometimes I am so lonely. It's hard being protected, you know. I want a little freedom while I can get it."

"You are protected for a very good reason, Serena. Surely you understand that."

"I guess. It's just a little too much sometimes. I'm hoping that you secure our position while I'm away, and when I return, I'll have a little more freedom."

"We'll see."

I turn my attention back to Purity and as I catch her eye, she smiles at me so sweetly from across the room I am struggling to breathe. I can't deny how much I am attracted to her, but I hate seeing her dancing in another man's arms, despite the fact it's only my brother who I trust with my life. However, I'm fast realizing that despite that trust, I really don't trust him with my wife.

CHAPTER 35

PURITY

This island is magical. I am living the dream and Killian's family is lovely. They have been so welcoming, and yet when I steal hidden glances at my husband, I have to pinch myself. He is so attractive and so sexy, I can't breathe. He stands like a king among his subjects and there is an aura surrounding him of power and influence.

Those smoldering dark eyes that stare at me with heated lust take my breath away. The dark stubble on his jaw is devastatingly sexy and his sharp suits and immaculate appearance adds to the mystery. But it's those eyes. Those turbulent, stormy eyes that tear my heart apart and leave it bleeding on open ground. I want to unlock those secrets so badly and I have a lifetime to pick the lock.

Shade is almost a carbon copy of his brother, the same dark brooding stare and words that give nothing away. I try to make conversation and say with interest, "Are you married, Shade?"

"No."

"Are you intending to marry?"

"No." He glances down at me and smiles with a wicked twist to his lips. "I'm having too much fun to chain myself to one woman."

I say nothing and gaze across at Killian dancing with his sister, and I wonder if he is regretting our marriage already.

Shade surprises me by saying, "Do you wish your parents were here, Purity?"

"Of course not." I stare at him in surprise.

"I couldn't wait to get away from them."

He appears amused. "Then we agree on something. Most people would consider that strange. Luckily for you, we share your disregard for our own parents."

"Killian told me they separated, and your mom lives in Australia. That must be a long journey to see her."

"I wouldn't know." He shrugs.

I never want to see her again. I'm sure you understand."

He points to nonna, who is swaying in Don Vieri's arms with her head on his shoulder.

"Nonna is all the mother I need and always was."

"Your grandparents are happy." I say, loving how they smile at one another as if there is nobody else here.

"They fell in love. They are the lucky ones."

Shade sighs. "I should return you to your husband if I value my life."

I turn and see Killian staring at his brother with a murderous rage and it makes me giggle. "He does appear angry. Perhaps Serena stepped on his toes."

Shade grins. "Something like that."

As we leave the dance floor, Killian steps forward and glares at his brother. "You took your time."

Shade shrugs. "Point me in the direction of another woman and I'll go. Your wedding sucks, brother. I thought the best man always ends up bedding the bridesmaid. Thanks for that."

He jerks his thumb at his sister, making me giggle at the hint of a smile on Killian's lips. "You're welcome. Now, if you'll excuse us."

He rests his arm around my shoulder and says loudly, "Enjoy the rest of your evening. It's been a long day."

A huge cheer deafens me, and I'm surprised when a loud bang makes me jump. Killian pulls me into his arms, and we stare in wonder at the fireworks lighting up the night sky.

I have never seen anything like it and clap my hands in delight as the music gets louder to serenade the display and I stare at a spectacle I have never seen the like of before. If I could bottle this moment and keep it to cherish, I would, and the tears fall as I stare up at the exploding sky. I am so happy, so sure I have done the right thing and I am fast on my way to falling in love with the man who made it happen.

Maybe one day he will feel the same.

* * *

After many kisses and congratulations, we head back up the stairs and despite my weariness, I am eager to be alone with my husband.

We did it. We signed the contract and now our life begins.

We reach the room and I squeal when Killian sweeps me into his arms and carries me through the door, kissing me deeply before placing me gently on the huge bed. The room is lit by lamplight, but the darkness in the man I just married excites me.

I watch as he removes his tie and unfastens his belt, tossing it to the chair before ripping off his shirt. I tremble with desire as he removes his pants and stands before me, naked and splendid, a definite feast for my eyes.

His body appears to have been crafted from granite, and I

love the dark hair covering his chest. He is a man in every way, and I feel weak knowing what happens next.

"You're a little overdressed, wouldn't you agree?"

He says with a wicked twist to his lips and prowls toward the bed with a devilish gleam in his eye.

I shiver.

I pant.

I savor the anticipation.

He tugs me to my feet and unzips the dress in one fluid movement. The fabric falling to the floor in a crumpled heap.

Then he stands back and stares at my body, the silk lingerie mere wisps of fabric touching my skin like a lover's caress.

The spark in his eyes excites me as he disposes of my underwear, leaving me standing before him with nowhere else to hide and he growls low in his throat as he runs those large hands over my body, saying with a growl, "Now you are all mine."

It's probably best I don't argue with him now about that because I already know I would lose, and I am fascinated by what happens next when a man considers the woman he married his property on their wedding night. Will it be different? Not forbidden anymore.

He spins me around and steps behind me, kissing my neck with a mixture of soft kisses and little nips with his teeth. It makes me tremble as I anticipate the pleasure and pain combining in a lethal cocktail of delight.

My legs tremble as my body responds, aching for more, aching for him.

"So beautiful, Bella. Pure and undamaged. Perfect for me."

His hand rests against my ass, smoothing the skin and causing me to groan. I love this adoration, crave it even because with Killian I am somebody of importance. I feel that with him, and I crave it like a drug.

His hands run across my entire body, touching me, holding me and wanting me.

Then he spins me around and kisses me deep and hard. I sense the ownership, and I love it.

The rings are heavy on my finger, the diamond choker still wrapped around my neck. The man who put them there holding me so tenderly in his arms as he claims my body in this soul draining way.

Then he eases me gently on the bed and cups the back of my head, staring into my eyes through the warm lamplight and whispers, "You *will* fall in love with me, Bella. You have no choice."

A fresh burst of wet heat is encouraged by his words and still staring into my eyes, he slides in, pushing in deep causing a soft groan to be the only sound in the still room.

The air conditioning provides a welcome breeze on our bodies, the ceiling fan doing a very good job of controlling the temperature in the room. Inside, though, I am burning out of control as he thrusts hard and deep, holding my head in place so I stare into his eyes the entire time.

It excites me, I want more and love it when his eyes gleam with danger as he thrusts harder, faster, with none of the gentleness of before. It's an amazing feeling knowing he is now my husband. The man I have dedicated my life to, the man I will grow to love.

As his cock rubs against my clit, I bite down on my lip, desperate to enjoy this for a little longer, and he growls, "You will *not* come yet."

I stare deep into those eyes as if he controls my body and I suppose he does because I tense, and the building orgasm passes as quickly as it came.

He whispers against my lips, "You will do everything I tell you. This body is now mine and I control it. I control you."

Once again, I'm not about to argue because right at this

moment, he does. I love what he does to me, the pleasure he gives, and I stare into his eyes and whisper, "I love how you own me, Killian."

If the atmosphere could get any darker, it shifts up a notch, and he groans as he pushes in hard and deep, whispering, "Then cum all over my cock and show me how much you love this."

Just his words alone have the power to make me cum and I scream as everything explodes in a sensation of pure ecstasy. It's as if I am flying, floating on those white fluffy clouds, knowing he will be there to catch me when I fall to earth.

There is no more powerful emotion than trust, and I trust Killian with my life, our children's lives and our future as a family. This is what I ran for. I knew it was out there waiting for me and for a moment the movie is forgotten as I settle into my role of being the perfect wife and nothing more.

I am complete.

I have gifted him my soul to do what the hell he likes with it, and nothing else matters more than that.

CHAPTER 36

KILLIAN

We are leaving Serenita and my family because life goes on and my business won't wait. My grandfather and nonna are sad to see us go, but I register the challenge in my grandfather's eyes and the weight of responsibility lies heavy on my shoulders.

As I bid farewell to my grandmother, she surprises me by whispering, "I have hope for you yet. Open your eyes and accept what's in front of you. Don't live in ignorance and guard your treasure well."

"You speak in riddles, Nonna." I whisper against her ear, and she laughs softly. "Do I? Remind me of that when I see you next."

Serena and Shade bid us farewell and I am happy they have accepted Purity into the family as one of us already. I overhear Serena whispering plans to meet up with my bride and the grateful happiness in Purity's eyes cuts me deep. She is so happy. It's obvious in her bright eyes and flushed face. She gazes at me as if she can't believe I'm real and that makes me fucking invincible.

The journey home is different from the one out here. For

the first hour I fuck Purity senseless and then, leaving her to sleep, I shower and head to meet Saint for business.

We spread out the contents of the folder my grandfather gifted me, and Saint appears as disturbed as I am.

"What's your plan?" He says as he holds the photograph of Gabriella waiting by the car handing Purity her business card.

"We need more information." I growl and Saint nods.

"This is unexpected." He says simply and I nod, the anger growing by the second at the betrayal this photograph portrays. It's like a punch in the heart and I sigh with exasperation. "It's a fucking disgrace. That's what this is, but we can't deal with it until we discover who the organ grinder is."

"Any ideas?"

"None at all. It will be a delicate operation to discover their identity."

"These photographs." Saint holds one in his hand.

"How did your grandfather obtain them?"

"A private investigator, apparently. He is a mistrusting bastard who enjoys having eyes and ears on his staff. For some reason, he chose Gabriella this time, and it paid off."

"I think it's more than that." Saint says with a puzzled frown. Rather than be angry at his words, I lean forward, trusting his judgment more than my own sometimes.

"It makes more sense that he was following her companion."

"I guess." I nod, the hatred twisting in my gut as I stare at the face of the hated man in the white suit.

Saint places the photograph down and leans back, reaching for the glass of whiskey that usually accompanies every business meeting we have.

"I will call on the guy I've had watching Gabriella. Demand a full report as a starting point." Saint says with a grim expression.

"Then get some eyes on her accomplice. I need to know his movements and who he calls. Put a tap on his phone and eyes on his movements, twenty-four seven. Any ideas who the lucky lady will be?"

"Not Gina. She is still working on Jefferson."

Saint pulls out his phone. "Polly, perhaps."

"Too rough. We need it to be believable."

"Portia. She has been quiet for a while and could be perfect."

"Good choice." I stare at the damning photographs and my blood boils. The fucking bastard. What the hell is he playing at?"

I spend the rest of the flight with Saint. My thoughts consumed by business rather than pleasure, as usual. Purity has already been relegated to my fuck toy while I carry on building my empire and yet as I stare out at the white fluffy clouds bouncing below the sun, I have an overwhelming desire to be with her right now. To hear her soft giggle and drown in those eyes that gaze at me with adoration.

She makes me feel like a king—her king—and I am fast realizing she is more important to me than I am comfortable with.

* * *

ONE HOUR BEFORE LANDING, I head back to the bedroom and my heart lurches when I see the sleeping form of my wife. Her white hair spills against the pillows as her soft lips smile with contentment. Her ivory skin shines as she stretches and turns, and my cock hardens with the need to be inside her almost as soon as I entered the room.

For a moment I wait and stare, marveling that this beauty is mine to keep. To build into my queen and to ruin at leisure. Just imagining the things I will do to her is almost an unbearable temptation, knowing what depravity awaits her is stoking the evil in my soul. She doesn't realize what I am capable of, what she will do under my command. I will test her sanity and her morals when I use her body to please mine.

But something is telling me it's more than that. It's not just sex with Purity. It's the way she lifts my soul, letting the light in and creating a freshness to my spirit that has probably never been there. I view the world through her eyes and share her excitement. She makes me see things differently and causes me to question my decisions.

I am conflicted, so as she stirs, I snap, "Get dressed. We will be landing soon."

"So soon." She yawns and the sheets fall from her body, gifting me a tantalizing glimpse of her pert breasts. It's an impossible situation that I must deal with to drive the madness from my heart and, so I say roughly,

"Go to the bathroom and bend over the vanity unit."

She looks up and yet says nothing, a hint of excitement lighting her gorgeous eyes.

I watch as she moves gracefully across the room in all her naked glory, and I follow her like a predatory animal about to tear her apart.

When I reach her, she is facing the mirror, her breasts grazing the marble, her ass in the air like a tempting red flag waving at me. I know I should hold back. Allow her some more time, but I need to regain control when I am around her.

I slip the tie from around my neck and approach, growling,

"Hands behind your back."

I note the excitement in her eyes as she stares at me through the mirror. She licks her lips, causing the blood to rush to my cock and as I bind her wrists, I unzip my pants, positioning behind her and holding her bound wrists down on her back, loving how she is spread out before me.

"Look at me, Purity." I say roughly as she lifts her head to stare at me through the mirror.

"Watch me own your body."

I love the excitement that lights in her eyes as I thrust in hard and deep. No foreplay this time.

Her eyes widen and she cries out as I pound relentlessly, holding her in place by her wrists, knowing how uncomfortable it must be.

Her eyes are wide as I purge her body from behind and with every thrust, the power returns to me. Her cries turn me on, knowing she is at my mercy and there is nothing she can do about it. I love this. The sense of power over another person is intense and darkens my soul.

I move fast and push deep, her strangled cry telling me this isn't as pleasurable as she thought it would be. I drown in the pain in her eyes and the fear edging inside as I move faster, relentlessly, as if to prove a point. My orgasm crashes through my entire body as I shoot hard and fast, knowing she has been denied her own pleasure this time. I am proving a point to her and to me. This isn't love. This isn't about her at all. This is all about me and it always will be.

I waste no time and pull out, my cum dripping on her ass, marking my territory.

As I unbind her wrists, I growl. "No shower. I want you to smell of me."

I try not to notice the questions in her eyes and the confusion surrounding them. Instead, I turn away with a cruel, "Get dressed. Make your own way to your seat for landing."

Then I zip up my pants and leave her standing there, alone and confused as to what the fuck just happened.

CHAPTER 37

PURITY

Well, that was different. To be honest, I'm not sure if I liked it or not. I feel sore, used and dirty.

As I attempt to wipe his cum from my body, I am mindful of his instruction, and it angers me a little. Surely, I'm in charge of my own body. I can clean up if I want to. The fact he left with cold indifference, angers me.

He used me.

I could see it in his eyes. He was on a power trip and had a point to prove. Well, that makes two of us.

I head across to the door and lock it, knowing I am safe for now and against his instructions, I stand under the hot shower, washing away his mark as he called it, replacing it with my own will.

As I soap my body, I still feel the burn. He wasn't gentle, quite rough really, so why did it excite me? He told me not to cum, he could try I suppose and as I stroke my own body, it's his angry eyes that stare back at me in my mind.

I disobey him.

I obey me and as my body responds to the image in my

mind; it awakens a sense of power that is new to me. I will not be owned. I ran away from that, and I will again if I must. My own power turns me on almost as much as his and as I cause my own release, it's with a sense of victory against him.

I dress in the same jumpsuit I came here in and brush my hair and clean my teeth. I feel good because I am in control of myself, not him, and it's important we discuss the rules again. Just as soon as we can.

As I make my way to my seat, I see him in the distance, his head bent over his phone, a glass of something in his hand. He doesn't even look up as I take the seat beside him and as I strap myself in, I lean back with a small smile gracing my lips. I am a wife now and with that comes a sense of purpose I've been searching for my entire life and I'm a little shocked when I hear a rough, "Why are you so happy?"

I open my eyes and stare at my husband and smile. "Because I'm your wife."

My response appears to shock him and then the darkness in his eyes lessens and he appears to relax a little.

His hand finds mine, and he twists our fingers together and whispers, "Yes. You are."

Then he raises my fingers to his lips and his scowl deepens when he says roughly, "You smell of soap."

"Do I?" I laugh softly and lean my head against his shoulder, whispering, "Then you will just have to mess me up again. Won't you?"

He says nothing and we make the landing in silence. It's not unpleasant, far from it in fact, if anything, it's perfect. He's perfect. My life is perfect, and I can't wait to see what my new job involves now I am returning home as his wife.

***

We make it back to the house and it's different coming home. I suppose it's because I think of it that way now I'm married.

I squeal when Killian sweeps me into his arms and carries me through the door again, kissing me deeply and whispering, "Welcome home, wife."

I gaze at him with adoration because he makes me feel so good. Even when he trying to push me away, I only want him more. I recognize he is lost. I am too and if I can help him with that, it may even help me too.

James is standing by to welcome us home and I flash him a brilliant smile as Killian lowers me to my feet.

"Congratulations, Mr. Vieri. Mrs. Vieri."

He nods with respect, but I register the amusement in his smile and Killian says abruptly. "Thank you, James. I trust everything is arranged."

"As requested, sir."

I'm a little confused, and Killian turns to me and says coolly, "You may want to freshen up. James has organized your new closet in the one next to mine. We share the same room now."

He nods to Saint, who is standing nearby.

"We have work to do."

Saint nods and as they head toward Killian's den, I'm a little lost because he doesn't even look back. I shake my head and say in a low voice to James, "He's a strange one."

James says nothing, but I can tell he agrees, and I say with a sigh, "Let's go and discover what he's talking about."

James follows me upstairs and as we pass the pristine art on the walls and tread the luxurious carpet, I pinch myself that I'm here at all. This house is too large for just the two of us and I try to imagine it full of children playing and family life. It settles my heart knowing I have purpose, but there is something telling me I want more. I always did and yet I don't know what 'more' is.

I turn to James. "Do you have a family, James?"

"No, ma'am."

"Please, call me Purity. You make me sound so old."

He appears shocked at my request and shakes his head. "I'm afraid I can't, ma'am. It would make me uncomfortable.

"Why?"

"Because I'm here to serve you. I am not your friend."

"Oh." I'm a little annoyed about that, and his words make me feel even more alone. I have Killian, but it's obvious he is a busy man and probably won't be around much during the day. I wonder what I will do.

We head into his bedroom and James says respectfully, "Please call if you need anything, ma'am. I will arrange for some refreshment in the dining room when you are ready."

"Thanks." I smile, but it's a little strained now because he has set the boundaries and pushed me firmly onto my side of the line.

I head straight for the second closet, on the other side of the bathroom that has two connecting doors. A 'his and hers' and I'm a little sad that even there we are separated. However, when I head into mine, I stare around in wonder because this is unexpected. When we left, this room was empty. Just bare rails and shelves and drawers with nothing in them.

I can't say that now because it's as if Killian ordered the entire store. The white interior is stuffed full of beautiful dresses, hanging on their rails, a tangible feast for my eyes. The shoes stand proudly on their slanting shelves and every type of purse stands proudly on glass fronted shelves.

There is a huge chandelier in the middle of the room, under which is a counter with a glass top, hiding gloves, belts and sparkling jewelry.

White fluffy rugs spill over the floor and the beautiful

velvet chair set by the small table provides a comfortable place to sit.

This room is heaven and is in direct contrast to Killian's masculine one a short distance away, where the walls creak with dark paneling and the suits hang lit by concealed lighting. His room smells of sandalwood, oud and musk. The leather from his shoes and belts making it a feast of masculinity that I inhaled with pleasure.

He was all around the room, and I suppose this is my own paradise.

I lift the nearest bottle of scent and spray a little on my neck. It smells divine and a shiver of pleasure passes through me. I've never owned anything before and now I have everything I could ever want. At least it feels that way.

For some reason, I fell into paradise when I ran from Heaven, and it's all because of a chance meeting with the man who made it all happen. He offered me a job, rescued me when I turned him down and has made me his wife. I am the happiest woman alive, but I'm conscious I am missing a vital ingredient from what I ran to find. Friendship.

The way James put me in my place only reinforced my loneliness. I like Killian's family, but they live so far away. I think about Gina, who was kind that night in the restroom. Maybe we could become friends. It's a start at least.

I physically ache to hear a friendly voice and then I remember the phone the biker gave me when I left. I should call Faith. I want to hear her soft voice so badly, so with a feeling of pure relief, I head back to the guestroom to find my purse.

CHAPTER 38

KILLIAN

Now my plan is in place, it's back to business. Purity will be kept amused while I work and will accompany me to the various charity functions I have planned as the shining light on my arm.

This weekend we attend our marriage celebration that will announce us on the social scene as the new power couple in town and all our enemies have been invited. I will not hide from them. I will ruin them, and I will do it by hiding behind a polite smile as I establish myself as the most important man in town.

Purity will do what she does best. Deflect any attention away from me because when she is in a room, everyone turns to stare. Her beauty and innocence are captivating. Her sweet smile and warm personality a dangerous drug that hooks you before you realize it.

She will give me the information I need as she weaves her magic spell over the women of this town. I will encourage her to spill their secrets, using that information to destroy their men, and she won't even guess she is working for me. Her excited chatter will be released with a few pointed questions. I will drop my requirements into the conversation that she will unconsciously use against my enemies.

Information is what I seek, and she will be starving for it. Purity is naturally curious and won't even realize I am manipulating her friendships for my own gain.

It will take time, I realize that, but Rome wasn't built in a day as they say and I am playing the long game, which is why I needed to marry my accomplice. Yes, Purity Sanders will soon become my most valuable asset as I use her to destroy the lives of the men who want to take my birth-right away from me.

I head to my den with Saint and as we settle into our usual roles, I hand him the glass of whiskey we enjoy as we ponder our problems. Most of our time is spent running over the business. Checking everything is running smoothly and dealing with any problems as they arise. It's exhausting and keeps us working long into the night. It's necessary because when you balance good and evil, it's important to keep them separated.

During the day, I take care of my legitimate business. Gold Hawk Enterprises, where I acquire failing businesses and tear them apart for profit.

At night, my attention turns to where the real money and power lie. My casinos, drugs operations, and prostitution. Mrs. Collins and her mansion are owned by me. She pays me a huge slice of her profits, which are considerable. I have many others around the state, not to mention the bars, the clubs and the protection services we offer. I run them all with an iron fist, keeping a watchful eye on my managers and employees.

My network of spies is immeasurable, and it takes a well-oiled machine to run effectively. Any failings in that machine are dealt with speedily and with no emotion if they threaten my business. Gabriella angered me when she allowed the legitimate part of my business to be compromised by the illegal one. She was careless and paid a heavy price.

However, business is suffocating me right now as I pull out the leather folder and slide the photographs out one by one. This is now the most important thing on my list because it threatens everything we have worked so god-damned hard for.

Saint sighs heavily. "What's the plan?"

"We set up a meeting."

He raises his eyes and I say irritably, "We go ahead with my marriage celebration as arranged. I have no doubt he will approach me then. I will arrange the meeting at Gold Hawk, and we deal with the traitor by staging an unfortunate accident as he leaves."

"Are you sure about that?"

Saint sounds uncharacteristically worried and I growl, "Of course I'm fucking sure. This is business and they have messed with that. There is no changing my mind."

"But–" He appears worried, and I pound my fist on my desk and roar, "I don't fucking care if you agree with this or not, Saint. Just organize the fucking hit and make it infallible."

Saint nods and takes a sip of his drink, obviously unhappy about my instructions. I'm aware he thinks I've made the wrong call. What he doesn't realize is, it was the *only* one. As soon as I saw the image of the man in the white suit, his fate was sealed. My grandfather knew it and so do I. It's just important that the man with Gabriella doesn't.

* * *

It's two in the morning when I drag myself to bed. As I walk into my room, I make out the body of my wife sleeping already, and I expect she's pissed at me. When I am working,

James knows not to interrupt me and I'm guessing she didn't like being left alone on our first night home. She will get used to it because Purity's job is to be my accessory and she will have every luxury she could ever wish for, except my time.

However, I am so fired up after going through our plan I need some form of release and she will do perfectly.

I head to the shower and wash away the stench of business and dress myself in depravity instead.

As I reach for the tools of my trade, I head into the room and take a moment to stare at the beauty who sleeps so peacefully, unaware of the demon circling her bed.

With a sense of anticipation, I secure her wrists, tying them together, causing her eyes to flutter and a soft, "Killian?" to pass her lips.

I drop my own to hers and whisper, "Wake up, Bella."

Her mouth twists into a gentle smile as her eyes flutter open and as she tries to stretch, she says in alarm, "What's happening?"

She struggles to move, and I press her down with a firm hand and say roughly, "Trust me, Bella. You will love this."

I take her bound wrists and raise them over her head and hook them on the bedpost, exposing her pert breasts to my greedy mouth.

"What time is it?" She whispers and I growl, "No talking."

My fingers prise her thighs apart and I bury my head between them, inhaling the scent of my woman, driving me crazy with lust.

Her soft gasp and burst of heat tell me she's ready for me and as I pleasure her clit, her small cries of pleasure calm my raging spirit.

I pull away before she can climax and run my hands across her body, savoring the soft touch of her skin. My cock throbs as it senses the pleasure waiting for it and I whisper in her ear, "You disobeyed me earlier."

"Did I?" She sounds almost amused and says softly, "Are you sure about that?"

"You washed away my scent. You disrespected my wishes."

"I don't know what you are talking about."

She smiles, not really understanding what she has done, and I say in a rough whisper, "Now you are lying to me."

I continue to stroke her body and she groans with pleasure as I arouse her to the point of total relaxation.

Her legs part and she arches toward me and as I fist my cock, I stare at the beauty completely at my mercy.

"You will learn not to disobey me, Bella. I will not allow it."

She says nothing and just smiles in her sweet, sexy way, causing me to groan and pump harder as I stare at her lying at my mercy bound for my pleasure. I reach for the second plastic tie and bind her ankles and kneel on the bed, my knees on either side of her body and pump furiously, loving the thrill of anticipation as she whispers, "I want you inside me so badly, Killian."

"Tough." I say roughly, causing her to stare at me in surprise and it's that precise moment that I cum so hard over her face and breasts. The spunk dripping into her mouth and down her face. Marking her, owning her, and claiming her. Teaching her not to fuck against my wishes.

She says nothing as I stand and as I head to the bathroom to clean up, I say coolly, "Now you will wear my mark for the rest of the night. You will lie in it, and you will become accustomed to it, knowing that I control you and if you disobey me again, your punishment will be more severe."

I pause and turn and with a wicked grin, say softly, "Sweet dreams, Purity. Welcome to hell."

CHAPTER 39

PURITY

I wake up in a very bad mood. It doesn't take long for the events of last night to remind me what an asshole I married. I feel dirty, used and cheap, and I need to wash as a matter of urgency.

The bed is cold beside me, which matches my heart. Why did I ever even like that man?

He has left already and at least he untied me and so I waste no time in heading to the bathroom and running a long and steaming shower.

As I stand under it, I plot his downfall. How bloody dare he. I will not allow it to happen again. I am fuming, so much it's probably a good thing he's left already because if I see him, I'm liable to serve time for murder.

It takes me a long time to cool down and when I head to breakfast, James is the only one around and I don't even greet him with my customary smile, causing him to say with concern.

"Is everything ok, Mrs. Vieri?"

"Not really, James."

"Can I help in any way?"

"Are you a divorce attorney?"

I stare at him with a hard expression, and he merely says, "I see."

"You see what exactly, James?"

I am so angry I can't help taking it out on him and he surprises me by saying gently, "Whatever Mr. Vieri has done to anger you, ma'am, I'm sure he deserves it."

"You got that right." I stare at him with a disappointed frown, and he shakes his head.

"Give him time. He's in new territory too and needs time to adjust."

It surprises me and touches me that he is so loyal. Caring even and worried about his boss. It disarms me a little and as he takes my breakfast order, I think about the man I married with a clearer head.

There is something they aren't telling me. Why does Killian live as if he's in solitary confinement? This whole setup is unusual and coming from a girl who lived her whole life in the shadows I experience a surge of empathy toward my husband.

As James makes to leave, I say quickly, "How can I help him?"

He turns and smiles. "Just be yourself, ma'am. That will be enough."

He heads off, leaving me confused. In fact, it's as if I've been confused my entire life. There must be more to life than serving a man. There must be.

When James returns, my mind is made up and I speak up before the idea fades.

"I would like to watch a movie if I can."

He raises his eyes.

"A movie?"

"Yes." I take a deep breath.

"I want you to show me where I can watch one."

He nods. "Of course. I'll make the cinema room ready."

"The cinema room?"

I'm surprised, and he smiles. "It's in the basement. Mr. Vieri doesn't use it much, so I will need to make it ready. It should be available as soon as you finish your meal."

He heads off to this mysterious cinema room, leaving me with my own turbulent thoughts. What on earth am I going to do about my husband? He is so cold, so distant, and yet when he touches me, when he looks at me a certain way, I forgive him everything.

* * *

THE CINEMA ROOM is my new favorite place. My eyes are wide as I peer around the space that is bigger than my childhood home. There is a huge screen on one wall and around eight seats that appear to recline, with tables set in the armrests and cushions and blankets to snuggle into. James has set a tray of popcorn and a large glass of sparkling liquid on one, and my heart sinks.

"Must I have more of that sparkling stuff? It's seriously disgusting."

He says with a twinkle in his eyes. "Try this. It has no alcohol in it."

Tentatively, I take a sip and my eyes light with pleasure. "What is it?"

"Lime cordial and soda. Lots of ice and a squeeze of fresh lime with mint leaves."

"I love it."

I am so relieved, and he appears happy at my praise.

"What movie would you like to watch, ma'am?"

He flicks a remote at the screen and it appears as if a thousand movies flash before my disbelieving eyes.

"May I?" I reach for the remote and he hands it to me with

a brief nod of respect. "Of course. Please call me if you need anything."

"I will, oh and thank you, James. I appreciate your help."

I smile, causing him to return it before leaving the room and I settle into the cozy seat and make full use of my new toy as I select a movie that appears to be just what I'm looking for.

* * *

Several movies later, many lime and sodas and a lunch tray that was delivered to my seat, the door opens, and I hear an amused, "So this is what you do all day?"

I glance up and hate that my heart flutters when I see my husband watching me with amusement from the open doorway. His tie is loosened at the neck and his jacket held over his shoulder, that he tosses on the nearest seat as he prowls into the room, closing the door behind him.

The gleam in his eye is almost predatory and my heart quickens as I sense he's about to pounce.

Standing quickly, I hold up my hand and say icily, "Stop right there."

"Why?" His smile irritates the shit out of me.

"Because I'm angry with you."

"Because–" he grins, causing me to snap. "Because you are rude, arrogant and think you have the right to do what you want to me with no regard for my feelings. Well, for your information, asshole, you can't."

I swallow hard as his eyes flash with danger, and he drops into the nearest seat and leans back, staring at me with an expression in his eye that should scare the panties off me.

"I have a contract that says I can."

He shrugs. "Your signature is on the bottom line, agreeing to it."

"No, I didn't." I say earnestly and he leans forward and says in a low voice, "Are you saying you didn't sign the contract, Purity, because we both know you did."

"Of course I signed it, but I didn't sign my soul away. I have feelings, too. If I wanted to be a man's possession, I would have stayed in Heaven."

"But you ran to me." He says with a wicked grin. "And you signed my contract. I fail to understand what the problem is."

Thinking back on the movies I have devoured all day, I flop into the nearest seat and say sadly, "I thought it would be better."

"What would be better?"

"Marriage to you."

His eyes flash and for a second, I almost believe he is upset and then his expression closes off and he says roughly, "I never promised you hearts and flowers, Purity. This is a business arrangement. You help me and I educate you. I fail to see what has caused you to be disappointed about that."

I stare at the frozen screen and regard the two actors staring lovingly into one another's eyes and I sigh.

"I have been learning about love."

The tears burn behind my eyes as I remember how good those movies made me feel. I smiled. My heart fluttered, and I cheered them on, hoping they would get the happily ever after that they worked so hard to achieve.

I lift my eyes to my husband's and say wearily, "I have learned a valuable lesson today."

He nods. "Go on."

"That it only works if you both want the same thing."

"What do you want, Purity?"

His voice is like smooth silk caressing my body and it gives me a moment's hope that he will agree with me.

"I want you to make love to me, Killian, because you want to and not because you are paying me to."

"Pretty Woman, if I'm not mistaken." He appears amused and my face flames as I realize he's right.

"If you like, but it applies to me too."

I look down and play with my fingers that sit nervously in my lap. "I just want to know what love is, Killian."

"It's a song by Foreigner, Purity."

I stare at him with mounting anger and snap. "Stop making fun of me. I'm trying to be serious here."

He sighs heavily and then, to my surprise, rises from his seat and drops down before me on his heels, taking my hands in his and staring at me with a soft smile.

"You want to know what love is? You are asking the wrong man."

I am compelled to look at him because the sudden sadness in his eyes curls light fingers around my heart and holds it prisoner.

"I don't know the meaning of the word. It has passed me by my entire life. You see, my life wasn't that different from yours."

He strokes my hand, and it feels so nice, and he stares into my eyes and whispers, "Like you, my parents ignored me most of the time. Unlike you, I had my grandparents to fill the void. Was it love? It didn't feel like it. You see, my grandfather is emotionless, much like I am, and my brother is the same. We were raised to have no emotion, no compassion and no tenderness."

"Why?" I stare at him in shock, and he shrugs as if it's of no consequence.

"Because of the world we were born into. To succeed in it you must park emotion somewhere and forget where you left it."

He reaches out and strokes my face tenderly, causing my eyes to fill with unshed tears as he soothes my troubles away.

"I can't promise you love, Purity, and I expect none in

return, but I apologize for scaring you."

"You did." I sniff as I stare at him through wounded eyes. "It's as if the minute your rings went on my finger, you became hard and unapproachable. You appeared angry with me and wanted to punish me for something, but I don't know why."

I take a deep breath and say in a whisper. "You scared me, Killian. You made me question everything and if this is what your idea of education is, I'd rather remain ignorant."

He nods and says fairly, "Your request has been noted and I will try to be gentler in the future. Unless you want me to revisit the harder approach when you become more accustomed to me."

"Why would I want that? The hard approach, I mean."

I'm surprised he even said it, and he grins, his eyes gleaming with a malevolence that holds me spellbound.

"Because plunging into darkness can be addictive. It is fascinating, thrilling and compelling. Not knowing what is coming, what kind of pleasure will challenge your ideas of good and evil. The thrill of something forbidden, knowing it brings you immeasurable pleasure. That is what I can offer you, Purity, but for now I'll take it slower and demonstrate a different approach. Gentler, more like your idea of love. Would that call off the dogs and redeem myself in your eyes, Bella?"

My heart physically flutters as he stares at me with so much adoration, I struggle to breathe. How could I doubt his intentions? He has been so kind and considerate up until now. Of course, I should trust him. He was just advancing my lesson, trying to give me pleasure. I'm not ready and I feel like a fool.

As his lips touch mine so gently, I cast my mind back to the movies I have watched all day and feel like the heroine in all of them. Desired, treasured and loved.

CHAPTER 40

KILLIAN

I wish I had time to fuck the fight out of her, but we don't have long. Her anger is an inconvenience I can't allow because tonight we must appear to be love's young dream. It's why I came home early because tonight is our marriage celebration before the entire town. All the most powerful people in Chicago and the neighboring cities will be attending tonight and I need Purity looking at me through a lover's eyes, not an assassin's.

She's pissed and I'm surprised at that. Most women crave the darker side of sex. They get off on the thrill and beg me for more. Her education in the pleasure it can bring may take longer than I thought, but I need her firmly on my side tonight, so I will be anything she wants me to be.

We head into the dining room where James has laid out a simple supper. This evening will be a challenge in more ways than bringing Purity back in line. It will also involve setting a few traps and I'm conscious things may not go as planned. They rarely do, but I have been over the arrangements so many times with Saint we have planned for every eventuality.

PURE EVIL

Purity appears calmer and eats her food with an appreciative smile when James serves her. For some reason, I'm glad she's forgiven me. When she stared at me with anger, a part of me died inside and I didn't know what to do about that. I was disappointed in myself because I had failed her, and I can't even process what that could mean. I don't care about women's feelings. I never have unless you count my sister's and nonna's. Perhaps it's because Purity is family now and has earned the right to my concern. It can only be that and so, as we head back upstairs to change, I take her hand in mine and smile gently.

"This marriage will take a lot of adjustment on both sides. We will be learning as we go along, and I hope you'll tell me if I'm doing it wrong."

The way her eyes shine tells me I have called it right and knew that with the right approach she would bend to my will, not even knowing I am playing a game.

We reach our room and I take her beautiful face in my hands and kiss her softly. A lover's kiss. Some may say true love's kiss and I laugh to myself when I see her eyes shining as she gazes into mine.

"Thank you." Her soft whisper makes me feel strangely good about myself and then she leans forward and kisses me so gently it stuns me for a moment because I like it.

If anything, it's so good I am tempted to cancel the event and I would if our future wasn't dependent on it.

She pulls back and whispers, "Do we have to go so soon?"

"Why?" I tease her because the meaning in her eyes is clear.

"Because I want to practice a little more."

She blushes prettily, which is like a red flag to a bull and tearing off my tie, I say huskily, "They can wait."

She stands before me and tugs her sweater over her head, revealing she is naked below and I groan out loud when I see her pert breasts begging for my attention. She steps out of her leggings and once again no fucking underwear, causing the blood to rush to my head. Both of them.

She surprises me again by stepping forward and saying with a cheeky smile. "You're a little overdressed. Let me help you with that."

I am shocked as the innocent angel I married turns into every wet dream I ever had and some I have yet to experience.

She reaches for my pants and, to my surprise, drops to her knees and pulls them down, releasing my rock-hard cock that dances suggestively in front of her face.

She nervously reaches out and touches it lightly and peers up at me with an anxious expression, causing me to nod. "Go ahead. It's yours."

"Mine?" Her soft smile warms my icy heart and I'm fast realizing I crave to see that smile directed in my direction.

Her soft touch on my hard cock is an unexpected pleasure. For a man who likes it rough and prefers to dominate, this softer approach is surprisingly addictive. I don't even breathe out of fear of ruining the moment and my heart leaps when she whispers, "It feels so good."

She raises those astonishing eyes to stare into mine, and the desire I see is new as she gazes at me with yearning. It makes me want to give her the fucking world and until this moment, I have never realized the power of a woman over a man.

It fascinates me and something strikes my heart when, with a mysterious smile, she drops down before me and presses her sweet lips to the crown. I try hard to picture anything else right now because this could become a very embarrassing episode for me if I lose control. I want to hang onto this moment and savor it. Explore it and test what it means to me. It's as if time stands still as Purity tentatively licks the tip and holds my raging cock in her gentle hands.

I groan deeply as she opens her mouth and sucks it in gently, as if testing it inch by inch. Her own soft moan of pleasure makes me hiss as she begins to suck softly with none of the urgency or polish of my usual partners. They know what they are doing, she does not and if I'm honest, I prefer this approach one hundred times more.

My heart is hammering and the sweat forms on my body as it struggles to maintain control. This is an unusual experience for a man who relishes control, and I give my entire body over to the woman bent on her knees, wielding her power over me for the first time. She's like a breath of fresh air in a rank depressed world and right in this moment I will do anything to keep her because there isn't a lot of good in my life and I recognize it now.

I want to hold on to it with an iron grip because I never knew it would make me feel so good inside. More powerful, as if I can take on the world and it becomes the most important thing in my life to make her happy.

I even surprise myself when I reach down and pull her flush against my body and she whispers, "Was I doing it wrong?"

Her eyes cloud with disappointment and I kiss her trembling lips with a passion I have never experienced before, whispering huskily, "You were perfect, Purity and you deserve the best. You deserve to be loved."

"Love?" Her eyes widen as she steps back and smiles, her eyes shining as she sees a different part of me.

I stroke her face softly and whisper, "Let me show you a different kind of loving."

She nods shyly and I lead her over to the bed and lower her gently down on the silk sheets. Touching her body with a lightness that causes her to shiver and sigh, "That is so good."

There is not an inch of her that I don't want to explore, and I press soft kisses over her entire body, loving the taste of my woman. Her innocence traps my own dark soul and washes it over it with a soothing balm that calms my spirit.

I fall under her spell, and I can't get enough as I lick and suck every inch of her skin, loving her soft cries and shocked gasps as I kiss her in more intimate places.

I am so powerful with her in my arms and this time as I slide in gently, I stare at her beautiful face as I ease in carefully, savoring every moment of a body I am fast realizing I can't live without.

She is special. The only woman I have ever thought of that way and my heart shifts when she whispers, "I love—"

Time stands still as her words hang in the air and my emotions scramble as they prepare for something they never realized they wanted.

She smiles and whispers, "This. I love this, Killian. It is so good."

If anything, I'm shocked at the disappointment I'm experiencing as she denies me the emotion I want from her so badly. As I move gently inside my woman, I am owning her, claiming her and marking her, but it's not enough. I want her heart as well and she is holding it back, denying me from owning the whole of her.

I want more, I want everything, and I understand it won't come easily. She can't pretend. She wouldn't know how and if I am ever to own the whole of my beautiful wife, I am going to have to give her something I don't even know is there. My heart.

CHAPTER 41

PURITY

I love this different side of the man who is fast becoming the hero in my movie. His dark sexy good looks and powerful personality are plunging me deeper into a world I know nothing about. I don't understand what love is and even the movies I've watched don't prepare me for my feelings, but when Killian stares at me with desire, I can't think of anything else.

I can't *see* anyone else because it's as if we stand in our own world where nobody else lives. We are alone and fixated on only one thing. Pleasing one another. I crave him, desire him, and want him. He angers me and sometimes I really believe I hate him, but then he does something so sweet and unexpected it brings me back full circle.

From the moment I set eyes on him while I waited for Miss. Sinclair, I knew he was a powerful man. I just didn't realize that power was over me.

Now, as he stares into my eyes with what appears to be love, I question my own emotions. Do I love him? Is this what it's like to love someone? To want them close and savor their gentle touch. To miss them when they're not around and wonder what they are doing.

I missed him today despite his treatment of me and when I watched the movies, I ached for him to be beside me. Could I love a man like Killian Vieri?

Should I even because I'm not stupid? He is a man with many secrets and dark corners that may conceal a monster with sharp teeth and razor claws who can tear my world apart.

But not now. Now I am experiencing the side of him I crave more than anything. His full attention and the pleasure only he can create. He feels so good inside me small flutters of pleasure pass through my entire body as he unlocks doors inside me that I never knew opened. I am blossoming under his touch, allowing him full access to my soul and as he kisses me softly and as if he truly loves me, a powerful orgasm hits me so hard I scream his name as my body convulses with ecstatic pleasure.

He tenses and with a roar and one hard thrust, powers his release deep inside my body, holding on so tightly as he pushes inside me deeper, harder. His muscles are rock hard in my arms. It stuns me as I experience emotions that could be the ruin of me and he becomes my number one addiction in seconds, as he hooks me on his line.

He stills and then rolls off me, dragging my body to lie flush against him and strokes my face while staring into my eyes, just like they do in the movies and whispers, "You are so perfect for me."

I smile with a happiness I didn't have earlier and truly believe we are heading on the right track and kiss him softly on the lips before whispering, "Thank you. I never dared hope it could be so good."

He pulls my face against his chest, and I hear his heart pounding as he strokes my back and says with a sigh.

"Tonight will be difficult."

"Why?"

"Because of the guests waiting for us."

"What guests?"

He lifts my face to his and smiles. "Tonight is our wedding celebration gala. The guest list is impressive, and everyone will be searching for the cracks in our relationship so, I need to you play the devoted wife."

"I am." I'm surprised he thinks I'm acting, and I guess my words stun him and a little of the darkness leaves his eyes as he whispers, "Then it is my turn to thank you."

"You don't have to thank me for being devoted to you. It's in the marriage contract."

"Of course." I hate that the light dims a little and he surprises me by saying, "What do you want from the contract, Purity?"

I consider his words carefully.

What do I want? I never really considered it before now and, pulling back, I sit beside him and say wistfully, "I want my life to count for something. I always have. You see –"

I turn and smile sadly. "I should have been happy with my life. I knew no different. It was all so simple, really. Do as I was told and that would never change, just the man telling me. First my father and then my husband. It was expected."

"So, what changed?" He strokes my back, and it's so nice. More intimate somehow than what we just did.

"I watched programs on the television that opened my eyes. I heard whispers of life outside Heaven that claimed many of the folk who ran past the mountain range. It became a myth, a legend and a dream. Some said if you ran, the devil was waiting on the other side to drag you to hell. Others said it was the promised land. When I saw Miss. Sinclair smoking a cigarette, leaning against the white car my world stopped turning. Right before my eyes was living proof of a different life. A more exciting life. One that I wanted so badly I could hardly think straight. When she spoke to me, I loved her soft, lilting voice. She seemed so kind, so self-assured and like nothing I had ever seen before. I wanted to be like her and when she dropped her card in my hand, it was as if she was giving me the keys to freedom."

I turn and Killian is staring at me with a strange mixture of interest and a deep yearning, and I recognize that look. I see it in the mirror when I gaze at my own reflection and impulsively, I touch his cheek and press my thumb against his rough skin.

"I wanted to discover what freedom tasted like. To breathe it in and let it wash over me. To make my own choices. To understand the whole of the world and not just Heaven. To experience the secrets that were waiting over that mountain range and one day to wear a smart dress and drive a white car. I wasn't interested in the cigarette though. It smelled kind of strange."

He laughs softly. "Good choice."

With a deep breath, I smile at him and whisper, "I took my chance, and I found you. Miracles do happen and I truly believe God directed me into your path. The devil wasn't waiting on the other side of the mountain range, after all. You make me happy, Killian, and together we will charm those guests and achieve good things. You can count on me."

He nods and then closes his eyes and breathes out a long-drawn-out breath, his hand finding mine and holding on tight. Is it relief or something else, I can't quite tell and when he opens them, I register the glint of power flashing in his eyes.

"We shouldn't keep our guests waiting."

In the brief second before we move, an understanding passes between us. We signed a contract. I have the rings on my finger as a reminder of that. This marriage will count for something amazing and if we fall in love, I will consider my life complete.

CHAPTER 42

KILLIAN

I never understood the power of words until I met Purity. She is like an open book and wears her emotions in plain sight. I know where I am with her and yet I'm not where I want to be. Her tales of home unleash the beast inside me because her father is drowning in hypocrisy. Preaching one thing and doing another and yet he has somehow molded her into the perfect woman.

My perfect woman. Strong, beautiful and brave. Qualities I admire and love to test.

We head to our respective closets after showering together and I loved her infectious giggle as we fooled around in the steam. I never understood the benefits of spending time with a woman. I suppose because I hadn't met her yet. Now I have, I want to keep her and if that is going to happen, I must make her fall in love with me. It should be easy. I can give her everything she desires, but what happens when she discovers the devil *was* waiting on the other side of that mountain range?

I have a bad premonition about tonight. Anxiety isn't something I'm used to, but I have bucket loads where it concerns her. The thought of her staring at me with anything but adoration is killing me inside because, as sure as I'm breathing, she will soon learn exactly what I'm capable of.

When we meet in the bedroom, words fail me. She stands like a vision dressed in white silk that flows around her body, touching her in places I am jealous of. Has it really come this? Jealous of a fucking dress, which tells me I'm fucked already. The unthinkable has happened and I am viewing her as more than a business contract now.

She is my most potent desire and the life in my veins. She gives my life meaning with a soft smile and the desire lit in her eyes. If only she felt the same, we would be invincible.

She twirls in the highest heels and grins.

"I've been practicing. What do you think?"

I gaze at the beauty before me, loving the sense of ownership as I stare at the diamond collar around her neck. Her white hair piled on top of her head, held in place by a silver tiara. She is wearing long black gloves that are in direct contrast to her smooth white skin and her make-up is amazing considering she's only just learning how to apply it.

"You are beautiful, Purity." I really mean that and can't tear my eyes from the vision before me.

"Thanks, honey, you look very handsome too."

She smiles, and it's as if the sun comes out, lighting the darkest part of my soul.

I reach out and as her hand finds mine, I whisper huskily, "Let's get this over with. I'm impatient to see what's under that dress."

She flutters her eyelashes.

"Nothing."

Then she pulls me after her with a mischievous wink and I swear every part of me wants to tear that dress off and fuck her and fuck the gala. However, years of putting business first overwhelms my wishes and with an irritated growl, I follow her out.

* * *

We are silent for the entire journey. Purity is pensive and I am struggling with unexpected anxiety. Tonight, could damage the relationship we are building. I'm shocked to discover that I want her to remain ignorant of my real world. For her to gaze at me with anything other than adoration is like a knife twisting in my heart and for the first time in my life, I want to be a better man—for her.

But I'm not and as we pull up beside the red carpet, I take a deep breath and try to fix the bastard in me back in charge.

Saint opens the door, and my men stand as guards as we exit the car, the flashbulbs of the paparazzi exploding in our faces.

This is always the most delicate part of any appearance in public. Anyone could have their sight trained on me and it would be game over before it got started. My men hate it. I hate it and now I have even more cause to worry because if anything happened to the beautiful woman holding my hand so tenderly, I am liable to burn this world to the ground.

When did she become so necessary in my life? I don't like it and I'm struggling.

With a deep breath, I play my part and hold her hand tightly as we head into the hotel that has been hired for this party only.

"Wow!" Purity stares in wonder at the huge glass sculpture in the center of the reception, flowers surrounding us with their heady scent. Soft music plays in the background and the waiting staff all smile and nod respectfully.

"I feel like a princess." She giggles adorably and my heart lurches. When I see life through Purity's eyes, I see things very differently. I have never noticed details before, but with her I see the beauty in everything. I love the sparkle in her eyes as she stares in wonder at the god-damned hotel reception, as if it's Cinderella's fucking castle.

It makes me want to give her the world just to keep that expression in place.

We head into the ballroom, and she gasps at the opulence of the finest hotel in Chicago. The people surrounding us are dressed in riches and dripping in jewels. The men stare at my bride with an interest that brings a scowl to my face because fuck if they desire what's mine. Just the thought of anyone's hands on her causes the beast to growl inside me and prepare to strike.

"Who are these people?" She whispers as she gazes around at a scene I doubt she ever believed she'd see firsthand.

"Businessmen and their wives or companions. Senators, judges, law enforcement officers and anyone of power in the state."

"You know them?"

Her eyes are wide as she smiles shyly at a woman nearby who is staring at her with undisguised jealousy. I like to believe it's because she has done the unthinkable and snared the most eligible bachelor in town, but it's not. It's because Purity is so god-damned beautiful it hurts to look at her.

"Not many, but the ones that count." I answer her question as Senator Gibbons heads our way.

"Killian, I must congratulate you on your marriage. You are one lucky devil."

He kisses Purity's hands and I thank God she is wearing gloves because the thought of his wet lips near any part of her skin makes me feral.

"Senator." I throw him an easy smile because my mission

is to charm, not to alienate, and I glance at his young wife who started life off as his assistant.

"Mrs. Gibbons."

I nod respectfully and note the desire in her eyes as she steps forward and kisses me on both cheeks, lingering a little too long, causing her husband to say quickly, "I must say we were astonished to learn of your marriage. I couldn't understand it, but I do now I've met you, Mrs. Vieri."

"Purity, please." She smiles, causing the Senator to stare at her a little too hard for my liking and I say abruptly, "If you'll excuse us, we must circulate but be assured of my continued support Senator and a large donation to your chosen charity."

He nods with a smug acceptance and as we move off, Purity whispers, "That was so lovely of you, Killian."

"What was?"

"Offering to donate money to his charity. What is it?"

The fuck if I know, but the proud expression in her eye is one I want to keep there, so I smile. "He has many charities and I trust him to direct it to the worthiest one."

Before she can reply, another well-wisher stops by, and I smile politely as they extend their congratulations. For the next thirty minutes we are swamped with well-wishers and Purity charms them all with a soft smile and an infectious giggle. The women appear as mesmerized by her as the men and I am unusually proud as I stand by her side, holding her hand tightly, wanting to keep her safely beside me and away from the predators who are circling.

The music starts and Purity stares in wonder, her eyes shining.

"I love this, Killian." She smiles with joy at the lights glittering across the dance floor.

"Then allow me." I kiss her cheek and pull her into my

arms and guide her across the dance floor while the guests look on.

"It's like I'm Cinderella." She whispers in my ear and her soft breath washes over me like a summer breeze. She feels so good in my arms. As light as a feather and knowing she is naked under the soft fabric is making concentration extremely difficult.

I can't help myself and taste her lips, deepening the kiss as we twirl around the dance floor in a slow and steady rhythm. It's almost sexual because as her body moves against me, it turns me on knowing that she is all mine and has never been with any man before. Nobody has touched my treasure, and that gives me a surge of power that I drown in.

She makes me powerful, able to move mountains and nonna's words come back to haunt me.

"Open your heart, Killian. Let emotion inside and stop trying to control every aspect of your life, emotions included. Only then will you be as powerful as your grandfather, because without love or emotion, you are weak."

It shocks me that her words have hit home because, for the first time in my tortured life, I am terrified of losing something. Good things never last — not in my world. They are fleeting like a rainbow on a showery day, or a wave breaking to shore. It makes me hold on tighter out of fear of losing something so pure it has burned a hole that could never be repaired if it did.

For the first time in my life, I am scared, and I don't fucking like it.

CHAPTER 43

PURITY

I am the princess in a movie, and my leading man is hot. So hot he burns with one smoldering glance in my direction and the slide of his hard body against mine. I can't look anywhere but into his eyes as he spins me around the dance floor, commanding all my attention and shutting the entire room out.

We are the only ones here. At least it feels like that as we dance to the music, his expert guidance preventing me from making a fool of myself. I wasn't kidding when I told him I was naked underneath this dress. I loved the slide of the silk fabric against my skin too much to place any barriers in the way of that.

However, now I'm regretting it because this could be extremely embarrassing if the wet heat between my legs connects with the fabric. Killian would probably love that. Knowing I am dripping for him. I always am though. There is something so intoxicating between us.

There was the moment he turned in the reception at Gold Hawk Enterprises and our eyes locked. It was right at that moment I felt it. A connection that had my heart racing and my senses screaming. It was as if our worlds collided in that split second, telling me my life would never be the same again.

The song ends, but we don't stop dancing. The next one begins, and Killian is in no hurry to return to his guests.

It's only when I see a man approaching that the atmosphere changes and Killian's mood changes in a heartbeat. He is tense, his mood evaporating quicker than ice in the desert.

I stare at the man and note the similarities immediately, and the low growl from my husband alerts me that this will not go well for the man heading our way.

He stops and pulls me to his side as the man moves closer and almost tucks me behind him as if he is protecting me somehow.

"What do you want?" He says in a low voice and the man smirks. "Is that any way to greet your father, Killian? Show some respect."

We have moved to the edge of the dance floor, and I note the curiosity of our guests as they watch.

"You earn respect and when a child grows up and learns his father isn't worthy of any, you forfeit the right to demand it."

An angry scowl appears on his father's face for a fleeting second, before he replaces it with an easy laugh and gazes in my direction.

"Welcome to the family, honey. I would wish you a long and happy life together, but sadly, it's never going to happen."

I stare with growing unease as the two men glare at one another and then a soft voice says to my left, "Purity. It's so good to see you again."

I turn and smile with relief as Gina stands beside us,

along with Jefferson Stevenson, her boyfriend. At last, a familiar face and I smile with relief.

"It's good to see you, Gina, Jefferson."

Killian grips my hand tighter as Gina says smoothly, "Allow me to steal a dance with the bridegroom."

She winks at me and whispers, "You appear to need saving."

She nods in Killian's father's direction, and I smile, grateful for the intervention.

Jefferson says warmly, "Would you do me the honor of dancing with me, Purity?"

I swear Killian growls beside me, but I realize this is the best way to diffuse the growing antagonism with his father, so I drop Killian's hand and smile warmly. "Of course."

As the group disperses, Killian's father shakes his head with amusement as he locks his eyes on mine. He nods and turns, disappearing into the crowd as Jefferson's hand creeps around my waist.

"You are beautiful, Purity. Killian is a lucky man. Then again, he always did have a talent for making his own luck."

"Does he?" I'm only half listening because my eyes are trained on the way Gina is flush against Killian's body as she whispers something in his ear. His eyes are intense and his expression dark, and a shiver passes through me as I observe them.

Jefferson whispers, "You know Gina and Killian were lovers once."

I stiffen as he chuckles softly. "She learned a lot from him. She is a tiger in the bedroom. He trained her well."

I feel sick as I stare at the way her hand rests on the back of his neck, her fingers brushing over his skin with an intimacy that tells me Jefferson isn't wrong. I swear my heart beats even faster as I watch my husband with a woman he was close to once upon a time.

PURE EVIL

It hurts.

I don't know why, but it does, and Jefferson carries on regardless of how uncomfortable I am.

"I would congratulate you on your marriage, but we all know it won't last."

"Excuse me." I pull back and stare at him in shock and he laughs. "He's using you. It's obvious. He does this. Takes what he needs from a woman and then casts them aside. In your case, he desires respectability. You are the epitome of that. His marriage creates the perfect smokescreen for his dirty trade that he keeps hidden behind the brilliance of Gold Hawk Enterprises."

I am shaking as his words wash over me and stifle my senses.

He is wrong.

Killian is a good man.

I have no reason to doubt that, but then the dots connect and images of the cold side of him chill my blood. I can't breathe as I notice him whisper in Gina's ear and she gazes at him with a smoldering expression of desire.

Stepping away from Jefferson, I say coolly, "If you'll excuse me, I need the restroom."

Without waiting for his response, I stumble toward the nearest exit and find myself out in the cool night air on a terrace. I hear the music behind me, but it's not sweet anymore. It's serenading my misery as everything that has happened swirls around me like a deathly virus.

"Purity." I turn and my heart drops when Miss. Sinclair steps out of the shadows and I gasp, "You!"

She laughs softly as she moves toward me, looking every inch the sophisticated woman who impressed me so much.

"You should have stayed where you were. At least it was obvious what you were there."

Her voice slides over me like silk on broken glass as she stands by my side, admiring the view.

"You lied to me." I sense the anger rising and she laughs as if I'm no consequence.

"I didn't lie. I found you a job. At what point did I lie to you?"

"But they were going to–"

"What, Purity? They were going to provide you with a room, a job, and food to eat. You would have earned well from it, a pretty young girl like you. You should have thanked me, but then Killian ruined everything by keeping you all to himself."

"He rescued me." I say angrily and to my surprise, she turns, a gleam of amusement in her eyes.

"He didn't rescue you, honey. He trapped you. Your marriage is a front to make him look good. He will use you, toss you aside and carry on doing what he does best which is ruining lives and souls."

"He's a good man." I say, but my voice breaks and she grins.

"Is that what he told you? Ask yourself who owns the establishment I took you to. Who pockets the profits of prostitution in this town? Who supplies drugs that ruin lives and lavishes the profits on impressing his new wife? And who murders anyone who dares go against him? Your husband does. He is the cancer that is destroying our country and all the wealth you enjoy is at the cost of the innocent. You are a fool if you believe his lying words because he is only telling you what you want to hear."

"You're lying. He's a good man. I know he is."

I step away, the tears raining on my parade as she carries on delivering every well-aimed blow.

"Ask yourself why he lives alone? Why he is so protected?

Why he hates his father and why he has no friends? Because he is evil, Purity. Pure evil and he will ruin you and leave you broken and disillusioned with life before reaching out and plucking a fresh face to replace you. I am proof of that."

She twists her lips into a wicked grin and hisses, "I was his fuck toy, too. He liked to tie me up and fuck me raw. Beat me, choke me, and whip me. I loved it. I craved it even because when a powerful man directs his attention on you, it's an aphrodisiac that hooks you bad."

I feel sick and turn away and her rough hand spins me around and she snarls, "Ask yourself why he is so cold. So distant sometimes. Because he will never let you inside his cold black heart. You will be destroyed, Purity, like everyone who has the misfortune of falling into his trap. If you don't believe me, ask him. Ask him about the whores he fucks and the ones he exploits. The wild parties where men use women as toys. The drugs they inject in them just like the one they injected into you. The way they are tied up and passed around a roomful of horny men and left with nothing but a wad of dollar bills stuffed up their ass."

She laughs out loud. "Congratulations, Purity, you married Lucifer himself. I hope you will be very happy."

She turns away, after having ripped the soul from inside me. I sag against the balustrade as her words do irreparable damage.

My mind is racing and my breathing shallow as I digest everything she told me and I choke on it. I want to disbelieve everything she told me, but something is telling me she's right. That place Miss. Sinclair took me to is owned by my husband and I wasn't rescued at all. I just swapped one cage for another.

I don't know what to do. I have no place to go, no one to turn to. Even the phone I had as my lifeline has mysteriously disappeared. The last time I saw it was on the island on my wedding day, but it never made it back with us.

I am cut off.

Alone and afraid because the man I trusted and was so close to falling in love with, has turned out to be the devil in disguise.

CHAPTER 44

KILLIAN

Gina tells me everything I need to hear and finishes up with a soft, "She's good for you, Kill. Hold on to that one."

"I intend to." I say, as I stare around the dance floor for her. I notice Jefferson on the side, raising his glass in our direction and my blood chills.

Where is my wife?

I break away from Gina and say quickly, "I must find Purity."

She looks anxious. "Isn't she with Jefferson?"

"Apparently not. Go and find out what happened."

I order her and, like the good little employee, she scurries off to do my bidding. Our conversation is forgotten already as I experience a moment of panic as I search for my wife.

I notice my father standing beside Gabriella and my blood actually boils as they smirk in my direction before turning and walking away.

Hand in hand.

It's as if all my senses are screaming at me and I experience blind panic as Saint heads to my side and says with concern. "What's wrong?"

"Purity." My words are rough and urgent. "Where is she?"

Saint touches my arm and nods in the direction behind me and as I spin around, I am awash with relief when she walks back into the room.

I waste no time in rushing to her side and I can immediately tell something has changed. She's been crying and I swear I summon every dark demon inside me as I prepare to punish whoever did this.

"What happened?" I waste no time and grabbing her arm, pull her back the way she came, the cool night air doing little to douse the flames burning inside me.

"Miss. Sinclair."

She says the two words I should have prepared for, and I grip her wrist tightly and hiss, "What did she tell you?"

"The truth, Killian."

It's as if I have wounded a fragile creature and I hate how that makes me feel.

"How do you know it was the truth?" I say roughly, and she shakes her head sadly. "Because it all adds up."

She sighs and stares at me with so much disappointment it shocks me.

"I thought you were a good man."

"What is a good man, Purity, because I'd like to meet him?" I reply with a dark edge to my voice. "Is it your father who taught you that good always wins against evil?"

I grip her wrist hard and snarl, "Because he was lying to you your entire life. At least I don't pretend to be anything else."

"What do you mean?"

Her lip trembles as I hiss. "Your father is a drugs dealer. He sells it for profit and then preaches the bible to counteract the evil inside him."

PURE EVIL

"He doesn't." She says, the anger in her eyes exciting me.

"He's a good man. He advises the reverend."

"Oh yes. Reverend Peters. The man who died for his sins. The serial killer who indulged his hobby by imprisoning young women and beating the shit out of them. I know all about your good reverend and let me tell you, he is better off dead."

"You knew him?" Her eyes are wide, and I shake my head. "I knew *of* him. My grandfather arranged a contract with him, but I knew enough to know I *never* wanted to do business with a man like that. I sent Gabriella to meet with your father to buy his drugs. She told me the latest shipment wasn't good enough, just like your father. Just like her, as it happens because Gabriella Sinclair has just painted a huge fucking target on her back by betraying me."

The power surges through me as my demon is released from where he has been hiding and it's almost a relief as I face her with full honesty for once.

"So, my darling wife, we will head back in there and play the game. You will honor the contract and we will work this out. You can ask me anything at all, but I want you to understand one thing before we head inside."

"What?" She glares at me with disappointed bitterness, but I ignore how it cuts me so deep inside.

I pull her roughly into my arms and hold her face in my hands, gazing deeply into those soulful eyes as I whisper, "I am everything she told you. I am the man you never wanted to find. No compassion, no morality and no fucks to give. Until you."

My eyes burn brightly as I stare deep into her beautiful eyes and I whisper huskily, "I need you to make me better, Purity. To show me how to feel. To teach me what is important in life and to make me a better man. As it turns out, you have the hardest job in the world because there is nobody who has fallen as low as I have. Help me, Purity because you are the only one who can?"

Her eyes fill with tears, and she sags against me, her lip trembling as she whispers, "I want to believe you, Killian. I want to see the good in you and I want to make this work. I will need some time to think about it though. Please give me that at least."

The tears spill across her pale cheeks and I lean down and lick them away before resting my lips against hers and whispering, "Trust me, Purity. I'm dealing with some serious shit right now and I need you to be strong. Don't let me fall."

To my surprise, her lips crash against mine and I swear my heart explodes. This kiss is urgent, desperate and a declaration. I tangle my fingers in her hair and devour her. It's as if I can't get enough and as I press my hard body against hers, she says huskily, "I can't walk away from you."

She trembles against me, and it becomes the most important thing to be alone right now and so I break away and say quickly, "Come. This can't wait another minute."

I pull her after me as if my life depends on it and as we take the elevator to the penthouse, I have only one thing on my mind.

Convincing her to stay.

* * *

The elevator doors close and I push her hard against the mirrored walls, biting, licking and nipping her neck as she gasps with pleasure. Her hands force their way under my shirt and her soft fingers graze against my chest as I press in hard against her soft, silk-encased body.

The doors open and we spill out into the finest penthouse suite the state offers and her eyes are wide as she stares around at the backdrop of the city through the floor to ceiling window.

"It's beautiful." She gasps and then squeals as I rip the dress from her body in one violent move, leaving her naked in the center of the room.

"Killian!" Her eyes are wide as I tear off my shirt, closely followed by my pants, and I growl, "Come."

I sit on the couch and pull her astride me, pushing up inside her with one violent thrust. Her eyes roll back in her head as I grip her shoulders and push inside, roughly and with a sense of ownership I desire more than anything.

I must know she is mine. Will always be mine. It's a desperation that won't leave me. Almost as if this act alone will be the lock that only I hold the key to. Her prison if you like, because she will never get away from me.

Her soft moans tell me she's turned on and I push her down to the white sheepskin rug and pound into her hard, her head bashing against the floor as I nail her to it. Then, holding my hand to her throat, I growl, "This is the monster you married, Purity. I am crazy for you."

Her breath quickens as she groans, "I can't fight you, Killian. I can't walk away."

It's what I needed to hear and calms the rage inside and as the relief settles over me, she drags my lips to meet hers and whispers, "I will help you."

I swear I cum so hard I see the white light of heaven as my world rights itself. She screams as her own orgasm joins with mine and her body throbs against me. I watch every magical second of her release, knowing that I caused it. Basking in the pleasure I brought to her, knowing she is going nowhere.

As she comes back to me, she stares at me with desire and the look of adoration I crave and she whispers huskily, "It would have been better if I heard it from you, but shit happens, I suppose."

It destroys all the tension between us and as she giggles in my arms, I almost tell her I love her. I stop because what the hell is happening to me? I don't love. I don't even know what it is, so I stroke her beautiful face and whisper, "You are everything to me, Bella. I will make you the happiest woman alive."

I wrap her in my arms and cling on tight, so scared that I nearly lost her. The trouble is, my life is unpredictable and I'm fully aware I must seize these moments while I can because nothing is for granted in this world I live in and the fear of losing her—what we have—only makes the beast inside me roar even fucking louder.

CHAPTER 45

PURITY

I am screwed in more ways than one. I can't walk away.

I should.

Thinking of how Killian makes his money goes against everything I have ever been taught.

Good and evil.

Right versus wrong.

It's not even because I have nowhere else to go. I ran once, I could do it again. No, the reason I'm here is that when Killian stared at me through those mysterious eyes, I saw the yearning inside them.

He needs me.

I could see it as plainly as my need for him. We shouldn't work. But something is telling me we need each other to survive.

Something is playing on my mind more than anything else I learned, and I whisper, "Tell me about my father."

It's almost as if I'm a disinterested onlooker, and not the flesh and blood of a tyrant.

"What do you want to know?"

He kisses my head and exhales an audible sigh of relief, and it melts my heart. For a man who doesn't show emotion, I can tell he is disguising the fact he has so much of it locked behind a wall of cold steel.

"You say he sells drugs. What are they?"

"Opium."

"What's that?"

"It comes from the poppy flower and is an addictive drug that is sold to users."

"A flower?" I think of the beautiful fields of poppies that grow all around our home. The same fields I ran in and played as a child. The fields my family helped cultivate, and it makes me sick that, unknown to me, I was helping in the manufacture of drugs.

"But he told us they were medicinal."

"They can be." Killian strokes my back.

"It can be used legally in the production of drugs."

"So maybe he didn't realize it was being used in the wrong way." I am so hopeful of that because it's as if my entire life has been built on a lie. Then Killian dashes any hope of that when he shrugs.

"No. He sold the drugs to the wrong kind of buyer. That man in the white suit. He was no executive from a pharmaceutical company. He was a man just like me."

I pull away and roll onto my back, staring up at the ceiling, and Killian turns on his side and watches me with a dark stormy gaze.

"The house you rescued me from. Is it yours?"

"Yes."

"So, you sell women for money."

For some reason, there is no emotion in my voice. I just want the facts so I know what I'm dealing with and Killian says softly.

"I won't lie to you, Purity. I have two sides to my personality. The genuine businessman who works legitimately and rescues companies or puts them out of their misery. The one who donates millions to charity and employs thousands of people. Then there is my family's business. The one my grandfather founded. The drugs, prostitution and gambling are a business too. They employ many people and exploit many others. Once again, I give people jobs. I give them options and they only need to fear me if they betray me. It's as simple as that."

"Betray you." I turn to face him, once again drowning in those mysterious eyes.

"What happens if they betray you, Killian?"

I watch as his eyes darken and the rage burns brightly inside them and he says casually, "I dispose of them."

"As in…"

"Remove them from life or from the situation. Take Gabriella, for instance."

"Miss. Sinclair?"

He nods. "She went against me. Betrayed me and took me for a fool."

"What will happen to her?"

"It already has. She lost her job, her position in my business, and her options. She didn't hang around and found alternative employment and that is what told me everything I needed to know."

"How?" I am fascinated by his world. It's something I have never even considered before, and how can I judge unless I know all the facts?

"She hooked up with my father, which some may say was punishment in itself, but I'm aware their connection goes back further than that."

He stares at me with a hard expression, and I can tell his next question is important.

"The day you first met her. Think about the man in the white suit. Did you see him tonight?"

I'm surprised at his question and yet something is niggling at the back of my mind, and I think back on the people at the gala.

Then I cast my mind back to that day many years ago and concentrate on the man I snatched a fleeting glimpse of.

It's as if I am seeing the scene with fresh eyes as the back story connects and as the man walks away from my house, I realize immediately who he was.

"Your father!" I sit up and say with a rush. "Oh my God, Killian. Miss. Sinclair was there with your father. Did you know? Was it planned?"

He sits beside me and locks his fingers with mine and says with a dead voice, "No, Purity. It was most definitely not planned. He is a traitor. It's why he wasn't at our island wedding. My grandfather told him never to return because in one sentence he sealed his fate and revealed where his loyalties lay. I wasn't aware at the time what my grandparents knew, but when we were there, my grandfather showed me a photograph. It was taken the day they came to your home. You were there talking to Gabriella when he emerged from the house. The man in the white suit was Benito Vieri, and he was negotiating his own deal with your father and cutting his family out."

"But he didn't do a deal. I told you what I heard."

"Yes. He is the monkey, not the organ grinder. So, all that remains is to find the man calling the shots and there are two people who can help with that."

He turns and stares at me long and hard and says darkly, "My father and Gabriella. It's why I'm preoccupied. Why I am closed off because I need to be. Living in my world is a dangerous place to be and I don't want you caught up in it. I want you to see the good side of me. The successful businessman who runs Gold Hawk Enterprises and helps charities with the profits. You are the good in me, Purity, and I want it to stay that way. I want you to stay because I never really expected you to become as important to me as you are."

I have no words. There is no comeback to that. It's as if he is laying his heart open for me to do with what I want. I am powerless against his honesty because he has neutralized every doubt in my mind and so I consider him with a blank expression and say with a small sigh.

"I'm not leaving you, Killian, but I don't want you to lie to me—ever. Even if I won't like what I hear, I want to know. I will be your wife as arranged in the contract that we signed. I will even try to love you, as agreed. But I will not tolerate secrets in our marriage. I am not that impressionable girl who left Heaven. I deserve your respect, as you will deserve mine."

If I thought he would be happy, I was wrong. If anything, he appears devastated, and it makes me nervous.

Then the shutters come down and he nods.

"You have a deal. We have a deal and so we must return to the gala and prove to everyone there that we are the happy couple–" he sighs heavily. "As agreed."

It's as if an emotional wall has been erected between us, which I hate but understand must happen to protect me. I can't allow my feelings for this man to develop further because I'm not sure if he's the man for me.

He has tricked me into something that suits him, not me and Miss. Sinclair's words are biting back hard. So, until he proves it's me he wants and not just a business arrangement, I will play his game, but hold back on emotion. Play him at his own game if you like because I'm in survival mode and until I can trust him not to dispose of me too, he doesn't get my heart.

CHAPTER 46

KILLIAN

It's been several weeks since the gala and we have settled into married life with a routine of sorts. I work most of the time but enjoy spending any free hours I have fucking my wife and hearing about her day. She has thrown herself into this marriage with a thirst for knowledge that impresses me. She is now running my home with James and has organized several changes already.

She is involved with many of my charities and is often attending meeting and functions with other women who do it so well. Purity is becoming everything I wanted her to be, but there is something vital missing.

Emotion.

It's as if she left it on that terrace of the hotel when she learned the true nature of my business. A little of the light died in her eyes that night, and I hate it. When we fuck, I try to reach in and grasp it, bring it back to me, but she is holding onto it so tightly I wonder if I will ever see it again.

My beautiful, innocent angel is learning and with knowledge comes a certain kind of disillusionment. I can't fault her on anything she does, but I want to see that spark in her eye

– that look she reserved only for me that I crave like the drugs I deal in. Almost hero worship and desire all rolled into one, but now all she gives me is what I asked for. A business deal.

However, today I can't think about my wife, my home or the charities that bring me a certain kind of power because today is judgment day.

* * *

THE AIR IS tense inside my office as we wait for the meeting that's been a long time coming. Saint is sitting, studying his phone and my mind is ticking over with the plan we have devised. It's almost too much to deal with because today I will step up and be the man my grandfather expects me to be, and today my father will learn what that means.

The intercom buzzes on my desk and my assistant says in her usual breathless voice, "Your eleven-o'clock appointment is here, sir. Shall I send them in?"

I already know he's here, courtesy of the call from security when he signed in and I stare across at Saint, who nods with a wicked gleam in his eye and I say roughly, "You can send them in."

Saint moves to his position against the rear wall of my office as my father heads inside, closely followed by Gabriella.

I stand as they enter, and my father's amused grin does nothing to calm the beast inside me as I contemplate what he has done.

"Killian. So formal. We could have discussed your problem over dinner. Not in this sterile environment."

He nods toward Gabriella.

"You remember Gabriella, don't you, son? She has been, um, helping me with business since you fired her so rudely."

Gabriella smiles with a sensual gleam in her eye as she bats her lashes and whispers, "It's good to see you, Kill."

I point to the two chairs waiting for them and say roughly, "Sit."

Saint's expression is blank because, like me, he has zero emotion when it comes to business.

As they take their seats, my father glances around the room and says amenably, "What, no refreshment? Perhaps you can ask your sexy assistant outside to rustle up a few drinks."

"Or we could conclude our business and you can fuck off out of my life forever." I say with a snarl, causing him to roll his eyes.

"See what I raised, Gabriella. A fucking monster. His mother would be so ashamed."

I'm aware he is trying to get a rise out of me, so I just lean back and shrug. "Who cares what she thinks?"

"She's your mother. You have been brought up to respect your family." He shakes his head. "If your grandparents heard you, they would be ashamed."

"Don't you dare lecture me about respecting my family. I won't take it from a man who turned his back on his many years ago."

I slam my fist on the desk and say roughly, "You screwed around behind our mother's back and drove her into another man's arms. You broke up our 'not so happy' family and couldn't give a fuck. Then you moved in your whore and screwed her with no regard if we heard you or not. You refused to take your position in the family business, preferring instead to build up your own empire. Your *rival* empire, taking deals that should have been ours and betraying your own parents. You are a fucking disgrace who doesn't deserve the name Vieri."

"I don't know what you've heard, but you're wrong, Killian."

He stares at me straight in the eye and says softly, "I have built an empire that is free of the sins of my father. I am respected, admired, and free from crime, unlike my father. You should applaud me for putting our futures first, instead of working in an antiquated world that will be a dinosaur sooner than you think."

I slide the photograph across the desk and note the disbelief in his eyes as he realizes he's screwed.

"Respect. Is this what you call building a business different from the one you grew up with?"

"That proves nothing." He tosses it back to me and I glance at Gabriella, who has turned a lot paler than when she came in.

"Do you remember this day, Gabriella?"

"I don't."

She shrugs and I laugh softly. "Well, I do. You were sent to Heaven to meet with Elijah Sanders to check out his shipment. If I remember rightly, you were sent there alone and when you returned, you told me the shit was bad quality and wouldn't pass the most basic tests."

"Did I? I don't remember."

I shake my head.

"Do you also not remember the call you took only last week from a man called Howard Montgomery?"

Now they both look uneasy, and she hisses, "You've been spying on me."

"I have." I shrug and say with a wicked grin. "It appears you prefer to do business under the covers now. Howard Montgomery visited your apartment and the surveillance we set up showed what an intimate discussion you had."

"You bastard." She stands and glares at me from across the

desk. "You should know, Killian. I screwed you enough times for information."

I say nothing and she stops as the words deliver her death sentence and she turns red and says quickly, "I mean …" She is lost for words and then changes direction and bursts into tears.

"I loved you. I wanted to prove to you that I was good enough —for you. I did everything you asked, and I would have killed for you. Then that girl showed up, and you cut me out. You fucking married her, Killian, so what was I supposed to do? I have needs, both physical and financial. I took a job with your father because he has proven to be a far better man than you ever were."

My father appears annoyed at her outburst and says roughly, "Shut the fuck up and sit down. You're embarrassing yourself."

She stares at him with pure hatred burning in her eyes. "Fuck you, Benito. You don't…"

A sharp sound like whiplash interrupts her delivery as my father strikes her hard across the face, causing her head to fall to one side. An angry red mark appears as he bellows, "I said shut the fuck up, you bitch. He's playing you. Are you so fucking stupid you can't see that? He is after information. Are you so dumb you've forgotten how this business works?"

She holds her face with her hand and sits sobbing in the chair and I enjoy a moment's satisfaction knowing she is defeated before I've even begun.

My father glares at me. "What's the point of all this, Killian? State the purpose of this meeting."

I turn my attention to my father and lean back in my chair, fixing him with an enigmatic stare.

"I want the name of the man you are working with."

"Who says I'm working with anyone? You've got to do better than that."

"It doesn't matter." I shrug and turn to Saint, who nods, replacing his phone in his pocket.

"I already know."

This time, I glare at my father and say bitterly, "I just wanted to test your loyalty and guess what, you failed the test."

I stand and nod toward the door that Saint has opened.

"Goodbye, father. Enjoy living with the choices you made."

He tries not to show it, but I note the suspicion in his eye as he tries to figure out if I'm bluffing or not.

He swings his gaze to Gabriella who stares at him with pure hatred burning in her eyes and then he turns to Saint who gives him fuck all back.

Then he shakes his head and says with a deep sigh. "I thought you were better than this, Killian. I really hoped you were, because now your grandfather's legacy is fucked."

He appears almost amused. "You know nothing about my business. How far my connections stretch and the power behind it. You think the Dark Lords will protect you? They hate you. They want to distance themselves from the Vieri family because you just aren't good enough."

He laughs as if the situation amuses him.

"Gold Hawk Enterprises won't renew your membership and your pretty, innocent wife heading up all the charities in the world won't give you respectability. They know who you are and what depths you sink to, and they are gathering to vote you and my father out. So, enjoy this life while you've got it, Killian, because the clock is ticking."

He smiles as if he hasn't a care in the world. "Say hi to your brother and sister for me. They know where I am if they want to join the winning side. You…" He shakes his head and hisses, "Made your choice when you sided with

Don Vieri over your own father. I'll see you in hell before I speak to you again."

He turns and snaps at Gabriella, who is sobbing in the chair.

"Come. You're an embarrassment."

As she makes to leave, Saint steps forward and pushes her back in her chair and she says with alarm, "What's going on? Let me leave."

My father snarls, "Let her go, or is imprisonment something you want to add to your increasingly long rap sheet?"

"On the contrary, I have an exit interview to conduct. When Gabriella was fired from my organization, I neglected to do one, so to stick to the letter of the law, we will have it now."

He rolls his eyes. "Do you take me for a fool, Killian? She comes with me."

"Then perhaps you would like to wait outside. This won't take longer than one hour, two at the most."

I stare at him with no emotion at all, no expression and no actual shits to give because when he walks out of this office, I will never see him again.

"You know what to do." He snaps in her direction and storms out of the office, and I swear my heart is pounding as I watch him go. I don't let emotion in, I can't because this is my cross to bear and I won't let my grandfather down.

* * *

As the door slams behind him, Saint follows him out, as arranged, and I turn my attention to Gabriella, who is trying to regain her usual composure.

"Thanks, Kill." She smiles softly and I sigh inside.

"For what, exactly?"

I lean back and she whispers, "For saving me from him. You don't understand what he's capable of."

"You think I don't know what my own father is capable of?"

I laugh derisively. "You forget, I've lived with the bastard my entire life and I have learned from the master. Your problem now lies with me, Gabriella, because the apprentice is about to become the master and I have learned my lesson well."

I fix her with a frown and say darkly, "Now about your exit interview."

CHAPTER 47

PURITY

I am so tired. Charity work is exhausting. I never realized what was involved in making connections and involving myself in this world. The women I meet scare me. The polished wives of Killian's business associates and the women in charge.

Endless lunches that appear to offer an opportunity to compare wealth. Handbags, jewelry and the size of our home. Where we're vacationing and who we regard as close friends and at the end of it, they deliver a speech about giving back to society and assure the recipient of several hundreds of thousands of dollars in donations before wrapping up the meeting and feeling good about themselves.

I want more.

I want to be involved. To learn where the money goes and the people it benefits. I'm not interested in possessions, but I am interested in honoring my side of the contract. I will become the perfect wife because, as hard as I try to ignore it, I want to stay with Killian.

When he arrives home from work, my heart flutters the

minute I set eyes on him. He only has to look at me, and I want him. There is so much I desire about him and it's not just sex.

It's him.

The way he makes me feel inside. The soft looks he gives me when he thinks I'm not looking.

The gentle touches he doesn't even realize he's giving me and the way we snuggle together to watch another movie of my choice.

He never complains. He watches anything I want and laughs along with me. Then there are the times we head out for a walk in the grounds of this magnificent home. The childish games we play and the stories he tells me about growing up with his siblings. I am hungry for life but starved of him. I want more of his stories, more of his touches and more of his desire-lit kisses. I want all of him and it saddens me to know I will never even scratch the surface of the enigmatic man I married.

* * *

I HEAD off to change before sitting down to the lunch that James has provided as usual on a table set for one. He always sets it in the window of the dining room so I can gaze across the ornamental gardens outside.

However, as I stand under the shower, I don't feel so good. If I'm honest, I haven't felt so good for a few weeks now. Mainly nauseous, but lethargic too. My fingernails keep breaking and I am drained most of the time and as another wave of nausea hits me, I run to the toilet and hurl inside.

I am so weak and sit, with my hand to my head, on the cool marble tiles.

I haven't said anything to anyone, but I have my suspicions and when I am less dizzy, I stand and head to my closet. I locate my purse and drag out the test I bought at the pharmacy on my way out of lunch.

With trembling fingers, I remove it and read the instructions, careful to follow them to the letter so there can be no mistake.

Five minutes later, I have my suspicions confirmed and as I stare at the solid blue line, it's as if every wish I ever had in life is granted in one heartbeat.

I'm pregnant.

I already know Killian will be happy about that. He's already told me he wants at least four children. I also know I'm ecstatic. I am so happy I could burst because we have made a life—together.

Then I experience the real fear that we are bringing a child into the world. A world of evil that could corrupt my baby's soul. It worries me that I won't be a good mother. That Killian will fail as a father and our child will be miserable.

Then a sense of purpose and determination washes over me. I won't let that happen. I will learn to love Killian, and I will adore our child. This baby will want for nothing emotionally, even if I die trying.

With a renewed sense of purpose, I fasten my hair in a ponytail and pull on a pale blue sundress. I want to tell my husband the good news and it can't wait another minute.

As I grab my purse, I race down the stairs and find James in the dining room.

"I need a ride to Gold Hawk Enterprises."

"But your lunch." He says with dismay, and I shake my head. "I'm sorry. It's urgent that I speak with him."

"I could call him." He says with a smile, and I shake my head vehemently.

"No. I need to meet with him face to face."

"I'm not …"

"James, please. I need a fucking ride as a matter of urgency."

He raises his eyes at my outburst, which makes me giggle, and then he grins.

"Of course. I'll arrange for Julian to take you."

I head toward the front door to wait for Julian, one of Killian's chauffeurs, and as soon as I hear the car at the door, I head outside and blink in disbelief.

"What's this?" I say in shock as Julian stands with the door open.

"It's your car, ma'am."

"Mine?" The tears build as I stare at the most beautiful white car I have ever seen.

James appears beside me and says with a smile. "Mr. Vieri wanted to surprise you. He had this custom-built and said it was your dream."

"But I can't drive." I am staggered and James says gently, "He has arranged for lessons. You begin next week."

"I do." My eyes are wide and James whispers, "He wants you to be happy, Mrs. Vieri."

For the briefest moment, I just stare, the tears burning behind my eyes.

I have my dream car.

A beautiful white sports car that is everything I would have chosen if I had the choice. White and black leather seats and a roof that folds back. It is small and sweet, and I can't even begin to imagine what the huge chauffeur will look like driving it, and it makes me giggle as I step into the passenger seat.

I'm like a kid on Christmas morning as I stare around me with happiness, inhaling the scent of leather and car polish with an excited shiver.

As the engine starts, the roar tears right through my body and I say with excitement.

"Let's see what this baby can do."

Despite my wishes, Julian drives us sedately to the center of town, to Gold Hawk Enterprises. The wind whips in my hair as I stare around me with a happiness I never really expected. This car is everything to me because Killian took note of what I wanted and made it happen. He always does and I have a warm feeling inside when I think about my husband.

We pull up outside his office and Julian says in his gruff voice, "I'll be in the underground carpark. Call me when you're ready."

"Okay, and thanks." I smile my appreciation and as I stand outside Gold Hawk Enterprises, it reminds me of the first day I arrived and placing my hand on my stomach, I experience a moments satisfaction that all my dreams came true because I took a chance on happiness.

With a spring in my step I head inside and this time the security guard smiles his welcome. I make my way to the reception desk and say 'hi' to Yvonne and she returns my greeting before saying pleasantly, "It's good to see you, Mrs. Vieri."

"You too, Yvonne. I hope the family is well."

"They are. Thank you, ma'am."

"I'm here to meet my husband." I say happily and her face falls a little.

"I'm sorry, Mrs. Vieri, he's in a meeting and we've been instructed to hold all his calls and under no circumstances to disturb him."

She appears a little awkward and to put her at ease, I smile.

"It's fine. I'll wait here."

As I turn, I notice his black car pull up outside and say

quickly, "It's ok. I'll wait in the car. It's obvious he won't be long."

As I head back the way I came, I am so happy. When Killian finishes his meeting, I will ask him to take me home so we can celebrate the good news together — in private.

CHAPTER 48

KILLIAN

Gabriella is shit scared and trying not to show it. She knows she's fucked up and the fact I didn't let her leave with my father tells her she's in deep trouble.

"You betrayed me, Gabriella."

I waste no time in getting to the point and she says with a wavering voice. "I could say the same to you."

"I doubt that."

I am irritated by her words, and she says angrily. "I've been your loyal assistant for years, Killian. You used me in every way possible and then tossed me aside for *her*. That immature baby who has no idea what she's gotten into. You don't need her, you need me."

Her eyes flash and I fire back.

"I never needed you. There are a million of you out there and only one of her. For your information, I couldn't wait to get rid of you. Let's just say old goods tend to stink after a while and you were seriously past your use by date."

"How could you be so cruel?" She sobs as I say icily, "You forget who you're dealing with, Gabriella. I would be a little more accommodating if I were you."

She glances up and I note the hope in her eyes, and it pisses the hell out of me because even now she is looking at me as if she wants to fuck me.

"Tell me the name of my father's contact."

"You said you knew."

Her eyes are wide, and I shrug. "I have my suspicions, but I need to hear his name from your own mouth before I deal with him."

She starts to laugh, and I watch a little of her old fire rekindled as she snaps, "You will get nothing from me until you reinstate me as your personal assistant, and we go back to business as usual."

"Business as usual." I sigh heavily. "Now, why would I want that when you have nothing I want?"

"You want a name."

She crosses her legs suggestively and purrs. "I could whisper it in your ear while you fuck me. Would that work for you, Kill? For old times' sake."

"You always were a cheap fucking whore, Gabriella and I would seriously consider my offer of employment with Mrs. Collins."

I sigh heavily. "Enough. I want his name now."

"I don't know who he is." She says with a sigh, and I fix her with a deadly glare and say roughly, "Then you will find it. You have exactly–" I peer at my watch and smirk.

"Four hours at a guess."

She looks confused.

"Why four hours?"

"Because that's how long the cops will probably take to arrest you for murder."

"I don't understand."

I go in for the kill.

"The murder of my father. Benito Vieri."

"What the fuck are you talking about?" She stands and I

watch the normally composed woman crumble before my eyes.

"I have it all, Gabriella. The arranged meeting with an assassin. The notes you passed him, the bank transfer from your account in Switzerland. An eyewitness placing you at a bar in town while you arranged the hit and a signed confession from the hitman himself. All I need is a name and you will be spared dressing in orange for the rest of your life."

"You're bluffing," she says, not really believing her own words for a second and then as the last word spills from her lips, a loud explosion rocks the building and she screams, "What's happening?"

I lean back and peer out of the window and say casually,

"It appears that somebody just attempted to assassinate me. It's just a shame they got my father instead."

"You fucking bastard." The tears stream down her face as she rushes to the window and stares out in disbelief at the scene below.

"You blew your own fucking father to hell. You're sick, Killian."

Moving behind her, I wrap my fingers around her neck and apply a hard pressure, and she gasps as I whisper in her ear. "Four hours, Gabriella and I would run if I were you."

I release my hold and like a frightened gazelle, she races for the door and, as she slams it behind her, I am empty inside.

I wander back to the window and lean my head against the glass and close my eyes because despite everything he was still my father, and I must live with this for the rest of my fucking miserable life.

I am disturbed by a text, and I glance down and note it's from reception. That surprises me because they know not to text me unless it's important.

I'm guessing it's telling me the devastating news, but as I open the message, my blood runs cold.

> Your wife is waiting for you in the car.

My entire world crumbles.

A sound comes from deep inside my soul as I roar like a wounded animal in the empty office. "Fuck! No!"

I have never felt pain like it. It's unbearable and I well and truly lose my shit.

Raising my chair, I hurl it against the wall, pounding my fists on the desk and scattering the contents to the floor. I roar with pain, and I tear at my hair as I realize what I've done. I killed the one person in my life who was innocent, beautiful, and brave. I destroyed the one woman I ever wanted to keep and as I sink to the floor, my back to the wall, I cry real tears for the first time in my life as I realize I killed the only woman I have ever loved.

My mind is struggling to cope and there is a huge gaping hole in my chest where my heart used to be.

Somehow, I struggle to my feet and as if I'm on autopilot, I move toward the door.

Every fucking step I take is heavy, as if the chains are tightening around my soul, dragging me down deeper into that dark, evil place in my mind.

I am a monster.

A cold, fucking, disgusting monster, who doesn't deserve to live among normal innocent people. I murdered the only thing that was good in my life. Extinguished any hope I ever had, because of what? A family institution that doesn't really count in the end. Was it worth my one shot at happiness? Ruling over a fucking society just to make my grandfather proud.

My assistant stares at me with fear as I pass. She heard the commotion in my office and knew better than to investigate. They hear the rumors and push all that aside because I pay them well. They choose to believe the whiter side of my image while turning away from the darker one.

Now there is no good left in me at all. I am fucking pure evil and will live up to my name. It's no wonder things went wrong for me because this is Karma at her deadliest.

I take the elevator to the ground and note the empty reception area. The glass at the front of the building is shattered like my heart. Broken pieces of jagged glass are forever scattered and will never be whole again. They cut deeply and cause pain—everything I deserve.

The sirens flash as the area is secured and as Saint appears by my side, he says with concern, "Fuck, Killian, what happened to you?"

I realize he is referring to my appearance and not the devastating scene outside where my car used to be.

Where Purity used to be.

Where my future used to be.

Where my heart used to be.

CHAPTER 49

PURITY

As I walk to the exit, I doubt I have ever been so happy. Knowing there is a child growing inside me is the most incredible feeling in the world.

I'm going to be a mom. Killian is going to be a father and together we will give this child the world. I will be the perfect mom and shower my baby with love and affection. Make them feel secure. Everything I was starved of as a child.

Killian will be a strong father, providing for his child, so they want for nothing. I may have to work on him for the emotional side, but I know he is capable. I just need to discover how to free it from the prison inside him.

We are probably the most emotionally retarded people I know, but we will work it out. I know we will and so, as I step into the sunshine, I turn my face to the heavens and love the sense of peace that washes over me.

I note the car waiting by the sidewalk and smile to myself. I will tell Killian the moment he steps inside. I will be waiting, and we will share a special moment alone, in private.

My hand reaches for the handle, and I briefly wonder where his driver is. Usually, he would be standing waiting and open the door for me. It doesn't matter. I don't need his help, anyway, and as I reach for the handle, I hear a loud, "Purity!"

My hand hovers against the metal and I glance up as a familiar voice makes my heart pound.

I peer in the direction it came from and blink as if I can't believe my eyes.

I take a second look and then drop my hand and head toward the person I have missed so much it physically hurt.

"Faith!"

I start running and dodging the traffic, I fly into my best friend's open arms with a sob.

"Purity." Her arms close around me and she hugs me so hard I think I will break and as my tears splash onto her shoulder, I sob with relief that she's found me.

"Oh my god, honey, I've been so worried." She says with a break in her voice. "You weren't answering your phone. I thought…"

She sobs on my shoulder, and we must be a crazy scene to anyone watching and as I pull back, I stare at her with a mixture of euphoria and tears.

"I've missed you so much." I blurt out, the tears cascading down my face as she smiles through her own. "Me too, honey. I've been out of my mind with worry."

I catch sight of Jonny, her man, out of the corner of my eye and his concerned expression makes me smile.

"It's good to see you too, soldier."

I smile through my tears, and he salutes me and whispers in his husky voice, "You too, princess."

He jerks his thumb in the direction of the coffee shop.

"You should talk in there."

Realizing we are quite the spectacle, I laugh softly, "Of course. Come, we have so much to talk about."

Faith links her arm with mine and we follow him inside

and Jonny heads off to order the drinks, while Faith and I huddle in a booth near the back of the shop.

She stares at me with concern.

"How have you been? What happened?"

As I fill her in, her eyes widen and when Jonny joins us, he listens with a feral gleam in his eye. They stay silent while I tell them everything, and Faith appears upset when she learns the full horror of my beginning.

I grasp her hand and smile.

"It's ok honey. I'm happy now."

The diamond ring on my finger sparkles as it catches the sunlight and she says with a worried frown, "Are you happy though, Purity? Do you love him?"

I say nothing because yes, I am happy, but I still don't know what love is.

"Of course." I take the easy route out and smile, deliriously happy because of the life growing inside me. I haven't told her that piece of news yet because I want my husband to be the first person, other than me, to know.

"What about you?" I say quickly. "Is he treating you right?" I fix Jonny with a hard stare, and he grins as Faith reaches for his hand and says happily, "I never thought life could be so good, Purity. They certainly never taught us that in Heaven."

"Thank God we made it out of there." I say with a sad smile. "Have you been back since?"

"No." She pulls a face. "I'm *never* going back."

"Well, I am," I say with determination, and she appears shocked at that.

"Why?"

"Because I want answers. My family has lied to me my entire life and I want to hear it from their own mouths. As soon as Killian is available, I'm getting him to take me there so I can have it out with them."

"Why bother?" Faith says sadly. "It doesn't matter anymore. They don't deserve any more of your time."

"Closure I suppose." I shrug. "You know me. I've always wanted answers and–"

I don't get to finish my sentence because the loudest noise rocks the coffee shop and Jonny yells, "Get under the table!"

He pulls Faith down with him and as I join them, I say fearfully, "What's happening?"

"Bomb." Jonny whispers, pushing both our heads down and saying urgently, "Stay where you are."

The sound of shattering glass rains down on us and the screams of our fellow diners ring in my ears. I have never been as terrified as I am now and when the sound fades Jonny say urgently, "Wait there."

He makes to leave and Faith yells, "No Jonny! It's not safe. Stay here."

"It's fine, darlin'. I'm used to explosions. You know that. It's my job."

Faith's eyes are full of terror as she watches him leave and then she reaches for my hand and whispers, "Are you ok, honey?"

"Yes, but what happened?"

"I don't know?"

It seems like hours before Jonny returns but can only be minutes and he drops down beside us and says with a worried shake to his head, "You can come out but–" he stares at me with so much pity in his eyes, I swear my heart stops beating.

"What, Jonny? What is it?" My voice trembles and then he breaks my world apart by saying, "Your car. It's in pieces."

"What?" I pull myself up and rush to the window and I swear every ounce of blood drains from my face as I stare at the remnants of Killian's car. The sirens and shouts fade into the distance as my heart shatters inside me.

"Killian. Oh my god, no!"

Without thinking, I race for the door and Jonny says, "No, Purity!" He reaches for me, but I'm quicker and wrench the door open as Faith screams, "Purity! It's not safe. Don't go out there."

I don't hear her. I can only hear my own ragged sobs and the sound of my heart breaking as I rush toward the scene, the tears pouring down my face as I pray, 'Please God, no. Please don't let Killian be inside that car. If I ask you for nothing more in life, please make him safe.'

I suppose in this moment something hits me I think I've known for a long time now. The pain I'm experiencing now can only mean one thing.

I love him and I probably have from that first night, he saved me from Mrs. Collins.

With an agonized scream, I race toward the building and then I hear a sound I'm wondering exists only in my imagination.

"Purity!"

I glance up and running toward me with so much emotion on his face, is the man I have only just realized I am deeply in love with.

I fall into my husband's arms and as they close around me, I sob on his shoulder as he buries his face in my hair and whispers, "I thought I'd lost you. Thank God, Purity. Thank God."

I can't speak because there are too many tears and then he pulls back and stares fiercely into my eyes and says with so much emotion it makes me cry harder.

"I love you. I love you so fucking much and if it takes me the rest of my life to prove it, I will."

I smile through my tears, marveling that deep pain can turn into joy so quickly and I say in a rush, "I love you too, Killian. I realize that now. When I thought I lost you, it hit me hard. I can't live without you. *We* can't live without you."

"We?" he stares at me in confusion as I reach for his hand and place it on my belly, and whisper, "I was coming to tell you, we're having a baby. You're going to be a father."

He stares at me in shock and then I see something I never believed he was capable of. His eyes change and the pain and secrets are pushed aside as they brim with tears of happiness. It causes the world to stop spinning as I witness a miracle and his voice shakes as he whispers, "I'm going to be a father."

I nod, laughing through my happy tears, and then he cups my face in his hands and kisses me so deeply, so emotionally and with so much love, I never want it to end.

CHAPTER 50

KILLIAN

I have never experienced relief like it. When I saw Purity running toward me, I couldn't get to her quickly enough. I went from the deepest despair to the purest joy in a second and as she fell into my arms, I vowed never to waste a minute of my time with her — to tell her I loved her — because I do.

I realized the moment I thought I'd lost her and when she told me she loved me, it made me believe I could move mountains.

Nonna was right. Love brings the greatest power on earth because I will do everything possible to keep it burning. For her and for our baby.

When she told me she was pregnant, I felt a fierce burst of love aimed straight at my heart. There were so many emotions battling inside me and my life changed forever. I have a purpose now. I have a family and I will make it my life's work to protect that with everything I've got.

The last thing I want is to let her go, but Saint appears at my shoulder and clears his throat.

"Boss. The cops want a word."

I stare at Purity and kiss her soft sweet mouth and whisper, "I must deal with this. Come with me."

I grasp her hand and she hesitates, causing me to stop. "What's wrong?"

"My friend Faith is here with her man, Jonny. I was about to get in the car, and she called to me from across the street. We were in the coffee shop when the car exploded. I thought…" She stares at me in obvious distress and yet as I look past her and see her friend waiting anxiously nearby, there is only one thing I must do. Tugging her with me, I cross the street and head toward the couple who are staring warily at me.

"Thank you." My voice is ragged and filled with emotion. They nod and I grip Purity's hand tightly and whisper, "You saved my wife's life. I will be eternally grateful to you and anything you need, you come to me."

Her friend stares at us and a huge smile breaks out across her face.

"We only want her to be happy." She says with a sweet smile, and I nod. "That makes three of us. Consider it done already."

I stare at the man with interest and note the battered leather jacket on his back and conclude that this man is one of the bikers who rescued them from Heaven.

"I owe you my gratitude–" I break off and he replies, "Jonny."

He stares at me with no emotion, only interest, and there is something about him that tells me he is no ordinary biker.

"What club are you from?" I am curious and he replies in a deep voice.

"Twisted Reapers MC." He stares me straight in the eye and I nod with a wry smile. "I promise you I'll take good care of Purity."

"That's all we want." He takes his girl's hand and says in a gruff tone. "Purity is family. We care about her."

He fixes me with a hard stare, and I nod, understanding the meaning behind his words, "As I said before, that makes three of us. You are welcome any time in our home."

Purity steps forward and hugs her friend and I watch the two women who came from the same beginnings cling to one another as if they can't bear to let go. Then Jonny removes a cell phone from his jacket and says to Purity, "We got you a gift. It appears you lost the last one."

He fixes me with a look that I acknowledge with a wry smile. As he hands it to Purity, he says softly, "Faith's number is here along with mine and Ryder's. We've also installed a tracking device, so if you lose it again, we will find it."

It makes me smile knowing they will be watching over her because how could I have a problem with that?

Purity grins and says with excitement. "Prepare to watch me travel the world because Killian has promised to take me." Faith stares in surprise as I slide my arm around my wife's shoulder and grin. "I never back out of a promise."

Saint is waiting and I'm reminded of the can of worms I've opened, and I say with a sigh. "Listen. I could be some time. Maybe you should all go back to the house and James will fix you some food. If your friends need to stay, there are many guest bedrooms that are always prepared."

Purity turns and her eyes sparkle. "Really. They can stay."

"Of course. If they want to, that is."

Faith squeals with excitement. "Oh my god, that will be amazing. We can catch up properly. Do you mind, Jonny?"

He smiles at her and winks. "Of course."

With a sigh, I turn to Saint. "Send another car to collect them. Make certain it's clean."

He nods and types out a text and turning to my wife, I whisper, "Duty calls, but tonight we talk."

"Just make it back home as fast as you can."

She pulls my face to hers and kisses me so sweetly, it takes all my self-control not to leave with them, but as I pull away, I stroke her beautiful face and whisper, "I promise. Let me tie things up here and I'll be home as soon as I can."

Almost before I finish my sentence, one of my cars screeches to a halt and two of my men jump out and hold open the door. Faith's eyes are wide as they step inside, but I'm guessing Jonny has seen this all before judging from the resignation in his eyes.

Yes. I know the Twisted Reapers, and it's not worth my life to fuck with them. They are the good guys, and I am not and taking them on would mean the end for me and I know it. I am more than happy to let them watch over my wife, knowing she is protected against any shit that is sure to head our way.

* * *

I WATCH them leave and as we cross the street, Saint says in a low voice, "Everything went as planned. Your father was the only casualty. The bomb exploded the minute he opened the car door, taking him out."

As I think about the hit we organized, I'm happy it went off smoothly. The plan was to swap his car license plate with mine and wire it up before bringing it around. The cameras will pick up my registration and believe it was an assassination attempt on me. My father would be so incensed when he left my office, he wouldn't be concentrating and the fact the street was empty and there was no driver wouldn't even cross his mind.

As soon as he opened the door, it was wired to explode, taking him out in a cruel twist of fate. The story that will hit the press is that I was the intended victim, and he was the unlucky one who was being given a ride home after visiting his loving son.

Now I must go through the motions and play the grieving son, knowing that Gabriella will send me the name of the man I want within four hours, or go to prison for life.

* * *

AFTER ENDLESS QUESTIONS and many condolences, I am alone with Saint in my office that was put back together before I returned. It's not the first time I've vented my anger and Saint arranged for it to be cleaned up.

The detective has left, and I exhale slowly, "What a fucking day."

Saint nods. "Are you okay, Kill?"

He appears concerned and I nod, glad I have someone on my side who I trust. Saint has been my number two since we were small boys passing through school together, and I trust him with my life.

"I was so scared I'd lost her, Saint."

I show rare emotion and he nods, a grim expression on his face.

"And your father?"

He stares at me with concern because we both know I ordered the hit on my own father, and it doesn't get more fucked up than that.

"He was a traitor. He turned against us, and my grandfather had word he was going to do the same to us, one by one. Clear the way for him to take over and wipe out his own family in the process."

"Now I understand."

Saint shakes his head and nods toward the decanter of bourbon on the side.

"May I?" He raises his eyes and I nod.

"We need a bottle each after today."

As he pours the drinks, he asks, "The cops. What's the plan?"

"Detective Conway is handling it."

"Does he know what to do?"

"Of course. He told me it will be reported as an assassination attempt on my life and my father inadvertently got in the way. All we need now is that fucking name, and then we can turn our attention to the organ grinder."

He hands me the glass just as my phone lights up with an incoming text, and noting Gabriella's name, I say darkly, "I wonder if it's who I think it is."

As I open the text, one name stares at me from the screen and I shake my head.

I hand it to Saint, who whistles out loud.

"Do you believe her?"

"Ninety percent, but she's a conniving bitch and I wouldn't be surprised if she's bluffing."

I laugh softly. "Either way, she's of no use to me now. You know what to do."

Saint nods as I drain the glass and then stand, grabbing my jacket.

"This day is done. I'm off to celebrate with my wife."

"Celebrate. Your father's death?"

Saint arches his brow and I smile. "No. The ending of one life and the beginning of another. I'm going to be a father."

Saint shows rare emotion as he reaches for my hand before pulling me in for a hug.

"I'm happy for you, Kill."

"I hope to do a better job than my father because any child of mine is bound to have a dark soul, and if I value my life, I'll treat him well."

"Him?" Saint shakes his head. "It may be a girl."

"Then she will be as pure as her mother. Either way, I'm happy."

As we head downstairs, I think about my father and hate what he did to his own family. Just imagining doing the same to mine leaves an extremely bitter taste in my mouth. Not fucking likely. I will be better. I *must* be better and if I'm not, I'm sure as hell Purity will pull me up on it.

CHAPTER 51

PURITY

It's been two weeks since the explosion and despite losing his father, Killian has been the happiest I have ever seen him. He is a changed man—for the better, and yet I sense the ominous signs of an approaching storm. When he thinks I'm not looking, his expression is tortured. His eyes are loaded with dark intent, and I am nervous about what he hides from me.

When Faith and Jonny left, I promised to visit them soon, and I meant it. We have come so far together; I will never lose touch with my best friend. She is family to me, and she always was.

Talking of which, I stare at the familiar scenery as it flashes past with a mixture of fear and trepidation. I am so nervous to be going home because I haven't spoken to my parents since I ran on the day the Reapers came to town to rescue Faith and Hope.

I kind of expect the welcome I'll get, but I am reassured by the man beside me holding my hand so tenderly. He is taking no chances and we are in convoy. A black cavalcade of menace as the three cars travels as one unit, the other occupants trained to kill to protect their boss.

It's taken me a while to understand Killian's business. I've googled the hell out of mafia and feel sick at what I read. I hate what he does, what his family built their empire on, but the side of him I focus on is the charitable donations he makes and the business he is so proud of. Gold Hawk Enterprises.

However, it's the other business I'm glad of now. The one that is following us to Heaven to demand answers. I need the darkness and I'm feeding off it because I am returning a woman, not the gullible, naive girl who left for a better life.

Killian works beside me, constantly on his phone and occasionally turning to kiss me softly or check if I'm ok. I don't mind. I love it when it's just the two of us. We can shut the world out and pretend everything is normal. It never will be. I realize that and so I treasure moments like this when I can snuggle beside him, glad we made it this far at least.

We took Killian's plane to the nearest airport. The one where the biker dropped me off when I escaped in the first place. Now I return a married woman with a baby on the way. Now I return with questions and a man who will make certain I get answers.

I return a lot smarter than I left and will not be fobbed off with vague answers and lies. Not anymore.

As the familiar scenery flashes past us, my stomach is in knots as the nerves take hold. Coming home may not have been such a good idea after all because with every kilometer we make, the memories come flooding back.

Killian pockets his cell and turns my face to his, staring deep into my eyes.

"You are strong, Purity. Remember that."

I nod, not really feeling his words and yet his dark flashing eyes give me the strength I sorely need right now.

His lips touch mine and he whispers against them, "You are my wife, and I will not let you fail."

"Let me?" I laugh softly. "There you go again. Telling me what to do."

His soft chuckle against my lips makes me smile as he whispers, "I can try, at least."

He kisses me softly and I swear my heart flutters every fucking time. I love the gentle moments with him almost as much as the passionate ones and there are a lot of those. Killian Vieri is a passionate man, despite his blank expression that he hides it behind. An enigma, a dark soul and a thousand personalities.

I never know which one will return home every night and I'm discovering I'm addicted to all of them. He has a softer side that I love, but the darker side of him excites me too. It would take a hundred lifetimes to work this man out, which makes for a very interesting relationship.

As we kiss, it's like the first, every fucking time, and my heart melts when he devotes his entire attention to me. I feel as if I'm the only thing in his world when he holds me tenderly and whispers loving words in my ear. When he kisses me with deepening passion and groans at my touch, those are the moments I cherish. He tells me often enough that he can't get enough of me, and I feel exactly the same.

Any doubts I ever had left me the moment I thought I had lost him, and it made us both wake up to what is important in our lives. Our family.

Now we are heading to meet mine and as I pull back, I say sadly, "Don't expect much, Killian. They hide their emotion behind disinterest. They always have."

"I can relate to that." He says huskily, as he kisses my lips once more and as his arms fold around me and he deepens the kiss, he chases away the fear inside me because with him beside me, how can I possibly fail?

* * *

I AM HOLDING TIGHTLY onto Killian's hand as the cars pull up in the yard. The familiar white wooden house, causing me to doubt everything.

We shouldn't have come. It's as if the angels are pulling me back, telling me that some things are best left in the past, but I disagree. I want answers because I have discovered my childhood was built on a lie and for a man who preached honesty, my father didn't practice what he preached.

Saint opens the door and Killian smiles. "Showtime baby."

He pulls me out with him, and I swallow hard when I notice the men who came with us are lining the route in. They are set at intervals around the house and if this doesn't scare the shit out of my family, they are bigger monsters than I thought.

We walk up the wooden steps to the veranda and as we reach the top, the door flies open and my heart drops when I see my father standing there.

"What–" He stares at me in disbelief, and I note the derision in his eyes as he witnesses Killian's hand in mine and then the blood drains from his face when he realizes whose hand I am holding.

For the first time in my entire life, I see real fear in my father's eyes.

"Mr. Vieri. Sir. This is an honor."

Killian snaps, "Don't you want to welcome your daughter home first, Elijah?"

He swallows hard at the venom in Killian's voice and turns to me with a dismissive. "So, you're back."

I gasp as Killian drops my hand and steps forward in a flash, grabbing my father by the neck and pushing him hard against the wall, causing him to gag as he hisses, "You will speak to my wife with respect, or you never get to speak at all."

A slight movement from the kitchen drags my attention away from the sight before me and I note the ashen face of my mom staring at us with fear in her eyes.

"Mom." I step toward her, and she whispers fearfully, "You shouldn't have come back, Purity. You are not welcome here."

"But…" I'm shocked as Killian turns his attention to her, still holding my father by the throat, and I watch her lower lip tremble as she whispers, "We have nothing here for you. Please go."

If anything, her reply makes Killian tighten his hold around my father's neck and he growls, "You don't get a choice, Mrs. Sanders, because guess what, this is judgment day."

He releases my father, who drops to the floor choking, his hands closing around his neck as he struggles to breathe and Killian nods to Saint, who grabs him by the arm and pulls him after us in the direction of the kitchen.

I am shaking as I follow them, and Killian pulls out a familiar wooden chair for me to sit on before taking the one beside me.

Saint thrusts my father into the one opposite and stands behind him, and Killian points to the chair beside my father and says, "Sit."

My mother drops into it with a frantic glance at her husband and Killian says in a dark voice dripping with intent, "I want the name of the organ grinder."

"The what?"

My father appears confused and Killian leans forward and hisses, "A few years back, you were visited by my father Benito Vieri. He attempted to set up a deal for the opium you supply, and you refused his offer. Purity overheard you on the phone telling the person on the other end you wouldn't deal with the monkey, only the organ grinder, so I will ask you again, who is the organ grinder?"

My father stares in disbelief and a small bead of sweat rolls down his face as he stiffens and falters. "I don't…"

Killian's fist thumps on the table, causing us all to jump, and he says darkly, "I would consider your reply very carefully, Elijah."

I watch in horror as Saint pulls out his gun and holds it to the back of my father's head and my mom screams, causing my father to snap. "Be quiet woman."

She falls silent and I stare at him with hatred as he proves to me every reason why I ran from this fucked up life.

"He will kill me." My father says angrily, and Killian adds, "And you think I won't."

His gaze falls to me and his lip curls.

"I might have known you'd disappoint me, girl. You always were rebellious, but this time you've gone too far."

The sound of the gun being primed electrifies the air and Saint pushes the barrel in deeper as Killian growls, "Tell me or die. It's your choice."

I watch the blood drain from his face and it's as if I'm staring at a stranger. This man isn't the powerful man I always believed he was. He isn't honorable, good, and kind. So, I speak up, addressing him with a hard stare. "Why did you lie to me all my life?"

He stares at me with derision. "I don't owe you an explanation, child. Remember your place."

I am mildly interested as Saint cuffs him around the head with the gun and the real fear in his eyes should bring out the compassion in me. It doesn't.

"You are no better than the men you warned me against. You deal in drugs and work with criminals. I hate you." I hiss, my voice loaded with venom.

My father says nothing and Killian surprises me by saying

in a dead voice, "He deals in more than drugs, Purity. He traffics women too. Think about all the missing women that have disappeared from Heaven over the years that many believe made it past that mountain range."

Mom's eyes grow larger, and I gasp. "What do you mean?"

My father says nothing, as Killian explains. "Those women never ran. They were abused and then sold like cattle on the open market. I have done some investigating, and your father was the man who made it happen. Reverend Peters broke many women in Heaven and, when they were no longer required, he established a trade connection with the Middle East. They were shipped off and their memory buried. They hadn't found freedom, they were halfway across the world at the time being abused and sold for profit, of which the Reverend and your father took a cut."

Still, my father says nothing and Killian snarls, "My contact told me they were expecting another shipment. The Reverend had taken a new wife and this one couldn't die because too many had before her. He would break her and then tell his congregation she had run away, leaving him free to abuse the next one in line."

"Faith!" My eyes are wide as I stare at my father. "You were going to do the same to Faith. You fucking bastard!"

I scream at him, and he winces at my choice of words, and I can't help myself and say in a cold voice, "Hand me your gun, Killian."

He says nothing and just does as I say, and I point it directly at my father's head.

"What about me? What was my fate?"

Killian answers for him as the wild panic in my father's eyes tells me I'm not going to like this.

Killian says roughly, "You were to be married to a man called Jethro Tunstall."

"You are fucking kidding me." I stare in disgust at my father because Jethro Tunstall must be seventy years old.

"He owned land that your father needed to expand his drugs operation and soon after the wedding would suffer a fatal accident. Then you would be sold after you apparently took your own life because you were so grief stricken. Your father gets the land and a million dollars for you. And they say I'm evil."

I can't even see straight. I am so enraged. My world has exploded like a nuclear bomb hit. There is nothing left. No feeling, no loyalty and no shit because these aren't my parents. They're devils in disguise.

My hand shakes as I point the gun at my father and I want to shoot him so badly. I am crying as I stare into his eyes, remembering the sick and twisted upbringing he forced on me. The demons are cackling as they surround us, and I have no sympathy for my mother because she went along with it.

"Tell him the name, you fucking bastard."

I'm surprised at the steel in my voice as I aim the gun at my father's head and Killian leans back with an evil smirk on his face.

"Lucas Stevenson."

My father lowers his eyes in defeat and only the small chuckle beside me tells me he's telling the truth.

Saint lowers his gun but mine stays where it is and Killian says almost conversationally, "Thank you, but I already knew."

"Then why?" My father stares at him with confusion, and Killian shrugs. "I just wanted to see how loyal you really are. Not very, it seems."

He nods to Saint. "Make the call."

"The call?"

My father appears worried, and Killian says with a smile.

"The woman who accompanied my father was my

assistant at the time. She betrayed me by working with my him. She is currently in custody on a murder charge. His murder. However, it will never go to trial. We all know that."

He turns to me and says with a deep sigh. "Lucas Stevenson is otherwise known as Judge Stevenson. He would be assigned her case and make sure she was set free."

"How can you stop that from happening?" I say in a whisper, and he laughs softly, but the sound of it chills my blood.

"Sadly, she will commit suicide in her cell. Such a tragedy as she believes she chose the winning side. The person delivering her food will discover she concealed a knife that went undetected. She will slash her wrists and then plunge the knife through her neck. He will raise the alarm, but there will be no saving her. Her cries of innocence will be silenced, and her secrets taken to the grave."

He leans back and shakes his head. "Such a shame that she told me everything I needed to know before she died."

My hand shakes as I lower the gun and he raises his eyes. "What's the matter, Purity. Has your thirst for revenge deserted you?"

I stare at my parents and tears fill my eyes as I whisper, "I can't do it, Killian. I can't be like him."

He nods, a gentle gleam in his eyes as he stares at me and whispers, "Would you like me to do the honors?"

"No." I shake my head miserably. "I don't want their blood on my hands. I want to forget they ever existed, and I want to make sure they can never do this to anyone else."

If I thought he would be disappointed by my decision, I'm surprised when his hand finds mine and he smiles with approval.

"Good choice, Bella. There are more ways to bring misery than death. Perhaps we should allow them to repent their sins for the rest of their lives and discover not everything works out in the end." He says over his shoulder to the guards standing by the door, "Torch the fields, the barn and the machinery."

"No!" my father makes to stand, and Saint pushes him down into his chair with an iron grip.

"No?" Killian raises his eyes.

"No?" He shakes his head.

"You speak as if you have a choice, Elijah." He leans forward and fixes my father with a dark glare.

"Let me tell you what will happen."

He turns to me and takes my hand and lifts it to his lips, kissing the wedding band he put there.

"Your daughter is married to me, and we are expecting our first child. I will make her happy and together we will raise our children to honor their parents and be loved. You will never see us again, or your grandchildren. Not that I expect you to be unhappy about that. Your daughter will want for nothing. She will travel the world and see what you warned her about first hand. The beauty, the pleasure and the excitement that this world offers, whereas you will be left with nothing. Your land now belongs to me, courtesy of a signature you made on the last shipment you arranged. You really should check what you're signing, Elijah, because you signed all your properties over to Gold Hawk Enterprises."

Realization dawns in my father's eyes as Killian continues. "The drugs operation will be shut down forever. The trafficking operation has already been terminated. You see, I am a very powerful man, more powerful than any of the clowns you have been dealing with and if you even attempt to sell the shirt off your back, I will know about it. Remember, Miss. Sinclair. Your own passing will not be so pleasant."

He turns to my mom, and she shrivels under his derisory gaze.

"You are just as bad as your excuse for a husband. You will live out your life knowing he failed. That *you* failed, but your daughter won. She will have the life you never dreamed of, and I will make her the happiest woman alive. Your own husband will make you the unhappiest because you will live out the rest of your days in poverty and be scorned by the very people you preached to when word gets out about your business. In a few weeks you will receive a visit from the sheriff who will arrest you both for your crimes and then you will be tried and found guilty before heading to prison for the rest of your miserable lives."

He shakes his head as if concerned and says with a sigh, "Terrible things happen to those in prison. Keep looking over your shoulders. I'd hate for you to suffer a similar fate to Miss. Sinclair. In fact, you will both wish that Purity had shot you. It would have saved you a lot of pain in your future."

He grabs my hand and pulls me up beside him and says pleasantly, "It's been a pleasure to meet you. We must do this again sometime, then again, let's not. Once was definitely enough."

He turns to me and says softly, "Say goodbye to your parents, Purity. You won't be seeing them again."

As I stare at the people before me, I see strangers. Then again, I always have, so I nod my head with respect toward them and say in a strong, determined voice, "I'm free now and just so you know, I'm glad I ran. I'm glad I exposed you and I'm glad I no longer have to see you, but most of all I'm glad none of my children will ever know you."

I spin on my heels and head outside, the acrid scent of burning forestation strangely satisfying.

As we step into the car, Saint follows and as we set off, I don't look back.

That part of my life is buried along with any compassion I ever had for the two people who brought me into their sick world. Now it's up to me to be better than they ever were, which won't be difficult because I already am.

EPILOGUE

KILLIAN

ONE WEEK LATER

I watch Purity laughing with Serena and nonna, and I can't tear my eyes from the scene. I don't know how it happened, but my life changed forever when she walked into my building one Summer's day and stayed forever. That I so nearly lost her makes me appreciate every hour we spend together, and I will never take that for granted.

I wasn't kidding when I told her parents I would make her happy. Give her the best life possible and treat her well. I'm a man of my word, as they have discovered.

There is nothing left of their business, and they are just lucky they still have a home because the fire burned long into the night, destroying their livelihood in one cruel twist of fate.

Their connections have been severed with all their business associates and the cops are due to pay them a visit any day now. They are just lucky Purity spared their lives, but I'm not so generous. They will live in hell for the rest of their days because I have no mercy. My own father was a casualty of that and with a sigh, I turn away from the happy scene and head to my grandfather's den.

They arrived last night from Serenita. My grandparents have a mansion in Chicago they rarely visit. Preferring instead to live out the rest of their days together in paradise. However, business always brings them back and when I head inside, I find my grandfather and brother already waiting for me.

The air inside his den is tense, toxic and dark and not just because of the many years of cigar smoke that cling to the walls, despite the yearly refurbishment. There are many memories in this office. Secrets that seal our enemies' fates and ensure the Vieris live another day.

They look up when I arrive and my grandfather points to the chair beside my brother, opposite his own carved wooden chair upholstered in black leather.

Their faces are grim, and I'm not surprised because despite everything, one important Vieri is missing.

He slides a glass of whiskey across the desk and in silence, we all raise our glasses as he says with a deep sigh.

"Today we mourn the passing of Benito Vieri. A son, husband and father who made the wrong choices in life. He turned his back on family, which was his ticket to hell, but despite his betrayal, he was one of us. May he rest in peace."

We drain our glasses and set them down on the table and my grandfather stares at me with his usual penetrating gaze.

"Are you good?"

"I am."

The faint nod of approval tells me despite the fact I murdered his son in cold blood, it was on Don Vieri's order and then he turns to Shade and asks the same question.

"Yes. I'm good."

The dark undertone in my brother's voice tells us we're all on the same page and my grandfather nods, apparently satisfied.

He leans back and an expression of distaste crosses his face.

"To be betrayed by my own son. I feel as if I failed."

I sense his disappointment from here. It's like a black cloud that has settled over this family that we are struggling to navigate our way through.

"My enemies I expected, but not family. Never family, which is why he had to die."

I couldn't agree more because when your own family starts plotting to kill you, all hope is lost. We learned that my father had ordered a hit on every one of us. Intending to clear the way for his own position as the head of the Dark Lords. We just got in first and now it's important we turn our attention to the next in line.

My grandfather smiles suddenly and says, "Congratulations on your news, Killian. It makes me happy knowing you are continuing the family line. May it be the first of many."

"It will." I say with a smile because if I keep Purity pregnant for the rest of her life, I will be happy. Just knowing a part of me is growing inside her is a power trip that will never get old.

I am looking forward to seeing her swell with our child, knowing that she is mine for life. I will never let her go and that means I can't give her a reason to want to. I must be the perfect husband to keep that smile on her face, and as it turns out, it's an easy assignment.

I love her and I never really expected that.

Shade reaches out and slaps me on the back and says warmly, "Yes, congratulations, Kill. You will make a good father. Be better than our own."

"That won't be difficult."

The two men nod with a grim expression and my grandfather says with a deep sigh.

"Lucas Stevenson."

We sit up and pay attention, our good mood shifting as we turn our heads to business.

"He is a problem to be dealt with."

"What do you know?"

I lean forward. Eager to hear the plan because, as sure as I'm sitting here, he has one.

"A man of many secrets and many personalities."

My grandfather taps his finger on the black leather box on his desk and then opens it reverently, removing a cigar, which he turns over in his hand without lighting it. We know this is his preferred thinking method. Only lighting it when his point has been made.

We watch the cigar turning slowly, almost as if it's mirroring his mind, and he says slowly, "We must destroy him from within."

The air is tense and laden with expectation as his eyes glitter with energy. A dark energy that tells us how much he loves this fucking shit.

"Outwardly, he is honorable. The family man who is loved and respected by everyone who knows him and many who don't. The grave face of justice and a man the government can trust. He has earned a good living at the top of his game, enjoying huge riches as a result of that. His children live an ivy league life, and his wife is the queen of society. They are considered untouchable."

He laughs with obvious pleasure. "The higher up they are, the harder the landing when they fall."

He turns the cigar and says in a rough whisper, "Then there is his other life."

I think both Shade and I lean forward at the same time, like salivating dogs on the end of a leash.

My grandfather grins as he senses our blood lust.

"He has another family. One that lives well but is hidden from view. A mistress if you like, but she is more than that."

The cigar turns as he says darkly, "She is the love of his life, and their children are the ones he dotes on more than his legitimate ones."

This is news and yet it doesn't surprise me. It wouldn't be the first time a powerful man was hiding another family beneath the rug with all his other dirty secrets.

My grandfather turns to Shade and grins. "The mother, Meredith Powell, is the keeper of all Lucas's secrets. Mainly his two illegitimate children, Rafferty and Allegra Powell. She married his brother who doesn't know they aren't his. The children's 'uncle' dotes on their kids and is protective of them. Lucas particularly adores his daughter because his wife only produced the disappointment that goes by the name Jefferson Stevenson."

We share a grin because my grandfather is right about Jefferson. He is one huge disappointment who believes he is untouchable. I almost can't wait to wipe that smug smile off his face.

My grandfather turns to Shade. "It falls on you to use the children to destroy them from within. Discover anything of help to bring them down and Killian–" He turns to me and grins.

"Jefferson is all yours."

My grandfather reaches for his lighter and leans back, lighting the top of his cigar with a dark gleam in his eyes, the fire reflected in them as he says with a finality to his voice that tells us this meeting is over.

"Tear his family apart one by one and watch the great

man fall. Use his secrets against him and discover what he holds over the rest of The Dark Lords. When you have all your information, remove him from life."

The end of the cigar glows like the ever-burning flames of Hell.

No mercy, no second chances.

Where your sins determine your everlasting fate.

My grandfather is the devil, and we are his loyal demons. We are the Dark Lords, and nothing will ever take that away from us.

Our revenge continues.

* * *

A Shade of Evil

Read Faith & Jonny's story in
Brutal Sinner

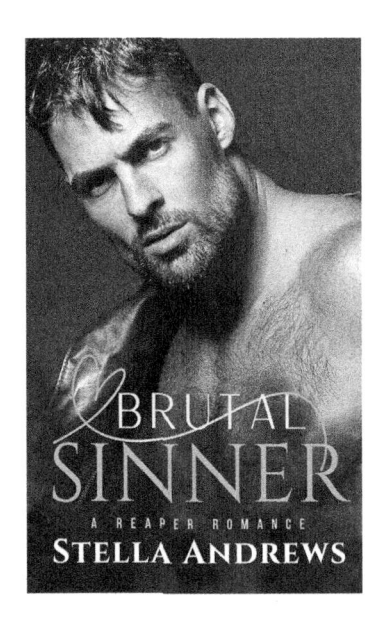

Thank you for reading this story.
If you have enjoyed the fantasy world of this novel, please would you be so kind as to leave a review on Amazon?

Join my closed Facebook Group

Stella's Sexy Readers

Follow me on Instagram

Carry on reading for more Reaper Romances, Mafia Romance & more.

Remember to grab your free book by visiting stellaandrews.com.

ALSO BY STELLA ANDREWS

Twisted Reapers

Rebel
Dirty Hero (Snake & Bonnie)
Daddy's Girls (Ryder & Ashton)
Twisted (Sam & Kitty)
The Billion Dollar baby (Tyler & Sydney)
Bodyguard (Jet & Lucy)
Flash (Flash & Jennifer)
Country Girl (Tyson & Sunny)
Brutal Sinner (Jonny & Faith)

The Romanos
The Throne of Pain (Lucian & Riley)
The Throne of Hate (Dante & Isabella)
The Throne of Fear (Romeo & Ivy)
Lorenzo's story is in Broken Beauty

Beauty Series
Breaking Beauty (Sebastian & Angel) *
Owning Beauty (Tobias & Anastasia)
Broken Beauty (Maverick & Sophia) *
Completing Beauty – The series

Five Kings
Catch a King (Sawyer & Millie) *

Slade

Steal a King

Break a King

Destroy a King

Marry a King

Baron

Club Mafia

Club Mafia – The Contract

Club Mafia – The Boss

Club Mafia – The Angel

Club Mafia – The Savage

Club Mafia - The Beast

Club Mafia – The Demon

Ortega Mafia

The Enforcer

The Consigliere

The Don

The Dark lords

Pure Evil

Standalone

The Highest Bidder (Logan & Samantha)

Rocked (Jax & Emily)

Brutally British

Deck the Boss

Reasons to sign up to my mailing list.

- A reminder that you can read my books FREE with Kindle Unlimited.
- Receive a weekly newsletter so you don't miss out on any special offers or new releases.
- Links to follow me on Amazon or social media to be kept up to date with new releases.
- Free books and bonus content.
- Opportunities to read my books before they are even released by joining my team.
- Sneak peeks at new material before anyone else.

stellaandrews.com

Follow me on Amazon

Printed in Great Britain
by Amazon